THE CASTLE

A NOVEL

SETH ROGOFF

TUSCALOOSA

FC2 is an imprint of the University of Alabama Press

Inquiries about reproducing material from this work should be addressed
to the University of Alabama Press

Book Design: Publications Unit, Department of English, Illinois State
    University; Director: Steve Halle, Production Interns: Georgeanne
    Drajin, Jessica Kreul, Kyu Kyu Thein
Cover image: Bolustck/stock.adobe.com
Cover design: Matthew Revert
Typeface: Adobe Caslon Pro

Library of Congress Cataloging-in-Publication Data is available from
the Library of Congress.
ISBN: 978-1-57366-207-9
E-ISBN: 978-1-57366-909-2

For Benjamin Rogoff Gideon, my brother.

FEBRUARY 1 (NIGHT)

I arrived at the village at dusk. I crossed the bridge and entered the abandoned, desolate space. From what I can tell, there isn't a single person here, no sign of human life. The structures in the village are crumbling, some already in ruins. Many of the roofs of the small stone houses have caved in from what, I assume, was the weight of year after year of heavy snow. I found an inn by the bridge. The wooden entrance door was locked. I managed to climb inside through one of the broken pub windows. The large ceramic stove on the far wall opposite the bar was, of course, stone cold—and I was afraid to light it out of fear of a chimney fire. The straw mattress was where I had expected it to be. The down blankets, worn but usable, guarantee I'll survive this brutally cold night. I write this by flashlight. The electricity, like everything else here, has failed to survive. *What could have brought me to this desolate place*, K. asks himself, *except the desire to stay*? I don't share this desire. I have other reasons for being here, other reasons—or maybe no reason at all. I suspect it is a matter beyond reason. I can imagine what Julia would say if she were to read this. She'd say there's no difference between reason and beyond reason, and if we erase the boundary between the two, she'd say—coming close to me, touching me, maybe giving herself to me for the last time, and every time was the last time—what's left is movement, what's left is the erotic intensity of flight.

FEBRUARY 2 (MORNING)

A single piece of paper ripped into dozens of pieces and then taped back together: if everything swirls around a single point, a vanishing point, then it could be that this paper is this point. It has led me here to this village to seek out an answer to the question it poses, though in truth it poses no question. There is a short statement on the paper: *Vom Schossberg war nichts zu sehen, Nebel und Finsternis umgaben ihn . . . Nothing was to be seen of the castle hill, fog and darkness surrounded it . . .* Fog and darkness, the landscape and atmosphere of a question that is no question: the question of whether there is a castle on the hill or not—the question of the status of reality here, the void of existence here.

The paper came from the Keter file, the declassified US intelligence file of Sidney Keter, the translator of *The Book of Moonlight* from German into English. The small piece of paper had an even smaller piece of paper attached to it with a corroded paper clip, which broke into three pieces as I worked to disengage it. The smaller paper reads: *Village of Z., 18 km NE of Spindelmühle.* The note is written in English with a black pen. The paper with the smaller paper attached to it with the (now broken) paper clip was filed with documents from the year 1952. A cover sheet from that year, originally classified as top secret, states: *Sidney Keter should be viewed as a radical. He has relations with communists and anarchists. It is possible that he is unstable and dangerous. If situation necessitates, his sister might be willing to commit him to an asylum. A potential receiving doctor is ready with the required paperwork. Keter was last seen heading north.*

Maybe I should say I fell asleep and woke up here in Z. Or, more believably, that I boarded a bus in Prague, which I thought was bound for Berlin but was actually headed to Spindelmühle—or, in Czech, Špindlerův Mlýn. It could be that the mistake had to do with the hour of departure, and (or?) the fact that I hadn't slept the night before. I'd gone to the bus station in the early hours of the morning directly after a long meeting with the writer Daniel Cohen. It was still dark when I boarded the bus in Prague. I immediately slumped down in my seat and fell asleep. And it was dark when I woke up in Špindlerův Mlýn—and so both explanations (boarding the wrong bus and falling asleep and waking up here) can be, in this way, brought together. The other travelers who got off in Špindlerův Mlýn lugged their suitcases and bags full of skis and equipment into town, tugging on stubborn or bleary-tired children as they made their way through the snow. I went in the opposite direction, following a sign that pointed across a field and into the forest: *Z. 18 km.* The snow along this path was heavy—knee deep for mile after mile—and in truth there was nothing much to designate it as a path. There was not a single bootprint or groove for skis on the trail that led over the ridge and into the distant valley.

The long walk from Špindlerův Mlýn to Z. happened yesterday and already it is half forgotten. When during the journey, for example, did dawn, which had just broken as I started down the path across the field, turn into morning light? At first, I had tried to keep my thoughts in order—to stitch together a story that would conclude in Z., or better yet, that would conclude at the castle on the hill above the village. I made certain statements to myself, strung together sentences. Then I'd lose focus and the story would start to fray.

I'm trying to piece it together now, buried with my notebook under three layers of eiderdown. It would be simple enough to say that it goes back to my translation of Jan Horák's novel *Blue, Red, Gray*, the 1,456-page samizdat masterpiece that occupied seventeen years of my life, occupied it like a foreign army occupies a conquered territory—permitting daily life to carry on within a framework of total domination, destruction, and violence. This is when (or where?) I discovered Keter, an important, if minor, character in the novel. This is also where I discovered *The Book of Moonlight*, that grandiose work of religious thought that transgresses and transcends all definitions, definitions like mysticism, gnosticism—even "religion" itself. That those two entities, the human being Sidney Keter and *The Book of Moonlight*, should slide their way from the pages of fiction into the materiality of the real shouldn't surprise anyone by now. What is harder to understand—even if it is not important it be understood—is how this materiality, this real, spread or seeped into other zones, infecting them, transforming them, until, at some point during those seventeen years, it pushed out all other notions of reality. It was in this state that I spent some months in the clinic Zelená Hora, seeking a "cure" under the care of Dr. Hruška. It was Hruška, who, during one of our late morning sessions, presented me with notebooks that contained Keter's complete diaries. Hruška claimed he got them from an old friend of mine, but this was clearly a lie. When I called him out on this deception, he brought up two points. First, he asked me if I thought it was a coincidence that the character Sidney Keter shared initials with Sy Kirschbaum, that is, that he shared them with me. Second, he quoted a passage from the PEN Translation Prize announcement that he was fond of deploying during our sessions. He read, "Kirschbaum's prose is so propulsive that it defies belief that the text is, in fact, taken from an original source. It is Kirschbaum's singular achievement that *Blue, Red, Gray* seems not to be a translation at all."

How did I arrive here? Could it be that I walked eighteen kilometers through the snowy woods over the mountain ridge and into this valley? There is no other way to get here—and even this way, the way I traveled, is impossible. There is no path to where I am. Yet, I am here in the village of Z., huddled under three layers of century-old eiderdown and writing this as the morning light cuts through the grimy, imperfect panes of glass, a light that seems to contradict the whole of this place—a strong, clarifying winter light.

The village of Z. was visible from the top of the ridge above it. Taking a break from the arduous walk, I gazed down at the collection of stone structures. I considered how ordinary it looked. It's a village one's eyes wander over without pausing on their way from one side of the valley to the other. On the other hand, it is amazing such a village ever could have come into existence in this valley. The gap between the mountains on one side and those on the other is narrow. The dense forests surrounding it cut off natural connections in all directions. When I descended from the ridge, I found and followed a small stream that cut its way to the base of the valley and then around the edge of the village and what had been cleared as its agricultural lands, long overgrown with trees. I continued on the path along the stream until it reached the wooden bridge. I crossed the bridge into the village.

Threads of a story twisted and frayed, formed and disintegrated as I walked through the snow. There is a fair amount of repetition in one's thoughts during a long walk like this. The wanderer drifts in and out of them, they are broken by sounds and plays of light, bodily sensations, tremors of consciousness. The day after I returned to Prague following a disastrous semester as a visiting lecturer at a college in my hometown, I took the Keter diaries out of my old steamer trunk. One volume begins just after Keter arrived in New York by ship from Europe in 1941. He had translated *The Book of Moonlight* from German into English while in Prague and had delivered the manuscript to the Workmen's Circle's publishing house in New York, which printed it in a run of one hundred copies. The copies were to be distributed to certain libraries, members of the circle, and to select scholars and critics. When the printing was done and the one hundred copies were bound and ready, Keter delivered one to the New York Public Library. He didn't even take one for himself. A few days later, the

Workmen's warehouse went up in flames, destroying numerous print runs, including the ninety-nine remaining copies of Keter's translation and the corresponding typed manuscript. There was nothing left of the book, Keter writes in his diary, beyond the original handwritten manuscript that he had hidden in his sister's apartment and the single copy of the Workmen's print run delivered to the library.

It is clear from his diaries that Keter was suspicious of the warehouse fire, even though the police report declared it to be an accident—an unattended cigar, it states (I have a copy), dropped burning embers onto a pile of newly printed syndicalist broadsheets. The fire, Keter wrote, had been set for one purpose: to destroy his translation of *The Book of Moonlight* before it could be disseminated. The plot was orchestrated, Keter thought, by those who saw the radical mysticism of the work as a threat to their materialist view of history. One of the suspected leaders of this arsonist band was named Esther Bird, who, I discovered, checked out *The Book of Moonlight* from the New York Public Library in 1946 and never returned it—Esther herself disappearing without a trace. One of Keter's notebooks has a pocket in the inside of its back cover. In this pocket, there is a black-and-white photograph of Esther Bird from the year 1945. The photograph captures her in profile as she stands over a table in the office of the anarchist newspaper *Freedom*, where she is one of the editors. She is leaning on the table. Her body is pitched forward, her head bent down to inspect some printed materials in front of her. The wide frame of her glasses cuts a black line across her cheek. Her thin arms and legs seem strained with tension. She is wearing a white blouse buttoned up to the neck, a garnet necklace, a dark skirt which flares out from her waist in a rigid line, making her thin body seen nearly flat, two dimensional, and this flatness works to magnify the tension in her body, her piercing downward gaze, creating power and energy in the photographic field. She is twenty-eight years old here, and at this young age already a dominant force in anarchist politics in New York. During the years since I tracked down the record in the New York Public Library, I had assumed Esther Bird took the book, the last surviving copy of Keter's *The Book of Moonlight*, to destroy it. In my imagination, I thought of Esther Bird herself as fire, as a flame hurtling through the sky toward its object. But now, after I have worked through the Keter notebooks more times than I can count, I have conjured another image. Esther Bird was not flame but wind, intent on conveying *The Book of Moonlight* out of danger. Saving it. Saving and hiding it—and hiding it meant hiding herself—until . . . until when? Until it could be found? Until she could live again? But she could never live again.

FEBRUARY 2 (NIGHT)

In the morning, I unpacked the food I brought with me and ate the remains of my loaf of bread. I found a large pot in the kitchen and filled it with snow, which I melted with the body heat I'd stored under my three layers of eiderdown. I drank this fresh water with delight.

I left the inn and wandered through the village. The streets were irregular, bending, intersecting, ending in dead-end alleyways—everything full of snow. Most of the houses—squat, plain—were shuttered, though occasionally a small window caught a reflection that blocked the gaze into those dark, tomb-like interiors. Damage to the dwellings seemed to have come from the top down. A roof would cave in, a hole opened by the swelling of ice. Once punctured, the process of natural destruction would begin, eventually creeping down to the house's foundation, eroding the bricks and mortar that kept the whole thing upright. Such, it seems, is the process of ruination here.

I found my way to the schoolhouse, which stood near the village center. The door to the schoolhouse was unlocked and led into one of its two rooms. The room contained a desk and pieces of old exercise equipment. I went over to a large window and looked out at the back garden. I could see some fencing posts, the fence itself having collapsed and disappeared, perhaps buried under the snow. The garden shed was in rough shape, its roof slanted, its door hanging from a rusty metal hinge.

I turned back to the interior and slowly made my way around the room. Under the large ceramic-tiled stove, a flash of white caught my eye. I went over there, reached down between the stove's legs, and pulled out a heap of bones, including what appeared to be the skull of a cat. The beast must have come to its place of maximal warmth only to have frozen to death there, a death now long ago.

The other room was filled with rows of desks facing a large slate board, which hung next to the teacher's desk on the far wall. I moved over to the desk and saw a stack of student assignment books, the cheap paper now yellow and brittle. I lifted one and opened it. The pupil had copied a single sentence down the length of the page. A rough translation of the

German: *Whoever lives and stays in the village, resides in a certain sense in the castle.* On the opposite page: *The village is the property of Count Westwest.* This line, too, was copied down the page a couple of dozen times. What useless nonsense, I thought, to teach kids to write in such a way, to teach kids to think in such a way. Better to remain illiterate, avoid reading and writing altogether. To outrun words, I thought, to escape the tyranny of statements like "the village is the property . . ."—perhaps this escape was possible on a journey between Špindlerův Mlýn and Z., where threads fray and nothing could be held together. But in Špindlerův Mlýn and here in Z.—no.

The desk was a solid piece of furniture. It had a spacious surface and three drawers to either side. I slid open the top right drawer and found a leather case or portfolio, which held sheets of mostly blank paper. The top sheet contained what appeared to be a diary entry written by the teacher. I peeled it off and placed it in my backpack.

I went out and checked the shed. It was full of chopped firewood stacked in piles and various pieces of garden equipment. I had thought I could make it to the castle today, but as I left the school's grounds, it was already starting to get dark. I hadn't yet located the precise road that led from the village to the castle, and knew from other small villages that the roads, once they left the cobbled streets behind and entered the forest, could bend and twist in unpredictable ways. Once lost at night on such a forest path, which would invariably split into countless other paths—forking this way and that—it would be impossible to make it back to the village or, likely, anywhere else, at least anywhere "mapped," even if Z. itself was unmapped, unknown to present times, lost in a crease or a fold of an archived notebook now stored—horribly—in Oxford, England.

The early onset of darkness—it seemed to be barely past noon and it was already getting dark. Or maybe it was later. I had left my phone at home in Prague and haven't owned a working watch since my grandfather's Patek Philippe stopped running years ago and I couldn't afford the cost of repair. I had considered giving the watch to my brother Henry, since he could easily manage the many thousands of dollars it would take to get it running again, but my grandfather had left it specifically to me—to me and not to Henry and not to my father—and I wanted to honor that. He had brought it back from the war. It was a mid-1940s chronograph, which my grandfather referred to either as his "piece of victory" or his "spoil of war." Nobody—myself, my father, my brother—knew the story behind the watch, nor did we appreciate its significance as a luxury object. When my brother figured it out around the age of forty, about the time he'd banked his first million while I was struggling through draft after draft of Horák's book, he tried to gently pry it loose from me. By that time, the watch had ceased being a watch for me (and ceased working) and had become a symbol. The Patek Philippe was history. It was a story of survival. That it didn't tell time didn't matter because the watch itself *was* time. It was beautiful. Intricate. Mysterious. In any case, I'd left the watch in Prague with the phone, remembering well the line from Jan Horák's Czech secret-police file, indicating that Horák had returned from a clandestine meeting in the mountains "without his watch." What does this matter? What does it matter that my brother Henry tried to get the watch from me, even if he never directly said he wanted it? What does it matter that my grandfather had left me the watch and not him and not my father? The only time I really wore the watch—meaning the only time I wore it as a status piece—was when Julia's father came from Rome to Prague while she was first living there. He was a businessman, a rich, stylish, beautiful human being, like his daughter.

"Can I take a look at it?" he said at one point during the dinner. "A piece like that has to be admired." I felt both proud and totally ridiculous as I stretched my arm out for him to gaze at the watch. Though he didn't say anything more about it to me, Julia told me later that he had wondered aloud how anyone could wear a watch like that and at the same time "those terrible clothes." He was right, of course. It was absurd. Julia's father was the kind of guy who was always right, right about everything, and yet at the same time was fundamentally wrong—wrong about things that one can't pin down, can't put one's finger on. Maybe Henry is like that. Totally right and fundamentally wrong. It could be that I am the opposite—wrong about everything and yet fundamentally right, right only if one avoids delving into what "right" actually means. Right by way of analogy, right by means of metaphor.

After another pass through some of the village streets, I decided it was time to return to the inn by the bridge. I was getting cold and hungry. When I was back in the pub, I feasted on a meal of hard cheese and dried figs. Tomorrow the food will run out. Three pathways are available to me. I will either have to leave Z. without reaching the castle hill, freeze to death, or starve.

The teacher's diary entry:

A man who calls himself a "landsurveyor" arrived in the village late in the evening some days ago and now is residing at the inn by the bridge. This surveyor claims that his assistants will arrive soon with his equipment. Needless to say, his arrival has caused a stir in the village among the peasants and others, including the village-council chairman, who has already summoned me to an emergency meeting, doubtless because of the pressure he is feeling from the castle gentlemen. The mechanisms for expelling the surveyor from the village immediately broke down. It is unclear why this is, but because of this failure the surveyor must be dealt with in a different way. The precise way, however, is not yet clear, at least it is not yet clear to me, and it is certainly not clear to the council chairmen. At the meeting, the chairman told me it could be that the arrival of the surveyor was the delayed result of an official process of summoning a landsurveyor that took place many years ago, a process he thought had been concluded with its loose ends tied up. It had been a strenuous—his word—ordeal. The chairman sent me to assess the situation with the surveyor and to report back to him with impressions. This is what I did. I found him, the surveyor, attempting to maneuver, making no real strides, primarily because he fails in all respects to understand the basic elements of life here. As I walked back to the council chairman's house that evening amid the heavy snowfall, I ran into Village Secretary Momus, seemingly in an abstracted or confused state of mind. When I asked him about the stranger, Momus bent down and whispered to me, "Teacher, this man who calls himself the surveyor carries on his body the mark of Cain." By the time I gathered myself to ask Momus what this meant, he had vanished into the snowy darkness.

FEBRUARY 3 (MORNING)

The mark of Cain—I think of the painter Josef Kostel, the main character in Horák's novel. At the end of the book, Kostel vanishes into the forest beyond the city of Prague. The reader looks on as he blends into the tangle of leaves and branches, becoming a specter, a shadow, a mist or vapor rising from the mossy ground. Dozens, hundreds of times, I revised those haunting final lines until they found a state of equilibrium—not perfection, never perfection, but balance, perhaps balance: *At first, we think we can follow his form as it weaves between the trees. Then not anymore. No longer. Nothing. Nothing exists but the traces of memory of a life that itself quite possibly never was, a body more water than earth, more air than fire.* I close my eyes and discover him again, this character through whom I saw the world for seventeen calamitous years. I see him coming through the woods and finding the stream under the mountain ridge. I see him follow it until he reaches an old wooden bridge. He crosses it and enters a village, transforming from Kostel to simply K. What does it matter if thirty years separate K.'s arrival and Kostel's vanishing? This is a flash into the future. K. has crossed the Acheron and arrived in the village of the dead.

Before writing this entry, I spent some time exploring other parts of the inn. There were rooms for guests, those for the chambermaids, the innkeeper's quarters. These spaces seemed more or less in proper order. The beds were made, the floors clear, clothes and linens neatly folded and stacked in drawers and closets. On a shelf in his room, the landlord had a bottle of plum brandy that was half-empty. I sniffed it, took a pull, and managed to swallow it. The attic, an airless space, had been made up for the chambermaids. Their trinkets cluttered the shelves and other surfaces—porcelain figurines, pieces of cheaply made jewelry, a ceramic water pitcher, a clumsily drawn picture of the castle hill. Lives abandoned. Spaces surrendered, given up, forgotten. I felt my breath pushing out into a place that had not felt the pulse of breath in a long time. I couldn't imagine what would come of this, my grave-digging. One should leave undisturbed, Horák told me once in a fit of drunken desperation, what has been buried in the past.

I made a significant discovery in the pantry next to the kitchen. There was a narrow staircase in the far corner that led steeply down into an underground storeroom. As I walked down the stairs, my beam of light fell on what seemed like an endless stock of canned foods—jar after jar of pickled cucumbers, mushrooms, carrots, red beets, and cabbage. There were canned fruits—blackberries, blueberries, plums, pears, apricots, raspberries, strawberries, and cherries. I hauled up as much as I could carry in one load. When I opened the first jar of carrots, I was struck by the powerful smells of vinegar and fermentation.

Whatever the nutritional value of the canned and pickled food is, it will be enough, if it doesn't kill me, to survive.

FEBRUARY 3 (NIGHT)

Searched in the morning for the road to the castle hill. Three paths seemed promising, but they either bent back down toward the village or meandered away into the wooded depths of the valley. It was a frustrating, ridiculous process. After giving up the search, I moved around some of the village houses, seeing if I could find ways inside. Most of these humble dwellings were still sealed tight—windows shuttered, doors locked—though occasionally the corrosion of metal or wood allowed me to press my body through. The interiors, like all else here, were spare, shut up in a certain way, seemingly concealing whatever it was that needed to be concealed, whatever it is that still needs to be concealed, revealing little or nothing, nothing that would begin to answer the primary question: What happened here? What force—if it was a force—destroyed this place, the human element of this place, and how could it be that life was snuffed out all at once and forever, as sudden and total as the flicking of a switch?

Since the teacher's note had mentioned the council chairman, I tried to locate his house and office, but though I came across various shingles for baker, shoemaker, metalsmith, carpenter, tanner, etc., there was none for the council chairman. Instead, I searched for the type of house that would have belonged to a villager of eminence, like the council chairman. Though this method was questionable (all the houses looked basically the same) it did lead me to one place with somewhat ornate brickwork above the door, including a small relief of a deer in profile, which was bending down toward a fox. I managed to push my way inside with considerable effort. To my surprise, there was no hallway or entryway. The door led directly from the street into what seemed to be a combination of a bedroom and an office. A small bed was placed with the headboard against the wall. There was a large cabinet across the room from the door. A tray stood by the bed, holding what seemed like various medical treatments and devices, including tubes and a hand pump for the administration of an enema. On the nightstand next to the bed, I found a short note: *Mizzi, it's time to burn the files.* I checked the cabinet. It was empty. I searched the rest of the house, which seemed much smaller on the inside than it had appeared from the street. The kitchen was narrow and cramped. A small sitting or living room contained, among other things, a wooden washtub. The one area that was relatively spacious was Mizzi's bedroom, which faced the back of the house and opened into a small walled garden. There was a sheet of paper on Mizzi's table. It contained only the word *landsurveyor* underlined in blue. I took it to add to my collection of documents.

I went back outside. It had started to snow, first gently, then more and more. I had found a wooden box of candles in the chairman's office, and when I returned to the pub in the inn by the bridge, I lit a few and placed them around the room. By this time, my whole body was shaking with cold, and it was unlikely that even the three layers of eiderdown could warm me up and keep me warm throughout the night. I decided I would have to risk making a fire in the stove. There might be a chimney fire that breaks out while I sleep, but for now, I am basking in the warmth as I write this, spooning globs of blueberry preserves into my mouth.

A village—canned for winter. I think back to the way here, the path, the lack of footprints in the snow. Doors that haven't been opened for decades, houses sitting idle for who knows how long without feeling breath, without heat, energy, light. History skimmed the surface, wiping away the village's people in a matter of days or even hours. How could the village have remained hidden—hidden in plain sight—only eighteen kilometers away from Špindlerův Mlýn?

The room is hot. I take a few pulls from the landlord's bottle of plum brandy and throw back the three layers of eiderdown. I set a stool at the bar and write this, now the lone remaining regular at a neighborhood pub, the one who has outlasted the others, the others who have somehow vanished into the night without saying goodbye. Without noise. Silent. Disappearing. For the first time since arriving here, I don't feel rushed. I know I need to slow down, to allow what is coming to me to come, that's it, to stop striving for a resolution.

While he was in Berlin, Keter wrote in his diary about a man named Isaac Mondschein. Keter had met him while staying in a boardinghouse on Auguststrasse in 1933 or 1934, before, that is, he moved to Prague. Mondschein, Keter writes, was from a town near Kyiv and had come to Berlin after the First World War. There was another guest in the boardinghouse named Avram Daud, a bookseller, who had traveled from the east with a sack of materials to sell in Paris and London. They were rare, priceless editions and original manuscripts. Daud befriended Mondschein and would read to him from a collection of mystical fragments that had been brought together and bound in Florence in the fifteenth century, eventually surfacing in Venice over one hundred years later among a small sect of Jews of Spanish descent who called themselves Rodrigans after their spiritual leader, the essayist Jacob Rodriga.

It seems muddled, but Keter is anything but muddled. He is crystal clear, as clear as air, but that is precisely the issue—it's so clear that what seems solid starts to break down, spaces and gaps emerge that you can see right through, resolution attenuates into a kind of diaphanous transparency—history as a fly's wing. One night in 1934, Keter wrote, passersby discovered Mondschein on the bank of the Landwehrkanal bleeding through his shirt. A stranger, a former field surgeon during the war, managed to bind up the wound with some cloth. They got Mondschein to a hospital, where the attending doctor sewed up the cut. By this time, Mondschein was out of his mind, delusional, paranoid. He was transferred to the psychiatric ward, the *Nervenklinik*, and placed under the authority of the Hereditary Health Court, which operated with a single mandate: to protect the German bloodline through forced sterilization of the mentally insane. Keter found Mondschein there and tried (unsuccessfully) to pull him back into reality. No success. Mondschein spent his nights standing on the room's desk chair and writing a long theological text on the ceiling. Keter couldn't tell whether the words came from Daud's recitations or whether they were Mondschein's own—or a blend of the two. In part, this was because the text was invisible during the daylight hours. But as night fell, the minuscule script began to glow with a pale blue-green luminescence until it was practically sprinkling down from above, as if Mondschein was caught in a fantastical, wondrous dream of his own composition, a dream spanning centuries, a dream in search of the essence of the divine. No record exists at the Nervenklinik for Isaac Mondschein, I've checked the archives a number of times. Keter claims in the diaries that the young man died of sepsis from a botched sterilization, but not before he'd finished his work, a text called *Das Buch der Mondschein*, what Keter calls, having somehow transcribed it (or, as he writes in the diaries, "captured it"), *The Book of Moonlight*.

It was through his lover Greta that Keter met Esther Bird. Greta was designing a graphic for *Freedom*'s masthead and brought Keter to the office when she presented her ideas to the editors, among them Esther. I feel like I have been chasing Esther Bird, in one way or another, for close to two decades now, a chase that started as a quest to retrieve Keter's translation of *The Book of Moonlight* and grew into a journey toward the very heart of existence. This is the journey that has brought me to the village of Z., that ends in Z., that seeks to find her, however unlikely, in Z.

FEBRUARY 4 (MORNING)

It wouldn't have developed as it did if I hadn't met Julia, though meeting Julia was one of the best things to happen to me. Despite that, and in retrospect, it is clear that meeting Julia was like ascending to the ridge in the mountains above Z.—the perfect moment, the most ethereal place—presaging the inevitable, disorienting, jarring descent. Julia had come to Prague in search of lost fragments written by Jacob Rodriga, pieces left out of *The Book of Moonlight*. I promised her I could find those fragments, a promise I knew already when uttering it would be impossible to keep. The fragments, taken together, formed what Julia called the Cain responsa, a set of writings, she claimed, that told a different story about the first human being punished for murder.

What do those months with Julia amount to now? Nothing. Or, rather, a great deal. It was Julia who established what could be called the northward line that ran from Venice to Prague, a route that wound its way through Merano and Vienna. The end of the route had to be, I told Julia on the night we met, in the cellar of the Strahov Monastery, below the rooms of its great library. That is where, I told her that night, I would find the fragments. I was sure about it, I said to her that night, I'd seen them, even if at the time I'd seen them I didn't know they existed. I assured her I could find my way back to the spot.

Julia believed in me—or, more accurately, she didn't believe in me, but wanted wholeheartedly to give over to the promise of the discovery of a lifetime. A lifetime! She was not yet twenty-five years old. She had found her way to Rodriga, and through Rodriga she accessed a whole counterhistory to the traditions of Western religion and philosophy, countertraditions that combined (for her) the sublime and erotic with transcendent truth, a truth not metaphysical but embodied— earthly, sensual, textural. When she left Prague—desperate, driven nearly mad (by me?)—she also left me. No surprise. Julia leaving me was as inevitable as Julia finding me had been. Years later, I received a document in the mail from her. The envelope contained a tear-out of an article she had published on the Cain responsa in the *Journal of Religious Studies*. A note written in blue ink with her tight, perfect script, thanked me for my "research assistance"—quotation marks in the original. That was many years ago. In response, I wrote two letters to her. In one, I told her about Horák, about the seemingly endless process of translating *Blue, Red, Gray*. I told her it was killing me, that in the process of finding the heart of the novel, I had utterly lost my way, lost the sense of anything I could call a destination. Aimless, rootless, I wrote, I was dissolving with the morning mist. In the second letter, I wrote to her that I regretted how it had been between us when she left, and that I wished I could have seen the bigger picture instead of just the walls closing in around me. I told her I should have gone with her. I wrote that I knew it was impossible for me to have gone with her, and that it was equally impossible she could have stayed in Prague with me. I wrote to her that if she had stayed, I could have found my way to believing more deeply, and with this belief I could have finally found what she had been looking for, palimpsests that led back to Abel's death, Cain's banishment—the beginning of a wandering that hasn't reached its end. I wrote that since she'd left, I had discovered pathways that led in various directions, that crisscrossed and came to dead ends, and trailed away, bending out of sight, beyond the imagination. I filled page after page with appeals, reproaches, self-reproaches, and expressions of longing and desire. I wrote I could still, a decade later, see every inch of her body, its gradations of color, its curves, could feel its smooth and rough patches, could inhale her scents, bringing her, if only in flickering outline, back to life, back to my small apartment in the center of Prague. But I couldn't send those letters, not because she couldn't receive them (though, I imagine, it would have been difficult for her to receive them) but because sending those letters would have thrown me back into dark, prisonlike chambers, hardly a candle for light.

I kept the letters in my apartment in Prague. I had them on the top of my desk, and they seemed to take up the whole desk, such that I couldn't place anything down next to them and had to leave the desk and leave the apartment to do my work. Soon, this leaving didn't matter. The thought of those words to Julia trailed me wherever I went, bursting to mind over and over like an unwelcome song. When I told this to Pepi, she said that the only way to rid myself of these ghosts would be to burn the letters. A couple of days later, I told Pepi I did burn them and that watching those haunted words go up in flames had been cathartic. But I couldn't bring myself to burn them, could never have burned them, even though plenty of times I had come close to them with a flaming match in hand. Burning them would have been burning me, and though there were times when I would have liked to ignite a self-immolation, especially during the last awful years of work with Horák, I knew I was stuck with those words—and with myself—for as long as I lived, a life among ghosts, a ghost story.

Julia appeared in Prague several months ago. She rang at my apartment around midnight. As she passed through the door, I noticed she was carrying a copy of the recently printed paperback edition of *Blue, Red, Gray*—the silver notification of the PEN award stamped on the cover. She was holding it between her forearm and bicep in the crook of her elbow. She saw that my eyes were drawn to the misty image of the Prague castle on the front, and said, as a way of greeting, "I thought the least you could do would be to sign a copy for me."

I managed an "of course," even though the statement unsettled me a great deal. The sight of Julia holding Horák's novel pressed firmly against her rich brown flesh provoked a jarring clash of opposite and antagonistic forces. If, somehow, Julia could be reconciled with Horák, it would signify a shift in the cosmology of my personal universe powerful or total enough to propel me on an endless yet irreversible trajectory toward the abyss. And now! Here I am in Z. Is Z. an abyss? Or is it, in fact, the antithesis of an abyss—a mountain that reaches upward toward the heavens, striving, climbing, pushing the limits of the imagination higher into the veiling mist, into the thin wisps of thought-clouds, those icy specks of certainty?

"What are you doing here?" I asked.

She looked around for a moment without answering, perhaps assessing what in the place had remained the same and what had changed during the many years since she had been there.

When she turned back to me, she said, "I'm back to finish the job."

"What job?"

"The responsa."

I was confused. Memories came to mind of those long hours in the cellar of the Strahov Monastery with nothing but a flashlight to guide me through the thicket of cobwebs and dust.

"That's not a job that can be finished."

"Maybe I'm inspired by your book. That was also a job that couldn't be finished. But I'm holding it right here. Pages bound by a cover, a cover signifying that the process is over. The straitjacket has been tied. Right, Sy? The unbound mind imprisoned by the constraining body."

"Those are different things. A book has a final sentence. A last word. A period at the end."

"And the Cain responsa?"

"A dream."

She laughed. "A dream. Good one, Sy. I'd say they are more like a seducer's chants, but if you insist on calling them a dream, well, then they're part of a shared dream that flows in two directions and transgresses the boundaries of sleep."

Julia's voice, sonorous and rich, seemed to have deepened over the years. It had a pleasant graininess that gave the English language a distinct quality, which I couldn't separate from either vertiginous abstraction or engulfing physical desire. In terms of appearance, while the bloom of youth had certainly been rubbed away, Julia seemed with the passage of time to have become increasingly herself—meaning even more captivating. Her cheeks, for example, had lost much of their smoothness and slight roundness, and were now sharper, more angular, creased and wrinkled on the forehead and around the eyes. Her hair— black, curly—was, as usual, snatched up from the neck and pinned on the top of her head with messy elegance.

She sat at my desk and ran her hand over the surface. She pulled open the top drawer and took out a pen. "An inscription, please," she demanded, holding the pen and the novel out to me.

It was hard to tell if she was being serious or playing games—and if it were game playing, it was unclear whether they were mocking games or a kind of foreplay. I was too tired at that point to do anything but follow along.

"Hand it over," I said and took the book and pen from her.

One banality crashed into another, mixing and jumbling into a useless mass of thoughts, or nonthoughts.

"This is my first time back in Prague since I left," she said.

"I'm surprised you would ever come back."

"It was nothing that bad, Sy, considering."

Considering what? I thought. I moved over to the desk and sat at the chair, which Julia had occupied moments before. Blankness. A blank page. Then another. Then the page that held the dedication: *For Ida Fields.* My translator's dedication. To Ida—to my memory of a lost affair. To my stubborn dedication to an enduring delusion. Julia turned back from the window and saw me paused over those words, saw my finger reach out and trace them. Silence filled the apartment. My hand felt frozen. The image of Ida Fields, appearing suddenly and fully—receding just as suddenly and totally—cut a scar into the space. It could be that Julia tensed up in anger, in resentment, with the memory of pain endured long ago—endured and conquered and sent back out into the world as a strike of lightning; what were the Cain responsa but a strike of lightning? I turned the page back to a blank one. I tried to focus. Then a glimmer of that buried past came to me. I uncapped the pen and wrote: *The crows assert that a single crow could destroy the heavens . . .*

This was it. Julia would understand it perfectly, meaning she would understand it as I did, meaning she would sense or intuit meaning—and in that way have total understanding—while at the same time, she would understand nothing, absolutely nothing, as I understand nothing. I stopped after writing this line. I knew if I added anything else, I would negate it—this understanding, this nonunderstanding—and yet I couldn't help myself. I wrote below it: *Love, Sy.*

I stared down at the inscription for a few moments, allowing the ink to dry. Then I closed the book, taking note that it was in pristine condition, that Julia hadn't read a page. It seemed strange that she would have come to me without having read it, especially with the book in hand. Had it been me, I would have already devoured it cover to cover. My fingers caressed the paper—as soft as skin, I thought, a beautiful body, and yet it was a testament to the utter destruction of my youth, leaving behind a life in ruins. With nowhere to go. It would have been fitting and dramatically satisfying if it were at this moment that the idea to find the village of Z. had come to me, if I had at that very moment left for Z. That's not the case, not with Julia there. No clear idea could have come to me with Julia there.

She reached out and took the book from my hand, whispering a thank-you I could barely hear. She sat down in the armchair beneath the standing lamp and read what I had written. I was sure she would get up and break for the door, but instead, after some moments of silence, she asked if she could have a drink. I poured her some whiskey and then took some for myself. I sat down opposite her on the edge of the bed. Julia grasped one of her black curls and twisted it around her finger, a gesture, combined with her downcast gaze, that indicated a search for elusive words, difficult words.

"The figure of Jacob Rodriga has come under attack," she said, "under suspicion."

"What do you mean?"

"His existence."

"How is that possible?"

"An Israeli scholar, Naphtali, claims to have unraveled a complex fraud. Calls Rodriga a phantom, says I made him up. He's out to destroy me. The University of Rome has opened an investigation. There's a panel of seven international scholars. They're combing through my book."

"Do you think," I asked, "that Naphtali is a hit man?"

"I'm not sure if he's working alone or at the request of others. Probably the latter. In any case, I need a place to hide out and make a plan. I had no choice but to come here. I have to find my way back to those sources, Sy, those palimpsests that you found deep in the Strahov's cellar."

I wanted to tell her there was no way back there, as there really is no way back anywhere, but I couldn't bring myself to do it. I felt myself on the borderline between a grandiose deception and a higher truth—stilled there, immobilized by a mix of confusion and desire. My second affair with Julia began, in other words, under the shadow of pending doom.

FEBRUARY 4 (NIGHT)

The heavy snow that fell all day today prevented me from getting to the castle. I had a large meal of pickled fruits and vegetables and set off into the village. I had a basic choice to make. Either I could stay in the inn by the bridge and haul firewood from the school's shed, or I could move to the school and haul food from the inn. Noting to myself how the move from the inn to the school might have precipitated K.'s decline, I opted for the opposite course, even though it meant carrying heavier loads. I discovered a wooden pushcart set on runners against a wall in one of the side alleys. I managed with great effort to dig it out from the layers of ice and snow and was amazed it could still move without immediately falling apart. I made my way to the school's garden and filled the cart with wood, then slowly pushed it through the streets to the inn—an exhausting exercise, but one that guaranteed heat for at least a couple of days.

I went out again and found my way to the second—and much larger—inn in the village, a square construction with an inner courtyard and a sizable stable for horses. The front door was unlocked. I went inside, followed a long corridor until it ended in the taproom. Unlike the inn by the bridge, where order reigned, the space here was in disarray. Dirty beer glasses and plates were bunched on the top of large wooden barrels. Filth, which had probably been tracked in from the horse stalls, was dried on the floor in long streaks. Disgusting. There was a door behind the bar. I tried the handle, but it was locked. I removed a small peg that plugged a peephole and gazed through it. Inside the room, I saw a plain desk with an armchair behind it.

I turned back to the taproom and surveyed the scene. On the side of the room was a small table, which looked out of place among the barrels. A single chair was pushed in—and under the table and chair was a scattering of salt and caraway seeds. This, I thought, must be the setting for the Momus interrogation.

Keter, according to his notebooks, had met Momus in the mid-1930s in Prague. By that time, Momus, Keter wrote, must have been in his mid–late forties, still a relatively young man with a powerful build. As far as Keter knew, according to the notebooks, Momus was the only survivor of the village of Z. When Keter met him, he lived in a large run-down apartment below the Prague castle in Malá Strana, as if his former position of village secretary of a castle official required that he set up again in close proximity to noble or regal dwellings, even though he had absolutely no connection to anything noble or regal in Prague, and, as far as Keter could tell, didn't even have a job. Momus claimed to Keter that he had left Z. with a trunk filled with the count's treasures, nothing exorbitant to be sure, but more than enough for him to acquire his spacious flat in the capital and to indulge his God-given calling: idleness. On the other hand, Momus wasn't dulled by his lack of work. This acuity was evident in their conversation in Malá Strana, Keter wrote, and came into full view in the report that Keter managed to convince Momus to allow him to copy. It was Momus's report of the arrival of a stranger to the village, a man who claimed to be a landsurveyor. Needless to say, the Momus report goes far beyond this single act of arrival of a stranger to a village one evening, a stranger who crossed a wooden bridge that led from the road to the village and who found a place to sleep in the pub of a nearby inn.

REPORT ON THE ARRIVAL OF THE STRANGER K. [UNOFFICIAL]
VILLAGE SECRETARY MOMUS
FEBRUARY 1, 1922

As many of the gentlemen of the count's authority know, a stranger arrived in the village some days ago. My attempt to interrogate the stranger for the official report failed. This failure was the result of the refusal of the stranger, known in the village as either K. or the landsurveyor, to cooperate in answering my questions. Nonetheless, the failed interrogation brought crucial information to light and revealed, along with this information, a certain perspective on village life and its relationship to castle authority. The rather sudden shift in perspective has provoked me to pen this unofficial report, in addition to (or instead of) an official one, even though I know such an unofficial report is prohibited by the castle's rules and traditions, and that it will certainly mean a demotion from the high position of village secretary to a perhaps lowly role above in the castle, if not a complete expulsion from castle service to the status of peasant—or worse. Such is life. Made from dust, gentlemen, to dusk shall we return.

As I said, the arrival of the stranger K. caused a shift in perspective on the relationship between the castle and the village. This shift was my starting point, which unfolded over the following days into a deeper inquiry. What's contained here is a study of the beginning of the end of castle power, an autopsy report delivered, in a sense, to a dying man. That the death of the castle system means the death of the village must be obvious even to you—and it is nothing to lament. Laughter might be the most appropriate response, though a laughter shaded with a certain gray spirit, or an anxious feeling that what is happening here is not only happening here, though having never left here—this village, I mean—it is impossible for me to say how far it spreads. It could be that when you, gentlemen of the castle, read this report, you will immediately have two thoughts. The first thought will be that you should burn this report so none in the village could ever read it—that after you burn it, you should find, capture, and kill its author, me, Momus. You'll discover I am long gone. The second thought, which will come to you quickly, following directly behind the bloodlust, is that this report has merely stitched together a story you already know—a story that has been told to you in thousands of fragments but never all at once. Thus, you know the story and you don't know it—and whether this failure to know it is your fault, as I suspect it is, or whether the story remained until now fundamentally ungraspable for you, well, I'll leave it for you to ponder. You will ponder this most irrelevant of questions even as the storm clouds gather and darken above your heads.

ON THE HISTORY OF Z.

As gentlemen of the castle, you are supposed to know something. Just writing this last sentence has caused me to shake with laughter—and indeed, you see I have smudged ink all over the page. It was once considered self-evident that the foundation of a gentleman's knowledge of the world rested on the bedrock of history. The castle authority—and this might come as a surprise to you, gentlemen—rose out of history, and it is this force, history, which you might experience as a steady wind swirling around you and the castle structure. It is this force, both material and immaterial, that propels the present time into the future. Long ago, gentlemen, the last of you lost connection—if you ever had it—with this energy. As a collective, you know nothing about the past, and as a result you are blind to the present. Allow me to try to pry your eyelids open a little bit to restore your sight. Just be aware, gentlemen, that even if you gain the ability to tell light from shadow, you will only draw the wrong conclusions from what you (think you) see. Everything will shock you, and you will lurch from one notion to the next—to the next—to the next—a hurricane of uncertainty ripping apart all stable ground. Poor gentlemen, how you will come to wish you had spent much less time horsing around in the stables!

I'll give you two versions of the founding of the village of Z. I would ask you to draw conclusions from each, but I'm reasonably certain you would draw the wrong ones. Perfect.

I'll leave you with those false conclusions. It could be that one of these totally wrong conclusions contains something right, something correct, and it would be amusing to me to watch you try to pluck this grain of truth from the sand. I'm not waiting around to see it. Just think: one of you has the correct idea, but you'll never figure out who knows it and what it is. This is the state of things, I'm afraid, among the gentlemen of Z.

The first version of the history of Z. begins deep in the past with the campaigns of Prince Teutonberg. Teutonberg was using the broader conflict, the war between Catholics and dissenters, to expand his domain. He had made gains in all directions, brutally punishing those who resisted and those who refused to accept what he considered to be the true faith and the traditions of Rome. His eastern flank was divided into four spears—two to the southeast led by his fiercest vassal, Lord Falkenheim. The two armies to the northeast fell under the command of Tugendhaber. Under Tugendhaber were the lesser vassals, the counts von Dornfeld and Westwest. It was Westwest who led his army into the Giant Mountains.

Count Westwest was unlike the other noblemen. He possessed none of Teutonberg's thirst for blood. He had little of Tugendhaber's crusading zeal. He had no interest in von Dornfeld's study of military strategy. Westwest was a man of letters, educated at the monastery school at Hügel-am-Fluss on his family's estate. When the war came, Westwest had no choice but to serve in one of Teutonberg's campaigns. It was his duty, bound as he was by his family's pledge of loyalty, a pledge made and renewed by generations of Teutonbergs and Westwests. When the time came, Westwest led the northeastern force to secure the mountain highlands and the valleys that lay between them. As a reward for this service (in addition, of course, to the continued protection offered by Teutonberg), Westwest would receive a stake in the conquered territory, thus extending his family's domain. Teutonberg had different plans. He knew, as everyone did, that young Count Westwest, unlike his recently deceased father, was no warrior, and that the campaign into the Giant Mountains was the toughest of the four, that the mountain folk were strong and stubborn, able to pick their spots, put up a determined fight, and vanish into the trees at a moment's notice. In other words, if Westwest and his army were cut down in the valley—the most likely scenario—the pledge with his vassal would be broken and Teutonberg could absorb the rich Westwest lands without provoking resistance among the other lords.

These were typical machinations, gentlemen, perfectly obvious to everyone involved. Westwest might not have been studied in the art of war, but he was far from a stupid man. He sensed that Teutonberg was setting him up for annihilation, that if he were to somehow survive, Teutonberg himself was prepared to finish the job. Westwest was familiar with the many stories of gruesome punishments meted out by Teutonberg on the slightest or flimsiest pretext. Westwest sent out two scouts in advance of his campaign. They made it to the first mountain ridge without trouble and then descended into the valley below. Here, the two men ran into some small groups of forest dwellers, who spoke an incomprehensible language. Despite their troubles to communicate with the scouts, the forest people were kind, inviting the scouts to join their camp, to eat their meat, to share their rock-hard wafers of bread. These were pagans, a people beyond the reach of time. The scouts reported back to Westwest: the valley beyond the mountains belongs to nobody, the landscape pure—a kind of barbaric Eden, outside, even, the gaze of God.

Westwest gathered his men. He told them about the campaign, the territory the scouts had discovered, about the evil intentions of Teutonberg to wipe out the entire Westwest family. The men pledged to support him against the lord and listened to Westwest's plan. He would lead his men into the valley between the mountains. He would negotiate a peace with the forest dwellers. The forest dwellers would allow him to build a fortress to repel future attacks. Westwest would promise to protect the valley from the coming storm, and they, the forest dwellers, would leave his people in peace. When the situation was stable, Westwest would send for the women and children. He would give up his estates in the west, settling permanently in the valley.

Two events happened not long after Westwest left his land with his men. The first was that Teutonberg, with his typical impatience and lust for conquest, wasted no time in seizing his vassal's estate, partitioning off corners and slivers to propitiate his other warriors. The women and children of the Westwest domain either ran for the monasteries and cloisters or they were divided up among Teutonberg's people, becoming domestic servants, stable boys, and common laborers. The second event, catastrophic for the stability of the region, was the advance of a peasants' army, a kind of ragged beast or swarm, a swarm of various grievances—land, taxation, justice—that when in motion contained an incredible energy. And this mass of energy hurled itself into the Teutonberg lands—including those that used to belong to Westwest—while Teutonberg was preoccupied with the eastern campaigns. There is a peasant chronicle of this short-lived campaign that cut its way into the Elbe valley and then vanished from the face of the earth. We have this chronicle in the castle archives, though most of you have no idea there is an archive at the castle. The anonymous chronicler savors the scene of the peasant fighters overtaking the largest, strongest, and most heavily fortified Teutonberg castle. The masses battered through the wooden and metal doors. They cut down Teutonberg's guard and seized hold of the lord himself. Teutonberg, the very symbol of the peasants' oppression, was marched out of the fortress to the nearest town. Word was spread a day's ride in all directions—and on the Sunday that followed, as if the execution were itself a religious act, a large crowd witnessed the axe fall on Teutonberg's neck. His severed head was stuck on a pike, left to rot and to be picked apart by birds. Such is a tyrant's end.

Of the fall of the house of Teutonberg, Count Westwest knew nothing. Though the peace with the forest dwellers had come quickly, the early and heavy snow, which covered the valley for at least eight months each year, had prevented the count from sending his scouts back for the women and children. Instead, the count spent his days roaming the forest, climbing (to the best of his ability and strength) the slopes of the mountains, in search of the ideal spot to build a castle.

Westwest narrowed down the options to three or four places. He had to wait until the snow melted to determine if the ground underneath could support a castle. The winter dragged on—days of heat punctuated with inexplicably heavy snowfalls and bitterly cold temperatures. Finally, in what might have been late summer, the last snow melted from the hills and Westwest could survey the grounds. His first choice was it—a strip of flat land on a hill above the valley, nestled between two mountains looming behind it, shielding it with high faces of rock. His men set to work at once, hewing stone and cutting logs. Westwest gave the gold and silver he had brought with him to pay the forest dwellers for their help. Among Westwest's men was one who had studied the building arts in Italy—and he, Pleicht, supervised the making of the blocks, the laying of the castle's foundation, and the erection of its walls. In the process of harvesting the timber, a certain amount of land was cleared in the valley. This land was sown with grain. It was in this way, little by little, summer after short summer, that the castle of Count Westwest was built on the hill above the valley.

Of course, stupid as you gentlemen are, lacking all imagination, as if the very capacity for imagination has been removed from your heads as a precondition for castle service, you cannot possibly fathom how such an original situation could evolve into the world you inhabit today, some three centuries later. Could time transform this valley—this earth—so fundamentally? Time has force, its own steady power. After a number of years, for example, the valley would be cleared of trees. Wheat was planted. Grain was stored in silos for the winter and for the lean years. Iron was mined and molded into tools, cattle brought from beyond the mountains, houses built, languages and cultures blended, children born with mixed lineages—part noble, part forest—a half-pagan, half-Christian Eden.

Everything seemed in perfect order until the sound of cannon fire ripped through the crisp mountain air one day, a day long distant from the time Count Westwest and his men laid the first foundation stone for a castle on the hill. It was three or four generations later—and the slow creep of history now came surging down the slope toward the valley like an avalanche. Or it seemed it would. Or the new Count Westwest imagined it would, or he wanted to imagine it would. It was this idea—this imagining—of the avalanche that set the stage for the reinvention of the valley.

This is a complex and baffling moment in the history of Z. The count and his men decided on an official language for Z., purging the language of what came to be called "forest adulterations." Unlike before, the count would now have total authority, in order, it was said, to prepare the valley for the inevitable attack from beyond the mountains. Labor needed organizing to reduce redundancies and to increase efficiency. A militia had to be formed and trained. Food production needed to be more rational, jobs distributed to cover the basic necessities of a people at war.

The attack never came. This didn't matter, because a future attack always remained possible, and even when the idea of an impending attack faded, the reality remained—the absolute authority of the count and the erosion of the status of the forest dwellers, until there were no longer any forest dwellers. They had turned into peasants.

I'll stop here and move into the second version of the founding of Z. If you, gentlemen, knew anything about the history of this region, you would know that around the same time as Teutonberg's campaigns, which were part of the bigger war between the Catholics and the dissenters, movements of people arose that sought to escape the brutality of this society and to create among themselves something purer. You are probably scratching your heads, gentlemen, because the word "pure" has no meaning for you, has never passed between your lips. Purity—it means the absence of imperfection, adulteration, or contamination. To exist in its God-given state, though I'm well aware you have lost connection to that higher power. In any case, one particular group of such seekers of purity came from the town of Breslau. Some of them were farmers, growing wheat for the market, vegetables and fruits for home consumption, processing animal milks, raising livestock for eggs and meat. Others were artisans—tanners, cobblers, stonecutters, masons, wheelwrights, and so on. Even a teacher from the church school was among them. The leader of this group from Breslau was a young man named Schwarzer, whose father had built the first printing press in town using the Gutenberg technique. The vast amount of work that came to him required that he train his son at a young age. Young Schwarzer, barely ten, began reading and typesetting books for sixteen hours each day.

It would have been easy enough for young Schwarzer to be swept into the movements for religious reform, to cling to one of those thinkers who was intent on reimagining a person's relationship with God. Around him, throughout town, such ideas were ripping apart neighbors and families—creating rifts between brothers, mothers and daughters, fathers and sons.

It could be that over time Schwarzer, too, would have been forced to choose between his father's Church and the radical dissenters, whose propulsive language he was coming to love. Schwarzer's father, as a good Catholic, was already feeling tremendous pressure to shut his press to radical literature, facing threats of ruination and excommunication from the bishop. Had it not been for the sympathies of the local lord, the elder Schwarzer's shop would have been burned to the ground.

One day, while his father was away on a trip to Nuremburg, young Schwarzer (now in his late teens or early twenties) began setting a collection of essays written in Latin by a Dutch writer named Jacob Rodriga. The Dutchman—rumored to be a Jew—claimed to have served as a navigator on two voyages to the New World. The essays were full of his impressions, mostly of the landscapes and peoples he encountered across the ocean. One essay, in particular, caught Schwarzer's eye. It was called "In the Hidden Valley." The essay was about events from his second voyage. Some members of the ship's crew, Rodriga among them, had cut their way into the interior of one of the islands, hoping to discover tradable goods to bring back home, at the very least to survey the land for future ventures, like a spice or sugar plantation. The island terrain was mountainous. Despite hardships and dense undergrowth, the men made it over the ridge and into the valley below. Here, in the valley, which, as far as Rodriga could tell, the natives called the Valley of God, the men discovered something extraordinary. The valley contained a whole other world—a village cut into the dense tropical forest. The people there greeted the men warmly, invited them to eat—fruit, nuts, a kind of hard bread made of types of grain Rodriga had never tasted before.

The sailors were interested in one thing: how could they profit from the discovery of this village in the valley? The men tried to ask about treasure—silver, gold, gems of any sort. Who was the king here, who was the prince? Who was the man who spoke with God? No method of communication, even the expert drawings in the dirt by one of the sailors, could convey the basic point, the point being: which people here were more important than the others?

Darkness was falling. The forest dwellers invited the sailors to stay the night, showing them to various beds made of some sort of stitched plant fiber. The next morning, the forest dwellers held an elaborate ceremony, which Rodriga describes in detail—the body painting, the costumes, the complex choreography of the individual and communal movements, the play of fire, which spread from torch to torch, pit to pit, as the masses of men and women swirled and twisted around them. The beauty of the ceremony left a deep impression on Rodriga, foremost the ecstasy, the joy, with which the forest people brought it to life. This was passion. This was love. And beneath it all, Rodriga sensed its animating spirit: absolute equality of every being, from the weakest to the strongest, from the oldest to the youngest, man and woman—in each spirit, the spirit of God, in each person, the whole community.

The sailors spent two more nights in the village. They witnessed how the people worked with this same communal joy—whether foraging for food, weaving fabrics, tending small gardens, or making clay vessels. Such was the people's love for each other that beyond a mother nursing her baby, it was impossible to tell how the families were constructed, or if the people even knew the concept of *family* at all. This social anarchy disturbed many of Rodriga's shipmates. They couldn't fathom how a society, so constituted, could function. What about jealousy, greed, and ambition? These, they thought, were basic human characteristics. And what about neighboring peoples— the peoples on the coast, for example, or in the next valley, or beyond? They would surely attack at some point—as they must have attacked in the past. How could this peaceful, joyous society repel the intrusions? The sailors tried to pose these questions, but the people did not understand them, and as far as Jacob Rodriga could tell, it was not language that prevented it but the absence in their minds of the foundational concepts: power, wealth, property, hierarchy, and war. Instead, the people *in-dwelt*, as Rodriga wrote, *with the spirit of Atah*, their primary god—a spirit that existed in everything from the tiniest seed to the looming mountains above. Where Atah dwelled—which was everywhere—was holy, thus all was holy, everything part of Atah's realm and design and blessing.

Schwarzer loved this essay. Its portrait of human nature and the possibilities of communal living awoke in him a desire for a better life, better than the dreary realities of Breslau, which was always being threatened by forces beyond one's control. While his father was away in Nuremburg, Schwarzer set this essay and printed one hundred copies. He began to distribute them. After some months, a small group of enthusiasts had formed, calling themselves Rodrigans after the essay's author, Jacob Rodriga. One member of the group translated the essay from Latin to German, and after Schwarzer set this in print, Rodriga's word spread even faster.

When the group around Schwarzer reached a certain size, local opposition to it started to grow. It was dawn of a warm spring day when Schwarzer led the Rodrigans out of the city toward the southwest, heading in the direction of the Giant Mountains. They were in search of a valley where they could create for themselves a society that saw the spirit of God in everything from the smallest seed to the highest mountain, a valley hidden in some lost fold of earth where the chance to start over was real, the chance to imagine and create a new way of life. Even you, gentlemen, might be able to imagine how the Breslau Rodrigans felt when they ascended those peaks, crossed the ridge, and descended into this very valley—a valley that had somehow escaped the human eye, the human hand.

Though now the village is known by a new name, or known, rather, by an initial and a period (Z.), it is thought that the original name given by that first group of Rodrigans was *Ziel* (destination). The valley was this destination, goal, or end point, just as heaven is thought to be the ultimate destination, the goal of a righteous life—a concept you might be dimly aware of, aware of, that is, if anything were left here of the grace of God. Fools! How foolish are you to think that this moral abyss, this swamp, his barn of rutting hogs, could last forever? Who knows what will happen to you when this village is no more, when the world of the castle has been swept away? When the fire and brimstone start to fall on your heads, just think of Momus. Imagine my mouth agape and my face alive with joy—joy at your well-earned demise.

The founding of Z.: The people—men and women alike—work to clear the trees. They mine stone from the mountains. They build houses, pave narrow streets, found a school, and plant fields.

We need to take one step further into the future. It is now generations after the founding of Z. Rodrigan society has flourished in the valley. There is just one problem, gentlemen. Village scouts have reported that the villages in a neighboring valley have come under the control of a certain count. The count has organized the men into an army. He has equipped them with new weapons. The villagers in Z. know that defending their valley from an attack will be impossible. A meeting is called to discuss the situation. The people of Z. vote to have one of their own, a man named Westwest, plan and build a castle on the hill above the village.

ON CASTLE AUTHORITY

You are free to decide, gentlemen, whether the castle created the village of Z. or whether the village of Z. created the castle. I can imagine your reaction to this proposition, and I take great pleasure in the confusion it must generate in each of you. You are scratching your heads, no doubt, asking why you have wasted your time reading the pages of this report. It is irrelevant to you, you think, what the correct order is—village/castle or castle/village. You do not care one way or the other, and you don't see why it would matter. You are charged with fulfilling a function. You have not been raised to think about fundamental things.

It is curious, still, that in the fulfillment of your functions, you have gleaned no real sense of the whole of castle power. I say "real" sense, because it would be impossible for you not to have any sense, though in this case the sense you have is completely wrong. Perhaps when you read the name Schwarzer, you thought of our young Schwarzer, the young man who wastes his days at the schoolhouse "assisting" Miss Gisa. Or you might have thought of this young man's father, the substeward Schwarzer, that humorless, vile man who surrounds himself with piles of documents such that none of you has seen his face. You might have gone to this Schwarzer at the castle, he might have received you, shouted at you from behind the stacks of paper, asked you what you wanted there. You might have told him. Invariably, it is something he cannot fulfill. He reprimands you for disturbing him in his important work. Then you leave. The next one of you enters and replays the scene. But what does any of this matter? Neither of these Schwarzers is connected with the original Schwarzer, though they are, of course, connected—connected by a kind of tradition that has lost all knowledge of itself. Our work, indeed, gentlemen, is a tradition that has lost all knowledge of itself.

Control—control over the connection between the valley and the outside world, this is the fundamental element of the castle system. The original system once it came into its mature form (remember I am basing this account on speculation and rumor) had three main tiers. There were the high castle officials, meaning those who served the count directly and were involved in making key decisions for the realm. Next, there were the diplomatic officials, those officials sent by the count to negotiate the economic relationship between the valley and the surrounding territories. These officials, the diplomatic officials, were usually the most talented, sharper and better educated than the high officials. As you can imagine, these confident young men were often at odds with the older, weaker high officials of the count—and thus I present to you one of the structural fissures in the castle system. And when there is a fissure, there are people poised to exploit it. The third group was made up of the liaison officials who moved between the castle and the village, the village secretaries. These secretaries were the lowest of the three tiers, poorly educated and tasked with keeping order in the village. This was not a job merely of enforcement of castle commands and rules, in fact, though you have no clue about this now, your predecessors were engaged in a highly sophisticated (so sophisticated they were unaware of it) campaign to build a culture, to set patterns of interaction, to produce customs, norms, taboos, etc.—in short, to shape the rhythm of daily life such that the village could, with minimal guidance, operate on its own while still being in accordance with the will of the castle.

I'll take each group in order, the high officials first. They served, as I said, the count directly. As time passed, it became their goal to shield the count from responsibility. The count became a figure no longer of any specific authority but of pure power. Because of this, the count's name would never be attached to any specific communication, to any idea—rather the count was invoked as the beacon of order, harmony, and meaning—the very center of power itself. This required the opposite to also be true: if the count was power, order, sense, tradition, etc., the absence of the count was chaos, disorder, meaninglessness, void. Over time, life in the village became synonymous with the life of the count, even if nobody in the village had ever seen the count, had ever heard the count's voice, had met a single person who had him or herself seen or heard the count, including the village secretaries.

You, gentlemen, might think you know Count Westwest. You have probably convinced yourselves you have seen him, maybe that you have spoken with him directly. You have not. Nobody has. This is primarily because it has been at least half a century since a Count Westwest resided in the castle. How could it be, you ask, that the castle and the village could survive without a count? I ask you to ponder the reverse: How could the village have ever had a count in the first place? If the count has left long ago, to whom, then, do the high officials report? Allow me to shock you once again, gentlemen: there are no high officials! The last of the high officials, a man named Klamm, is said to have left the castle years ago and vanished into the forest. Or perhaps he was killed. Since many of you think you serve under Klamm, this fact will surely surprise and unsettle you. Many of you have seen Klamm—have raised beer glasses with Klamm. I myself am officially a secretary of this same Klamm, and I can tell you that there isn't just one Klamm but many, dozens of Klamms, hundreds of Klamms, a Klamm for each and every villager's imagination. The image of Klamm, as the high official for village affairs, matters even more than the image of the count.

Despite your ignorance, gentlemen, you know a world exists beyond this valley. When you read this, I will be in this world. You have heard the names of the great cities: Paris, London, Rome, Jerusalem. In these places, you will find our officials and perhaps our count. They might have never stepped foot in the village. Imagine for a moment one official, who had a grandfather who had been a high official of Count Westwest. This grandson, now an elderly man, has a house in Paris and receives his annual salary from the count's domain. Or it could be that even this isn't true, that it's made up by those wily diplomatic officials to slander those on high so that they can, in the meantime, pack away as much of the valley's wealth as possible before castle and village alike fall into ruin.

I'll turn to them now. This is the most important group, the diplomatic officials who are charged with establishing and maintaining connections between the valley and the outside world. In the early years, this meant primarily managing the timber trade, selling logs from the valley to those who could pay in silver and gold. Important here is the figure of Sordini. He was an Italian man working for a foreign count. In his negotiations with Z.'s diplomatic officials, Sordini realized he was dealing with unsophisticated men. He convinced one specific diplomatic official, a man named Blau, to bring him to the valley so he could discuss arrangements directly with the high officials—and in this way could forge a more productive bond between Westwest and his master.

There are two theories about Sordini that I've encountered in the archival record. The first is that he organized the diplomatic officials to purge the high officials, and then arranged the village secretaries, your ancestors, to purge the entire diplomatic corps. At the end of this bloody mess, as Sordini was getting ready to remake property relationships in the village—he had already summoned a landsurveyor from abroad—he was murdered by a faction of villagers, the Brunswick faction, which itself was vying for power. The second theory about Sordini is that he, in fact, encouraged the rise of the Brunswick faction in order to quell rising dissent among the villagers, dissent led by the master cobbler and his daughter Amalia. Sordini realized that the power of the castle would always be far less than the collective power of the village and that to control it in perpetuity, the village would need to be divided, the powerful interests there (on all sides) allied with castle officials. The most important element was to make it seem as if the villagers were acting purely in their own interest without any connection to the castle. In any case, whatever version you believe, Sordini is long dead. The central question about the diplomatic officials is this: do the diplomatic officials exist or don't they? Is there an heir to Sordini? Is the wealth that the village generates—if it is, in fact, generating wealth—staying in the village or flowing abroad?

I am a village secretary, a village secretary of the powerful high official Klamm. As a village secretary, I can write with confidence about my peers, with whom, however, I share very little in common. Let's start with the most basic. What is the purpose of a village secretary? It is, of course, to represent the interests of the castle in the village and to represent the interests of the village at the castle. But how do the village secretaries determine "castle interests" and "village interests"? Already, we have hit an irresolvable snag. Or perhaps it's better to say (or suggest?) that the answer is both impossible and self-evident: the village secretaries are aware of castle interests without any direction whatsoever. How? Castle interests are unchanging: the castle is interested in protecting the power of the castle system. And how does a village secretary determine how to do this? It is automatic—the villagers themselves lead the way and the castle's village secretaries only need to be present to support them. Not that this support is deliberate. Most of the time, the village secretaries are completely unaware of supporting anything. They (we) arrive at the Gentlemen's Inn. We go to the taproom and drink beer. We eat. We have sexual relations with the villagers. We have meetings with petitioning parties from the village about various matters. To each request or question, we respond that the answer will come from the high officials at the castle, though we know these high officials will give no answer. Eventually—and how this process works remains a mystery to us—the petitions work their way to the council chairman, head of the village council, who will preside over an official decision in the name of Klamm.

To conclude this section, what we find here is a hall of mirrors, gentlemen, reflections and reflections of reflections, shadows of shadows. And the villagers, well, they are convinced, as you are, by the movement of reflections and shadows, mistaking these beings for people of flesh and blood. Funny enough, these reflections and shadows are not of any specific castle authority. No. Each villager casts a reflection, creates a shadow. Each villager creates the illusion, which he or she obeys.

THE ARRIVAL OF THE STRANGER

As most of you know by now, a stranger arrived in the village some days ago. The typical methods of dealing with such an arrival took place. Though many of you blame the landlord of the Bridge Inn for not getting rid of the stranger immediately, this is a mistake. He acted appropriately. It is incorrect to expel a man at night into the forest, especially under such conditions of cold and fog. Castle protocol is clear on the matter. As such, Schwarzer, son of the substeward, should have left the man alone. This was the first error. If he had been left to sleep, in the morning he would have been gently taken from the village and put back on the road. Still, despite Schwarzer's unfortunate assertion of himself into the scene, the order remained basically correct. The man arrived. The landlord provided him with lodging. He was asked for the papers (though at the wrong time), which would prove he had permission to reside in the domain of Westwest. The fatal mistake, my friends, was the phone call. Most of you know nothing about the nature of telephone systems—and I myself used to know very little about them before I was assigned to conduct this investigation. It is said that one of the diplomatic officials, in awe of a telephone system in a neighboring village, arranged for one to be installed here, primarily to connect certain points in the village with corresponding castle officials in charge, theoretically, of handling daily affairs. In addition, this particular diplomatic official believed the lines would connect castle offices with other castle offices, allowing for the fastest and most rational flow of information through the castle authority. Eventually, so the vision went, a call could be rerouted higher and higher until it reached the count's residence, even if, as you know from this report, the count had not lived in the castle for many years. If we accept the premise that the high officials were also gone and that the diplomatic officials were by definition mostly away from the valley—at times for years—and that village secretaries are often in the village (at the very least half of the time), you start to see what a tangled mess a phone call would cause when, finding no answer, it is forced to change directions dozens of times before it can locate a hand to lift a receiver and a voice to say hello.

It is possible that Schwarzer's call about the landsurveyor caused great commotion at the castle—that is, if anyone was there to receive it. But someone did pick up, right? Was this in the castle itself? Was it in the area just outside the castle's walls? Or was it in the heart of the village? A stir was created, at the very least in the pub where Schwarzer agitated the villagers by waking up the surveyor. This was bothersome, as even you can imagine, but it was not decisive. What, really, did it matter that this man, this stranger, had come? And what did it matter that Schwarzer, a total fool, had made an ill-considered phone call? On the one hand, it didn't matter a bit. On the other hand, it mattered a lot. If Schwarzer had said to the person who answered the phone at the castle (or elsewhere) that a stranger had crossed the bridge and arrived in the village and wanted to spend the night at the Bridge Inn, the response would have been an obvious yes. One night—and in the morning the stranger would either have to be granted permission to stay or he would have to carry on. But Schwarzer didn't say this. Instead, gentlemen, he told the person on the phone, a Mr. Fritz, that a man had arrived "who claims to be a landsurveyor summoned by the count." It is beyond hilarious to think about how Mr. Fritz would have reacted to hearing this from Schwarzer. Panic, riotous panic must have washed over him. In his many years of service, he has not made a single independent judgment—like all of us—and now he is being asked to verify a decision made directly by the count, a man he has never seen, never heard. Fritz's reaction was to reject everything: no surveyor!

Stop for a second. It is the nature of our phone system that communication flows not only from the initiating point, point A (in this case the Bridge Inn) to point B (the place in the castle (or elsewhere) where Mr. Fritz was located) but that it also splits off and can be received at any other point. In this particular case, because the call had searched so long for a connection, many people picked up the phone at the same time as Mr. Fritz, but unlike Mr. Fritz, they were afraid to speak. Nonetheless, these many people overheard the conversation between Mr. Fritz and Schwarzer about the landsurveyor. Could it be that Sordini himself heard that the landsurveyor he had summoned long ago had finally arrived? Stupid men— Sordini was long dead, if he ever existed in the first place. This is the most mysterious moment, gentlemen, it is truly hard to explain, even for me. It seems as if someone who had overheard the conversation between Mr. Fritz and Schwarzer called Mr. Fritz directly after he had hung up the phone and instructed Mr. Fritz to call Schwarzer back and to tell him to accept the surveyor into castle service. Mr. Fritz did as he was told, and then, following procedure, recorded the matter in a file and sent this file to the office of the high official for village affairs, Klamm, which meant that I, Momus, was assigned to accept this file, conduct a thorough investigation of the matter, interrogate the stranger, and issue a report to be read and submitted into the official record by Klamm himself.

That the case fell to me, Momus, was lucky only for me, because it provided me with the opportunity to gaze into the near future—that is, to perceive the cloud of doom that now hovers over our valley. Upon receiving my instructions, I went directly to see the chairman of the village council. The council chairman told me about his meeting with the surveyor, a meeting that had greatly weakened him, an already sick old man. In fact, the chairman is not that old, but the stress of being the connecting point between the castle and the village for so long had aged him well beyond his years. You can see his wife, Mizzi, though the same age as the chairman, is still a young woman, while he is already a feeble old man, bedridden with gout. In any case, the chairman might be weak and infirm, but he had a clever idea. The idea was to dig up from his records and display to the stranger a paper with the word "landsurveyor" underlined in blue. This was his defense, but unfortunately, the paper could not be found, despite Mizzi's assistance. The stranger, for his part, shook a letter, purportedly from Klamm, in the chairman's face, though in truth it was a letter that could have been written that day or deep in the past by Klamm or someone else, someone without the knowledge of Klamm's existence. In short, gentlemen, everything was unclear, muddled, confused—but in this muddle, danger was lurking. The chairman, sensing the danger but not understanding it (I also didn't understand it yet) resolved on one thing: he had to divert the stranger away from the job of landsurveyor, even if it seemed like this position was recognized by the castle and by Klamm. At stake, as the chairman saw it, was the inflaming anew of the Brunswick faction and, potentially, its chief opposition, the cobbler and his daughter Amalia.

Illiterate man—the council chairman—illiterate men, all of you! You and he can read words. Fine. You can trace letters one after the next—forming sentence after sentence. This "reading" will yield for you a basic understanding such that you could even repeat the words aloud. But, my fools, this reading achieves nothing. It would be better not to read the words when you read the words in ways directly opposed to their true meaning. Yes, if you were not so stupid, you, too, would be able to read in the opposite direction—right to left, so to speak, instead of left to right. Let me tell you this: if you invert your gaze, read right to left, read inside those mere shells of words (those brittle husks) and toward meaning, then you'll start to see what I, Momus, see. You would see that nothing matters, not Klamm, not the letter, not the paper with the word "landsurveyor" underlined in blue, not Sordini, not the Brunswick faction, not Schwarzer or Mr. Fritz or the landlord or even the count. And certainly not the castle on the hill.

THE STRUGGLE AGAINST THE INTERROGATION

I sat across from the stranger, the landsurveyor, K. I asked him if he would submit to the interrogation. He refused. In truth, though I pretended otherwise, I didn't care. For one, I knew the interrogation was a sham. Second, I already knew, based on my preliminary investigation, that K. would not submit to the interrogation—that he would resist attempts to "control him," at least when it came to the mechanisms of what he deemed to be a tyrannical officialdom. I would have wrapped it up immediately if it weren't for the looming threat of Klamm's censure, however illusory (even the illusion of Klamm's censure was powerful), and the pressure being applied by the council chairman, pressure exacerbated by his precarious state of health.

Will you, in short order, be called to final judgment? No. There is no final judgment for you, just an ordinary, mundane destruction of your life. A force is coming that will clear this valley and scatter you beyond the mountains, where you will live out your ugly, pathetic lives until your miserable deaths. That's one possibility. The other is more sudden—a thunderbolt, so to speak, a strike of fire.

Let me back up. Jacob Rodriga, in his book of essays, had another piece called "The Mark of Cain." I know, gentlemen, I have already tested and far exceeded your ability to focus on a single thing for more than a minute or two. Such is the training we receive as the servants of the castle. That I, Momus, have soared above you in intellect and ability is due to my internal capacity and not, as you might imagine, to my proximity to Klamm. There was no proximity. In any case, I'll quickly summarize Rodriga's essay on Cain. I discovered the essay not long ago while searching through the castle archives, thinking already of writing a report about a pending doom that was still invisible to me but felt as a sensation, a sudden and momentary chill on the skin. We know that in the village snow can fall even on the hottest of summer days.

Rodriga wrote that a certain work of seemingly great antiquity had come into his possession. The work had been given to him by an old man named Avram Daud, who claimed to have brought it (along with a case of other documents) from Spain. The documents originated, said Daud, in a Jewish principality or *taifa* called Eden, which had been located in a valley of the Ebro River. Eden had been invaded and destroyed in the thirteenth century, but the case of documents had survived—first through the efforts of the mystic Hiob Halevi. They eventually ended up in a Jesuit library in Madrid.

This is how Rodriga tells it: There was a man named Cain. Cain was the first son of Adam and Eve. He had a brother named Abel. As the brothers grew older, it was clear that Cain was the stronger one. And because he was the stronger one, Adam assigned him to work in the fields, while Abel would tend to the flocks. The earth was rocky, hard, and dry. Rain fell unevenly throughout the year—a desert for months, days of deluge would wipe away the topsoil. Year after year, Cain worked this ground, growing wheat for the family. He cleared away the rocks. He dug trenches that would drain the fields quickly when the floodwaters came. He built a stone cistern that would hold water when there was no rain and a well so deep that he could draw from it over the entire year, even after months of cloudless skies. The work was exhausting, backbreaking. It taught Cain that every variable mattered when it came to the success or failure of a crop. He had to be aware, to plan, to anticipate—to anticipate the very circumstances he feared the most. It took years to increase his yields, but eventually Cain's crop became abundant. He built a silo to store the surplus grain.

One day, Adam and Eve came to their children. "Cain and Abel," they said, "it is time you made offerings to the Lord." The brothers knew the importance of this moment, the chance for them to directly honor the Lord for the first time. Abel went out to his flock and selected his choicest beast—young and fat—for the sacrifice. Cain walked his fields until he came upon stalks that were the strongest, healthiest, tallest of the lot. He drew his blade and cut them down. He tied them into a bundle and hauled them over to the altar, where his parents had made their offerings every week for as long as he could remember. As the older brother, Cain came forward first. He placed the cut stalks on the altar and set them on fire. He fell to his knees as the smoke swirled around him. Tears came to his eyes, and Cain trembled with love for the Lord, his God. As the fire died down, Cain let out a piercing wail—it was a call to be heard in the heavens, a call for God to open up the heavenly gates and to gaze down directly at His creation, a call for God to honor His creation with His gaze as His creation worshipped Him.

Abel approached as Cain drew back from the altar. The lamb, tender and plump, was bound by the legs and still. Abel placed it down on the altar and drew out the blade he had carved from bone. He opened up the lamb and spilled its blood—giving the blood back to the Lord. After the blood was drained, Abel positioned the body of the animal on top of a bunch of dried olive branches. He lit the branches, and, like Cain before him, he dropped to his knees to honor the Lord. Unlike Cain, however, Abel remained silent, and the fire grew and consumed the offering.

God had heard Cain's wail. Some say it woke Him up from slumber. Others say He was luxuriating in Eden when He heard the noise and was greatly disturbed by the clamor. Who could be bold enough, God wondered, to call out to Him in such a violent manner? As the Lord gazed on the altar and saw Cain's offering, He was shocked. Had He, the Lord, not cursed this very ground as punishment for Adam and Eve's transgression—their eating of the fruit from the tree of the knowledge of good and evil? And yet, here was Cain, their oldest son, reaping a bounteous, beautiful harvest.

Furious, God rushed to the house of Adam and Eve and called out to the family. When they were gathered there, He spoke to them. "Cain and Abel, brothers, sons of Adam and Eve, you have made your first sacrifices to your Lord. Abel's offering has pleased the Lord greatly. He selected the choicest lamb from his flock. The smoke from the burnt offering reached heaven, pleasing God and His angels. Cain, your offering has displeased the Lord. You gave nothing but a bundle of useless stalks. The smoke from your offering vanished in the wind and did not reach heaven."

Adam and Eve were terrified. Cain, their firstborn, had lost favor in the eyes of God. They went to Cain, pleaded with him to make another offering, perhaps by taking a beast from Abel's flock. They spent days discussing the ways Cain's offering might have been inferior to Abel's, the way Cain acted at the sacrificial altar and how it might have angered God. Despite this counsel, Cain was unmoved. He had made a proper offering to the Lord, he said, and had taken the best of his harvest. He had called out to the Lord with love—and the Lord had responded, incomprehensibly, in anger. It was the Lord, Cain said, and not he, who was at fault. He, Cain, would make no second offering to God.

One day, Cain was out in the field and lay down to rest. He fell asleep and a dream came to him. In the dream, he spoke to Abel, though he could not hear his words. They were out in the field, away from the house. Above them, a bird of prey was circling, and Cain looked on as it described wide arcs across the cloudless sky. When he looked down again, he saw that his hands were covered with blood. It was lamb's blood, he thought, and looked around him for the body of the beast. But there was no beast. Instead, Abel's blood poured into the ground beneath him, and Abel lay there lifeless, his neck cut with a blade of bone. Cain fell to his knees and grasped his brother's body. He put his fingers to Abel's neck in hopes of staunching the flow of blood, which was being soaked up by the dry, thirsty ground. Abel was dead. Cain wailed, louder and louder until the noise and his shaking ripped him from the deepest regions of sleep. When he woke, there was the body of his brother—lifeless, drained of blood.

How could this be? Cain thought. Could he, Cain, have done this to his brother with his own hands? He loved Abel. He had protected him, taking the most arduous labor upon his own shoulders. It was his charge, and this charge filled Cain with pride and passion. With passion he harvested and winnowed the grain, with pride he milled the grain into flour, which his mother mixed with lard from Abel's flock to make the hard cakes the family ate throughout the year. As tears streaked down his face, Cain considered his brother. Abel was a being as light as air, as soft as cloud—and it seemed that if one looked hard enough, one's gaze could pass right through him, obliterating Abel's physical form, leaving behind only his spirit, a spirit that rose like vapor from the ground, that dissipated like mist—a spirit that could pass into another body and shake the other soul it touched, making this other soul somehow more vibrant, alive, better. Never had Cain so much as lifted a hand against his brother. Never had his brow furrowed in anger at something Abel had done. Cain wept over his brother's lifeless body. Cain searched the deepest regions of his soul, trying to discover what it could have been that might have caused him to lift the blade against Abel. He found nothing. His heart was devoid of hate. Cain found there only a purifying love.

At that moment, as the love of Abel pulsed from his core, Cain knew that the dream he had dreamed had not been his. Or it was his, but it was a false dream, a kind of confused vision planted in his mind from beyond. While he slept and dreamt of murder, someone else had killed his brother. Just as he had this thought, Cain heard a noise behind him. He turned and saw a storm approaching. The Lord emerged out of the swirling wind and spoke to Cain. "Where is your brother Abel? His blood screams out to me from the ground." Cain was frightened and remained silent. The Lord spoke again, "Since you have spilled your brother's blood on this ground, this ground will be cursed to you. You will wander the earth ceaselessly. You will find no place to plant roots. You will have no home."

"Allow me, first, to bury my brother's body," Cain said, "and to mourn his loss with my mother and father." As Cain spoke, he took a step toward Abel's body, but found himself suddenly cut off by a wall of fire, which stretched from horizon to horizon. Cain spoke again, "My Lord, I have done nothing wrong. I did not kill my brother. I am falsely accused. And now, You wish to banish me, to condemn me to wander from place to place without rest. You know that wherever I shall go, I will be hated. At the first place I arrive as a stranger, I will be killed."

God thrust his arm from the storm cloud. Cain turned away in fear, and God's finger struck him on the back of his neck and burned a mark. The Lord spoke, "All will know when they see this mark that it is the mark of God. The people will hate you, but they will not dare to kill you, for they know that if they do, they will invite my wrath and they will be destroyed."

Cain turned away from the wall of fire, away from his fields, away from his house and his parents. As he left his homeland, he thought about whom it could have been, if not he, who killed his brother. Was his failure to protect Abel—that innocent, pure, vaporous one—equal in guilt to having thrust the blade of bone? He thought of his father, now a weak old man, a man full of regret and delusion. He constantly talked of the Garden of Eden, the forbidden fruit, and especially about the expulsion— unable, after all of these years, to reconcile with its loss. No, Cain thought, despite his flaws, Adam was a peaceful man. And his mother? Eve was the stronger of the two. She had led the rebellion against the Lord and had eaten first of the forbidden fruit. She had befriended the serpent—but she, too, was good, kind, and peace loving. She would never have lifted her hand in hate against her son. That left only one possibility—the murder of Abel had been committed by an angry, jealous, vindictive being—the Lord. But why would the Lord, the source of all creation, strike down his brother and place the blame on him? Was it, Cain thought, to sever him from his family—to cut the branches from the trunk of the tree? Was it to divide humanity in order to more easily rule over His domain?

Thoughts of the past came to Cain as he made his way across the wide, barren expanse. The Lord had tried to prevent his parents from attaining knowledge. He failed. But in failing, He had cut them off from immortality. He had banished Adam and Eve from Eden, the land of plenty, hardening the ground for his father beyond it so that the ground yielded little in return for his backbreaking labor. He had afflicted his mother with pain in childbirth and with a position of subservience to his father, despite her superior character. He had made the serpent their enemy, created hostility between nature and humankind. And now this—murder! And now this—deception! At this moment, Cain knew his fate. He would be, forever, the enemy of the Lord. "I must reach beyond the Lord," Cain told himself, "into the pure spirit of life, the same spirit that gave breath to Abel, that coursed through the veins of my mother Eve as she ate of the forbidden fruit." Then he cried aloud for the world to hear, "The Lord is a tyrant, and I, Cain, am His foe."

Cain wandered for many years until he came to a city called Enosh. It was the first city on earth. Not long after Cain arrived, the city was afflicted with strife. The rulers blamed the stranger Cain, and he was forced to leave and continue his restless, ceaseless wandering. After leaving Enosh, he came to the city of Irad. Again, soon after Cain arrived, the city was afflicted with strife. The rulers blamed Cain, and he was forced to carry on. Time and again this was repeated—in Mehujael, in Methusael, in Lamech, in Jabul and Jubal. Finally, Cain came to the city of Tubal. At once, as in the other cities, the people's eyes were opened and they saw, as if by miracle, the force that was oppressing them. This force was not as they would have expected it to be. It was a force emanating from them, existing within them, a desire—a desire to be dominated, to submit, to be ruled, to be subordinated. While it remained unconscious, even half-concealed, this desire was experienced as comfort, as a kind of love. Once the desire entered the people's consciousness, nakedly exposed, it became intolerable, and the people sought to destroy its object, to seize power, to remake their city and themselves. The chief of Tubal knew that the source of the people's enlightenment was the stranger Cain—the stranger who carried the mark of God on the back of his neck. The chief, ignoring the mark, attempted to have Cain killed—and the Lord, in His fury, wiped Tubal from the face of the earth.

CONCLUSION

Because of the general degree of stupidity among you, gentlemen, you will be unable to draw lessons from Rodriga's work, and, truth be told, those lessons remain obscure even to a superior man like myself. They are as ungraspable as clouds. Or, I should say, these lessons would have remained veiled in the kind of heavy mist that often fills our valley if I hadn't seen with my very eyes what none here in the village could see—the faded, now almost imperceptible mark on the back of the stranger's neck. Yes, I saw it. I saw it as the landsurveyor refused to submit to my interrogation and turned to leave. It was the mark of Cain.

When he left, I sat back in my chair and sunk into thought. I had a pretzel in front of me and pulled it apart while in a daze, not caring about the salt and caraway seeds that scattered over my papers, the papers that would eventually come to hold this report. I took a long drink from my beer. K.—*Kain*. Kain has crossed the bridge and arrived in the village, I whispered to myself, and whether he knows it or not, doom follows closely behind him. This is the basic fact, the proximity of doom, and in all likelihood, gentlemen, K.—*Kain* has known and forgotten this basic fact countless times over these thousands of years of wandering. I tell you this, gentlemen, not to try to preserve village life and most certainly not to protect the castle. I, Momus, am telling you this so that when the fires blaze, when the time has come, you can pause for a moment and know it is meant to be this way. It has always been meant to be this way, even before Kain arrived here. It takes talent to escape one's fate. I'm sorry to tell you that, unlike me, you do not have this talent. Please, then, take this final chance to allow a total understanding to wash over you. Let it sink in. Explore the depths of its certainty, its combination of complexity and utter simplicity. When you find the center of this understanding, pause there, linger, fall silent and listen carefully. Do you hear it? Do you hear the noise coming from a mysterious place beyond these borders? This, gentlemen, is the sound of the end.

Farewell, gentlemen.
Village Secretary Momus

FEBRUARY 5 (MORNING)
It was late evening when K. arrived. The village lay deep in snow. Nothing could be seen of the castle hill; fog and darkness surrounded it. Not even the faintest light indicated the existence of a large castle.

I eat an entire jar of preserved strawberries, savoring, despite a nauseous feeling, the mild taste of fermentation.

FEBRUARY 5 (NIGHT)
I found a carriage road that left the village and, I had assumed, continued until the castle. As far as I could see, given the course of the stream and the nature of the rocky face of the hill below the castle, the road was the only approach from this side of the valley. It might be possible to come at the castle from the other side, but this would require a long arc of many miles.

The road, however, did not lead back over the stream, as it should have, but instead cut its first leg in the direction of the ridge opposite the castle hill. I can imagine that this has to do with the course of the stream and where it has been bridged for a second time, but I can't confirm this. I made it around the first bend in the road, which already seemed to be in total wilderness, but no farther. The snow was deep, the steps precarious. Had the snow been more stable, maybe I would have tried to continue. After falling to my waist for the second time and struggling to dislodge my body from the chasm this created, I gave up and turned back. This is a very bad development. I need to get to the castle. If Momus's report is proof of the existence of something like the Cain responsa, this means the other Cain documents might also be here, meaning that the whole of *The Book of Moonlight* has been deposited, collected, stored, archived—whatever word one wants to choose—at the castle, which means, finally, that the castle is the heart of a great textual universe, which is to say that this place—now unreachable—houses what I have been painstakingly trying to discover for decades: the core of a tradition of radical otherness, a tradition that challenges tradition, a tradition of rupture, disruption, and revolt against the thousands upon thousands of mechanisms that have attempted to restrain these counterstories with the straitjacket of an intolerably limited meaning. What will happen when this "meaning" breaks free into the freedom of meaninglessness? What will emerge in this chaos? There will be truth. Yes, meaning is untruth. Meaninglessness is true, but only at its core, only its essence, because on the border of meaninglessness is a lie. I am tired. I need sleep.

Yesterday, toward evening, I returned to the schoolhouse. I searched the teacher's desk and discovered a notebook. I stayed up late into the night reading it. It contains a detailed record of the teacher's observations of other villagers, including (and especially) his assistant, Miss Gisa.

Pages full of Miss Gisa, cataloguing everything about her—the cut of her long skirts, the styling of her thick, blond hair, the buttoning (and unbuttoning) of the blouses that seemed to choke her neck, her austere, sharp movements, the pain she inflicted on the students with her favorite tool of punishment, the ruler, the way she stroked the plump schoolhouse cat. Besides the lavish attention paid to Gisa, the teacher has pages on Schwarzer; on Brunswick and his wife; on Barnabas and his parents and his sisters Olga and Amalia; on Lasemann; Gerstäcker; the council chairman; the landlord of the inn by the bridge and his wife, Gardena; on the landlady of the gentlemen's inn; Frieda; Pepi; and so on. A curious document—full of useless detail, overflowing with spite, pulsing with anger, hate, and envy. Even the schoolchildren are not spared. To the contrary, they get the worst of it. Stupid. Ignorant. Foolish. Little animals. The insults rain down from the teacher's pen in tight, flawless letters.

Included in this informant's notebook is a lecture on the castle structure. The following indication is at the top of page: "To Be Repeated Each Year":

> Students, as you know, you have the honor of living in
> the territory of Count Westwest. Though you might

never see the count, know he is watching over you and is aware of everything you do, even what you think. It is said that the count knows what you dream about, that he has methods of seeing into your mind as you sleep. The count's total knowledge of his subjects enables him to rule his territory with enlightened perfection. He does this through his officials, who work to carry out his plan. Each official in the count's system, from the lowest secretary to the highest steward, has a precise function and carries out his function flawlessly, like a well-oiled gear of a clock, never missing a tick, neither behind nor ahead but in perfect rhythm with the world. That you do not perceive the functioning of this mechanism says nothing about its perfection. It indicates only your very lowly station as a village child. No villager can see the whole of the village at one time. Only the count can do this by looking down from his window in the castle turret. From there, he can see all things, the whole domain, the relationship between one entity and another, including the distance—from your perspective infinite—between himself and you. What is unfathomable to you is within reach to him. What is incomprehensible to you is simple to him. It is your fate as children of the village to unburden yourselves by giving up questions about the count or the castle structure you will never be able to answer. Instead, immerse yourselves in love for the count. Look out at the castle above you as you look upon your father and mother—here merged into a single, venerable body of stone. This body is the form of absolute authority. Embrace it with unconditional love, as it embraces you.

FEBRUARY 6 (NIGHT)

"What now?" Julia asked as we lay in the darkness, naked, expired.

I could tell by her tone that, freed of desire, she was in a pensive, melancholy mood. I turned to her. Her black hair was tangled around her head. The brown skin of her shoulder pushed out from the white sheet. I had recently returned to Prague from a semester of teaching in the US. The course, Introduction to Literature, hadn't gone well. The dean's final letter to me, which arrived in Prague a week or two after I did, was a tirade of abuse—the words "you failed" littering the page, as if their very repetition would pound the point deeper into my brain. Failed to provide . . . failed to assign . . . failed to respond . . . failed to attend . . . failed to submit . . . A tedious document. Pointless.

"What now?" I repeated her question. "The only possible thing. I'll find the Cain responsa."

This pleased her. She rolled over and pushed her head against my side. "And after that? What about life? Your future? Will you do another translation?"

"It's impossible for me to translate anything again."

"That can't be true. Isn't this what you learned from Dr. Hruška at the clinic—how to start again, how to break free of Horák, to escape his book?"

I wanted to tell her that I didn't go to the clinic for those reasons and hadn't learned anything like them there. There were no reasons for going to the clinic. I went to the clinic because I went there, or, rather, I went there because it was the only place I could go. I went there because my past twenty years were there, Daniel Cohen was there, Milena was there, Dr. Hruška was there, and the Keter diaries were there. A vortex had been forming around me, and I could either have been swallowed up by it or go to the clinic. I went to the clinic. This was an end point, which is why the moment I got there I needed to find my way out. But I didn't find my way out. I was incapable of finding a way out. Milena found the way out and I followed. But this following wasn't easy. It took everything I had. I had to pour my entire existence into this following. How dare the dean focus on procedures and protocols and processes and performance after this escape? How could a man like the dean hope to understand that when I stood at the podium to give those lectures I was fighting for my survival?

I didn't say any of this to Julia, though I suspect she knew it. She knew me, after all, and I think she knew me well. I hoped she did. And if she didn't know me in some deep way, all of this—Rodriga, *The Book of Moonlight*, the Cain responsa—didn't matter.

"I went to the clinic," I finally managed to say, "to remember—to remember in order to forget."

"What's left after remembering and forgetting, Sy?"

"Nothing," I said. "Nothing is left. But it's a light nothingness—a nothingness that's weightless and bright. But it's still nothing."

"There's never nothing," Julia said and kicked her leg out of the blanket in search of some cool air.

"You're right," I said, reaching my hand out for her, "the state of nothingness can't last. Things pour in from all directions. Then, before you realize it, you're back to where you started."

FEBRUARY 7 (MORNING)

It was still dark when I woke up. It was many hours before daybreak, but since I have no tool for measuring time, I have no way of knowing how early it was. When I woke up—suddenly and with a fright—the idea to return to the other inn came to me and I couldn't shake it. The feeling I'd had when I was there the other day had been similar, it occurred to me, to the feeling I'd had while on my way to the clinic Zelená Hora. I had arrived in the town in the valley below the clinic late in the evening and had to find lodging there for a night, since it was clinic policy to receive new guests only between eight and ten in the morning. The place I found was called the Hotel Koruna, likely constructed around the same time as the other inn in the village of Z. There was a neglected nobility to each place, also a dissipated, tawdry quality, not to mention the presence of filth—not messiness, but deeply ingrained dirtiness. Disgusting places—though they were somehow able to overcome this disgustingness through a kind of will, a will to project importance, to be themselves, to be centers of power. The Koruna certainly didn't disappoint in that regard. From evening until late into the night, the pub was jammed with people of all types, from people whose look bordered on homelessness to the local elite wearing a kind of pompous attire long out of fashion in Prague, Berlin, or elsewhere in the civilized world. To my surprise, this elite, after two or three beers, was much worse behaved than the others. They cracked racist "jokes" about Romani, Arabs, Jews, and others. They subjected the female waitresses and patrons to gross sexual harassment—verbal and physical. I'd found a spot above the fray, so to speak, on a high stool at the bar.

The bartender that night called herself Mara, a small, pale woman of indeterminate age, though I'd guess in the range from twenty-five to forty. She wore an ugly white blouse with sequins on the sleeves and down the pleats in front and a silly, juvenile lace collar. It seemed like the kind of garment an eight-year-old village girl would wear to a local Easter party. Her skirt was no better—nothing more than a formless gathering of gray cloth embroidered with hideous golden thread in the pattern of a faux-medieval crest. When I asked if the crest had any significance, she told me, to my surprise, that it did. It was the crest of the family Sternberg, the dynasty that had built the castle on the hill called Zelená Hora, naming it the Grünburg am Grünberg because of the coat of ivy that covered its walls. With various additions and subtractions, this was the structure that now houses the psychotherapeutic clinic run by Dr. L. Hruška. When I told her that I was on my way to the clinic in the morning, she paused in her endless task of washing out dirty beer glasses and told me that many people on the clinic's staff come to the pub for food and drink. Often, she said, so many clinic people are at the inn that the inn itself feels like part of the clinic. It wasn't an exaggeration, she said, to say the pub and the inn couldn't exist without the clinic—and, of course, the clinic depended in various ways (I was an example) on the inn. Nonetheless, she said, the relationship between the clinic and the inn was an unpleasant aspect of her job because of the awful behavior of the doctor and his "followers."

"Even the doctor comes here?"

"Quite often," Mara said. "He was here tonight, not long ago. You've only just missed him. His assistant, Králová, was with him."

"You mean Dr. Hruška?"

"Who else? There is no other doctor here."

I drank my beer slowly, watching Mara turn and twist and struggle her way through the room with half a dozen glasses of beer to deliver—through that sea of arms and hands and fingers, which seemed to wrap around her, catch her, and then break apart time and time again. It didn't help, I thought, that the tables were arranged close together.

"If Dr. Hruška comes in so often, you must know him well," I said when Mara was back behind the bar with a fresh load of glasses to clean.

"Yes, I know him quite well," Mara said with a slight twist or pucker in her expression. After a pause, she added, "I'd say I know him better than most. Or knew him. Now, he barely looks at me. He just orders his beer and then rushes over to the little room behind that door where he smokes his Virginia cigar."

I was too exhausted to think through the implications of what Mara was saying. The past months were trailing behind me in a cloud of murky haze. At some point during this time, I'd finished the translation of Jan Horák's *Blue, Red, Gray* after seventeen years of work on it. I'd sent the finished manuscript to New York, to the editor Carl Glaser. That moment of placing it into the cardboard box, taping it up, packing it into another shipping box, pasting on the address, bringing it to the post office, sending it away—away from me, away from Prague. And after this? What else? What came after that moment? This was the issue. The issue, more precisely, was what led to the absurd scene in which a man resembling my brother Henry came through the door of my small apartment in the center of Prague and ripped me from my life (or my death). Real life slipping into phantasmagoria—or a train to Zelená Hora. And between the real and the fantastical—terror. And beauty. Terror and beauty—the poles of literary breakdown.

It was dark, silent as I walked through the village of Z. on my way to the other inn. New snow had fallen in the night. The footprints I'd made during the previous days had been filled in. The village again appeared untouched, uninhabited. This was where the gentlemen from the castle stayed while they were here—the gentlemen's inn, the center of castle power in the village. The center of castle power! It was nonsense to use such a phrase many decades after the fall of the count's authority and the ruination of the village. I gazed into the darkness. The castle was out there on the hill. The castle was set above the village on the castle hill. On clear days, the castle came into view. There was nothing grandiose about this castle, and the very use of the term "castle" to describe it reduces language to an absurdity. It was, in fact, no more than a miserable assemblage of sorry stone structures, far humbler, if I could trust my vision, than even the village itself. There was a tower at the center of the cluster of structures, but even this tower had little in common with the lofty spires and elegant, proud turrets of other noble or godly places. This tower was a monotonous round building, notable only for its high terrace, which seemed to be crumbling away. I couldn't shake the feeling that there was something crazy—totally mad—about this castle, about this round, squat, ugly tower. In this respect, the gentlemen's inn was a more imposing piece of architecture. It had high stone walls, large windows, a wide inner courtyard with an arched mezzanine, and stables for the horses. Inside, the place was a maze of corridors, countless rooms of all sizes, a taproom, a kitchen, maids' and landlord's quarters, larders, and who knows what else. I pointed my flashlight in the direction of castle hill, words encircling me: *the longer he looked, the less he recognized, and the deeper everything sank into twilight.*

As I made my way to the taproom I felt Momus's presence around me and could almost hear the young man's voice resound through the empty space—"In the name of Klamm!" *In the name of Klamm*—a ridiculous declaration. Yet, it contained a threat, or an ominous warning. A desperation that contradicted nearly everything in his report. In the pub, I found Momus's interrogation table. I sit at the table now as I write this, every now and then looking at the door across the way, the door behind the bar, the door to Klamm, the door to Dr. Hruška, the door to a theater of delusion.

In this theater, there's a scene at Sladkovsky's bar in Prague. I am there with the writer Daniel Cohen, whom I knew in Berlin and met later at the clinic Zelená Hora when we were both guests—patients—at the same time. I'm the first to admit a blurring of lines between myself and Cohen. How could it be otherwise? Our whole relationship had been based on such a blurring, beginning as it did with our drinking together of a cloudy yellow liquid one night in the basement of a Grunewaldstrasse apartment building, an act, however poorly thought through or juvenile, that pushed both of us beyond the borders of ourselves.

I've brought him back the manuscript Milena had stolen from him. I've taken it out of my bag, and I've slid it across the table to him. He takes it, pages through it, discovers the text written over his text, the novel-in-the-novel, Milena's marginalia. By the time he's done with his cursory review, Cohen isn't looking good. His face is pale. He runs his hands over his cheeks, through his hair. It's clear he's lost, doesn't know what to do, it's clear the marginalia have not only covered up his text, but they have also trapped him, framed him, obliterated him, they have muted his voice, erased his authorial presence. Or only partly. Or they have just injured him, wounded him.

When he's done, Cohen puts down the manuscript and pushes the pages to the middle of the table. I can't tell if he is offering them to me or just moving them away from his body, as if he can't physically tolerate their proximity. It is a complicated moment. I'd tracked Milena to Venice, to the Hotel des Bains, and had retrieved the stolen manuscript from her. I'd brought it back to Cohen, fully intact, despite the marginalia. I had expected he would be ecstatic, euphoric—grateful. Instead, he is distracted and morose.

"What's the matter?" I ask him. He doesn't respond, keeps staring past me across the bar. I continue. "How long have you been out of the clinic?" He doesn't say anything, takes a drink from his beer.

I start to feel a rising anxiety. His look, his mannerisms, his silence, his reaction to the manuscript—I wonder if Cohen has lost his mind. At the clinic, it seemed like nothing was wrong with him. He was too healthy to be there, a tourist among us. Or a writer on retreat in the clinic's library to work on his next novel, a novel now sitting on a table between us, belonging to neither him nor me, a novel called *Guests at the Hotel des Bains.*

Eventually, Cohen starts to talk—and when he does, words rush forth with unstoppable force. I go to the bar (in the gentlemen's inn) and find a bottle of schnapps to see me through this entry. It's a walnut brandy or something like that. I take a few shots. They steady me against the unbearable cold. I can barely hold my hand still—but here goes:

He had a vision while still at the clinic, Cohen tells me. In the vision, a large column of stone rose from the ground in front of him. There was a kind of terrifying joy, Cohen says, in watching this column grow higher and higher, driven upward seemingly only by the force of its own internal energy. At first, Cohen says, he was alone. In all directions, the landscape faded away into a murky twilight. It was both there and not there—or there in pale outline, itself coming in and out of view, dissolving and solidifying. There he was, alone, taking in the sublime pleasure of experiencing this awesome pillar rising suddenly and forcefully from the ground. It was as if the inner force of the earth, Cohen tells me, was thrusting it high into the air, proud, erect, strong. Cohen stood there awestruck as the rough stone slowly began to gain a smoothness, a polish, as if by miracle the ordinary stone had transformed into a rose-hued marble. He reached out and touched the pillar. It was radiating an inner heat, a remnant, perhaps, of its metamorphic process. As if I'd surmounted some invisible boundary, he tells me, when I touched the pillar, I felt something like total love. Or maybe, he says, it was something else. The neighbor of love: envy. The neighbor of love: lust. I felt it move through me—into every part of my body. Filling me with a kind of wild ecstasy, an ecstasy coupled with dread, like the friction between love and envy, love and lust. I fell to my knees and pressed my chest against the marble. The heat coming from the pillar intensified until it started to burn my skin. It hurt, the pain increased, was unbearable. At the same time, the pleasure increased in equal or greater proportion. It felt good—good and painful—and I couldn't bring myself to let go, to pull away, and yet I knew if I didn't, I would burn to death. Finally, a woman came. It was Milena. She grabbed me by my shoulders and pried me loose. I fell to the ground, writhing, screaming, my skin feeling like it was on fire. She told it was over now, that I was fine. Nothing was wrong with me. In that moment, the pain faded. I touched my skin; it was back to normal—there were no traces of the fire. The pillar, too, had gone cold. I touched it again and it was as cold as ice. I noticed that around us others had gathered. I knew some of them, but some were strangers. I have no idea where they came from or why they had come here. They pulled me back, maybe ten or twenty steps from the pillar. All at once, they pointed to the top of the structure, which was by now (it had kept growing) very high—maybe five or six stories. As I looked up, pieces of the marble surface started to crack and began to flake off. It was as if the whole thing were being sculpted by some giant, invisible chisel. The top of the pillar slowly transformed into the shape of a human head, upon which sat a giant crown of gold. The head itself—flat faced, sharp chinned, wide eyed, also seemed to be made of gold. Then the chest emerged from the pillar, flanked by two powerful arms pressing into the body's sides and ending with enormous hands. The chest and arms turned from marble to silver as they took shape, creating a jarring contrast, Cohen says, with the golden head, as if the figure was not one body but an assemblage of bodily pieces. Beneath the chest, a stomach and a set of thighs emerged from the marble and immediately turned to bronze. Legs came next, formed of iron, then came feet of clay. Though it sounds hideous, Cohen says to me, the statue was an incredible sight. Around him, he says, people fell to their knees to paid homage to it—to the gigantic figure looming above them. It was unclear why we loved it—because of its size? The perfectly crafted features? The shimmering surfaces? The contrasts between the materials? The scale of value running from gold to clay? None of us seemed to know, and none of us cared. More people kept coming and bowing down to the statue, filling the space and blending into the darkness. Milena remained next to me the whole time. I didn't look at her, because I couldn't peel my eyes from the statue's head of gold, but I felt her by my side.

Then something started to happen, Cohen tells me. The atmosphere began to change. A tremor passed through me— and it moved into her, I could sense it, and then to the others gathered there. It must have been caused by the energy of a mass forming, a great boulder that seemed to have been made of stone but couldn't possibly have been made of stone. How could a boulder of stone of such size have come hurtling through the sky toward the statue's feet? It was stone and yet not stone, Cohen says. An otherworldly substance, he calls it, flung by a cosmic slingshot—shot from the hand of God. The sound of the impact was deafening. The ringing in my head made it feel like it would explode. People might have been screaming out at that moment, but the whole world was muted and shrouded by a cloud of dust. I looked over at Milena. Tears were streaming down her face, as they were streaming down mine. Why was I crying? I didn't know. Then the dust swirled in the wind, and she was gone. The rest of the people vanished, too, Cohen says. Everything was silent and clear again. I looked up and saw that the statue had been obliterated. The rock sat in its place, that boulder of an otherworldly sort. As I looked on, it started to grow. It was growing so quickly I had to move back, first slowly, then turning to run, fleeing the rising of a great mountain. When it had finally stopped growing and had spread itself out along the landscape I stopped running and turned to perceive it. I thought for a moment about this succession of occurrences. I gazed upon the mountain, hoping it might hold the answers to my questions. One question crowded out the others: how was I to live in this new world?

She was gone, Sy. The vision vanished. The wilderness faded. The mountain thinned and disappeared. My room in the clinic slowly materialized. I was hot, feverish, but at the same time stone cold. I called out for Milena. I needed her. But she'd left the clinic during the night. You know this part. She'd taken the manuscript. She knew you'd come to track her down. She took it to lure you, Sy. Maybe I should have gone after her— after you. At one point, I resolved to do it. I put on my clothes and made it as far as the entryway of the clinic's guesthouse. That's where my fever spiked, and I needed help getting back to bed.

Daniel. Daniel. Daniel—voices pierced my sleep, he says. Images flickered back to me. From stone pillar to a king—the king who contained all kings. The resplendent golden king, the less-radiant silver king, the practical bronze king, the hardened iron king, the earthy and fragile clay king. The rock—hurtling into the feet of clay, pulverizing the foundation of the king of kings. The whole structure comes crashing down. The rock, the object of destruction, swells into a mountain. What is this mountain, Sy? Is it the incarnation of good? Of evil? Which mountain hermit dwells there? Which god roams around its peak? You can imagine what Hruška said when I told him about the vision. He was thrilled. We've broken through a major barrier, he said. It's been tough, a long slog, Hruška said, but we're finally getting closer to the truth. Was he right? Maybe you and Milena leaving helped rip down the barrier. The dam broke, so to speak—the river flowed. And when it flowed, it cleared everything out of its way. You might find this hard to believe, Cohen says to me, but during those feverish weeks after she left, I hardly thought about the manuscript, about the Hotel des Bains, even though I suspected she would go there along the route through Vienna and Merano. She had to go there, just as you had to follow her. She'd been there before. Didn't you know it? It was decades ago. I saw her there for the first time. She was on the beach, wearing a blue-and-white striped bathing suit. She was pushing the sand around with her feet. Hruška told me that the different parts of the statue's body represented different kingdoms, and the stone that grew into the mountain was the kingdom that has no end, that can't be destroyed because it doesn't exist in our time. I asked him if this meant death—the kingdom of the dead. Our process would reveal it, he said.

The visions kept coming, Cohen tells me. Each time I lay down to sleep, it was something else, or the same visions repeated but with new elements. Sometimes, Milena would pull me tight against her body and I'd be on the cusp of an orgasm when the rock would fly through the air and crush the statue's feet. Other times, there was no statue. Instead, there was a tree that grew seemingly to the heavens, its branches stretched out wide, its leaves as large as sails. Drooping from these three-fingered leaves were luscious fruits, but each time I reached out to pick one it would vanish. As I looked on, the tree started to grow sick. First, the fruit shriveled into black lumps. Then the bright green leaves turned yellow and brown and fell from the branches. Then the branches themselves grew brittle and began to break off from the trunk. Finally, the trunk of this great tree was blown from its roots by a strong gust of wind. These visions, Cohen says, didn't last a single night. They did not last mere seconds, but years. Years during which the grasses grew higher where the tree had been. Years of rain, years in which moss covered everything in sight. Then came the terrors. Lions with eagle wings swooped down on me. Three-fanged bears stood upright and loomed over me, ready to crush me. Leopards with three wings and four heads ran at me to rip me apart. Then there was the most horrifying creature, Cohen says, a beast I can't fully describe, because it would never come into full view. It was half in my field of vision and half beyond. I could tell its teeth were made of iron. Horns grew on its head. Some were small, others as long as swords. This beast would come at the end of the vision. It would come first as a savior, ripping apart or devouring the other beasts that threatened me. It would ram its sharp horns into their bodies. It would tear their flesh with its iron teeth until their blood had been spilled and their lifeless bodies lay in a crumpled pile in front of me, shaking with the last gasps of life. But this gave me no relief. A moment later, the iron-toothed beast would turn its head toward me. The beast's terrifying gaze would meet my gaze. At this moment, Cohen says, I'd feel a strange transfer of energy—as if this beast was longing to become me and I was longing to be it. Words came to me, words I could barely understand—*wrath is at an end.* When I whispered these words, the whole scene was swept away, and there I was, trembling, cold, drenched with sweat. I'd go to the dining room in the morning for breakfast, but I couldn't eat. I'd come back to my room and fall into bed in a state of total exhaustion, but I couldn't sleep. I'd close my eyes and come right up to the border—and there they were, those beasts, waiting for me to enter to start the whole thing again. The border zone—the land of fog and darkness. I was alone there. Trapped. Trapped and yet free, free to remain there, trapped by fear, fear of the fog, fear of the dark landscape beyond the boundaries of sight. In this fear, in this trapped freedom, I had a wild thought, Sy. I know you'll understand it. The thought was this: Hruška was conjuring these beasts and then releasing them into my dreams. That's why I had to get out of there, Cohen says, why I had to get away from him.

There's more, Cohen says. Milena was there. You were there, Sy. Others. Walt Myserson was there—the entire Berlin scene. When I told Hruška I had to leave, he protested. He said my condition was deteriorating. I said of course it's deteriorating, he was sabotaging me, he was out to destroy me. I can hardly remember leaving. It was days or weeks ago, months or years ago. I don't know. I can barely remember anything. Colors pulling apart into white light—disappearing. Everything disappearing until my eyes close and the visions erupt, growing more intense by the day. Those words encircle me—*wrath is at an end*. What does this have to do with the manuscript? Was it merely a coincidence that the visions started on the very day the manuscript disappeared from beside my bed? The loss of a story, or now that I see it in front of me, a story's transfiguration. The story broken apart, breaking into pieces, its arc bending toward some distant and foreign terrain. You of all people know what it's like, Sy, to lose control over a story. No end in sight. Nothing in sight. Blankness of a page neither empty nor full—a page resisting every gesture, every mark. Do you understand what I'm saying, Sy, what I'm trying to tell you? I'm talking about the end point—not an ending, *the ending*. The story ends when time ends, time stands still, history is no more—an eternal present without past or future. This is the story of the withdrawal of God away from His creation. But then God turns. Then God faces again what He created. Then He begins to move back toward us. This is when time halts. This is when everything is still, everything waits, waits for the possibility of a kingdom that cannot be destroyed. There is great energy in God's turn, Sy. The very first, tiniest movement back toward humankind provokes the furious struggle for survival. It's impossible to imagine. Yet, it's there in those visions—beasts ripping apart beasts, bloody, violent, enraged, uncontrollable fury. This is the bestial force of humankind, Sy, the bestiality of the moment immediately preceding the end point. The end point, judgment, wiping away all that came before, the creation of a new kingdom on earth. It's happening, Sy, the spiral has begun. I can feel it—I can see it. But there's one thing I can't see. One question remains unanswerable. What if there is no end point? What if the end of wrath never comes? What if God's kingdom never materializes? Or, think about this, Sy, what if the end of wrath simply means an end of existence? What then? Nothing but emptiness, Sy, a yawning emptiness without hope, without fear, without joy or anger or love or hate—a nothingness horrifyingly complete.

I see myself walking, Sy, through a denuded forest. Around me, the trees have been infected with disease. They are dried, brittle skeletons. Below them, the ground is littered with fallen branches, patches of yellowy dried moss. It is silent—not a sound of a bird, a buzz of an insect—not a movement of an animal across this barren ground. The stream that used to flow through here has dried up, its bed now a desiccated combination of rock and mud baking in the sun. I move through this landscape for hours. I feel a rising anxiety—a feeling like I might never see anything—plant, animal, human—alive again. I consider the following: if everything is dead around me, how am I still alive? Toward evening, I come to a field and see a wooden bridge that crosses the dried-out streambed. I hesitate before crossing it, knowing, somehow, that to cross is an irreversible act. It is an entry into another world. I feel the shiver of this otherness, which is, at the same time, only a reminder of sameness, that although the other side of the bridge and this side represent two discrete (and perhaps opposing) realities, they also constitute one realm, one space, one territory—the internal defined by the external, the shape by its dividing line. I cross. I gaze up and see, through the fog and darkness, a structure that appears to be a castle on a hill, though the longer I look, the less clear my vision becomes, the more everything slips away into the blurry darkness surrounding me. Across the bridge, there is a small village. Its structures are made of stone. Many are falling apart—some are just heaps sunken in on themselves, ruins. There are no people in the village, Sy. It is deserted—most likely for decades already. How am I here? What am I supposed to do in this place? Has God's wrath found its way to me? Have I found my way to it—its center? The center point of the coming end. A precursor. What happened here? It occurs to me that the answer lies in the castle on the hill. Perhaps, I think, the castle itself—the structure itself— is the answer to this question. Or it is the shell of an answer, the promise of an answer. The vision is fleeting, Sy. I open my eyes and it's gone. I open my eyes and I see the sun, the clouds, the blue sky, the crowns of trees, magpies and twittering finches, walls and buildings, a city, a universe, and there's a hand on my shoulder, and there's a voice calling, "Cohen, Cohen."

FEBRUARY 7 (NIGHT)
I unfolded the paper as I walked through the long, narrow corridors of the gentlemen's inn. Sidney Keter: radical, dangerous,

threat. The note clipped to it: *Z., 18 km NE of Spindelmühle. Heading north.* Communist, socialist, anarchist. I found a dark hallway, its ceiling sloping down, narrowing the space as I passed through it. Doors lined the hallway to either side. The walls facing the hallway stopped a few inches from the ceiling. I could feel something there, sense something around me. I tried the handle on a door to my left. I was surprised it wasn't locked. It swung open. I entered. It was nearly completely dark in the room; only the faintest light seeped through the small window at the end of the hallway, which faced in the direction opposite the courtyard. I switched on my flashlight and looked around. It was a small room with nothing in it besides a narrow bed. I lay down on the bed and looked up at the ceiling, moving my flashlight in and out of the cobwebbed corners. I thought about the Nervenklinik, Isaac Mondschein's blue-green letters, his spirit, his spirit that came sprinkling down on me from the heavens, from above, from somewhere. Cobwebs and dust—the play of light, glimmers, sparkles, sparks of imagination. What if this door shut? What if it locked from the outside? I would be trapped in here. Nobody would hear me scream. Nobody would ever find me—not me, not my bones, nothing. I tried to calm myself down, to arrest the panic that was gripping me, quickening my heart, pulsing through my blood. Rooms becoming cells, spaces of detention, spaces of interrogation, spaces of torture. What did Keter discover here in 1939 after he escaped Prague as the German army rolled in? I switched off my flashlight, closed my eyes to think about this, and might have fallen asleep for a minute or two. Or maybe it was longer. When I woke, the thin light from the corridor had vanished. I gathered my backpack and flashlight and left the room. I continued down the hall and turned into a second room. I was getting close, nearer, approaching the center, the heart of the inn. There was a small desk with two chairs on either side of it. I turned away. Another room had a desk with just one chair—and another only a single chair with no desk at all. Here. I entered this room and flashed my light around. Graying walls. Dust, cobwebs. The air felt heavier. Energy as memory, I thought. A room emanating energy into a space as stones give back the sun's heat into the cooling evening air. Communist, socialist, anarchist, Jew. The words tumbled; they gathered. Sidney Keter. I stared at the single chair and an image started to flicker. Or form. No, it emerged and started to solidify, even if it remained always an apparition, a ghost. Or something between a ghost and a delusion, between dream and nightmare. I saw a young woman—she was the woman I've been searching for. She was thin, had black hair, had glasses. She was wearing a plain gray dress. Her skin was dark. She tried to get up, but she couldn't. She was restrained. I looked at her arms and saw that her wrists were bound to the chair with rope. I moved a step closer to her. The image started to blur. Closer, the image started to fade. I was losing her. I reached out and she was gone: *18 km NE*. I shone the beam of my flashlight through the paper. For the first time, I saw traces of erased words. I gazed through them, not quite trusting my eyes. How could it be that I've never penetrated to the interior of this paper before? In this room, this room with its single chair, a chair for restraining her. For interrogating and torturing her. The erased violence. The underlying truth of the inn's history, village history, history—violence. Power and violence, two spiders spinning a conjoined web, a web around Keter, which also ensnared me. I read those erased words: *The crows assert that a single crow could destroy heaven.* No. No. Not that.

I turned back into the corridor. I moved quickly and soon found a door that led outside. I stood in the frigid air as icy snowflakes fell around me. The sky was covered by clouds. The wind was picking up. I returned to the inn by the bridge.

The fire burns in the stove as I write this. The pub is hot. I eat a mix of pickled mushrooms and sauerkraut. I long for something fresh, a fruit or vegetable with structure, with internal density—with crunch. Time erodes crunch. Time erodes substance. I think about the single chair in the room, the ghost body. There was only one person it could have been. It was Esther Bird. She had checked out Keter's translation of *The Book of Moonlight* from the New York Public Library in 1946 and never returned it. She never returned. She vanished. She vanished from the city, from her life, from history. Anarchist. Communist. Socialist. Jew. Feminist. Radical. Mondscheinian. Rodrigan. A single Esther Bird. A single Esther Bird could destroy the state. A single Esther Bird could destroy the structures of power. But the structures of power would never permit an Esther Bird to enter their domain. They tried to catch her, to cage her, to crush her. She fled, she flew. Beyond the realm, beyond the sphere of power. She wriggled free of the chair and soared above these mountains and valleys. The state means no Esther Bird, the impossibility of Esther Bird.

She wrote a piece in the newspaper *Freedom* called "The Eschaton." It was printed in June 1946. Keter writes about it in his journal. They had spent time together since they first met when Keter went to the paper's office with Greta. Evidence from Keter's journal is the following. January 15, 1945: *Saw Esther Bird today.* February 2, 1945: *With Esther Bird at the Workmen's Circle.* February 4, 1945: *Walked with Esther Bird on Broadway past the newspaper's office.* February 5, 1945: *Invited Esther Bird to the reading circle. She met me on the sidewalk, and we went in together.* Or this one, undated: *Watched as Esther Bird crossed the street toward me, her body appearing and disappearing in traffic.* Or this, from December 2, 1945: *Esther B. waits for her coffee to cool and then drinks the entire cup with one tilt.*

She wrote in *Freedom*:

After thirty years of world war, the old revolutionary politics has lost its truth. It could be that it never had any truth, even though I used to believe in it with all my heart. I believed in the inevitability of capitalism's collapse under the weight of its own contradictions. Workers would rise up and take back the value of their labor. I believed that states constructed by emancipated, dignified workers would never go to war against other states so constituted. The revolutionary's task was to pave the way for capitalism's collapse, for the rise of the workers' state, for socialism. Now I see that what I had taken as the fundamental problems in society and the fundamental dynamics of history were merely superficial manifestations. The crisis is deeper. The nature of this deeper crisis is both general and individual. The individual crisis is one of atomization, separation, and distance. The human being, over the last one hundred years, has come to understand itself as independent of the totality, from the wholeness of being. The individualist understanding of selfhood drives the subject toward maximizing material gain in the form of capital and property. This is the economic imperative of the day: the race to acquire the means for self-gratification and to aggrandize one's power, or at least the feeling of empowerment. This movement, this seeking impulse and the competitive drive that feeds it, provides the underlying energy for capitalist society to function. Possession. Power. Even the socialists and communists among us feed off and contribute to this same energy. Competition. Possession. Power. These flows of energy come together in a single channel, and this channel is violence. Individual violence. Social war. The two great wars of the last thirty years were enormous eruptions of the concentrated energy of capitalism. Competition, possession, power: the coal and oil of collective violence. For such a massive social phenomenon like war to come about, however, requires that individuals, atomistic selves, do not remain separated and isolated but rather that they join together in common purpose, perhaps a seemingly greater purpose. This is the second dimension of the current crisis, the general or social dimension. Individuals, understood as rigid selves independent of the whole, can only come together as a group through the yearning for the imposition of hierarchical, authoritarian, and tyrannical structures. These structures promote a false consciousness of autonomy of selfhood, when in fact they work to crush this autonomy completely. You are free, these structures tell us, yet you must serve. You are in control of your lives, except that you are also under our control. Your interests reign supreme—if they don't conflict with our interests. Your freedom is guaranteed precisely through your submission. The liberation of the self is achieved through the imprisonment of the self. The power of the people is aggrandized through their humiliation. This is the formula for today's social reality. It guides our politics, our economy, even our culture, a culture debased and under political and economic control. The primary representative of this structure of power is the state, without which such collective violence, the likes of which we've lived through for the past thirty years, would have been impossible. This is the meaning of the underlying reality of the atomic bombs the United States dropped on Japan. Each bomb contained the compressed energy of tens of millions of individuals—tens of millions of individuals striving, fighting, competing for their own personal gain. The genius of the state was in developing a technological expression of this collective energy, the ability to compress it into a tube of around ten feet in length, weighing close to ten thousand pounds, resembling a small whale, and to transport this whale across the world by air in order to drop it on its enemy. Everyone knows the result. It is the result that the state calls victory. The victory of death. In this way, we can understand the simplicity of modern war despite its complexity. Modern war is the following equation: victory is death. This statement opens up another: the state is death. And this leads to the next statement, which might shock you, because while you will resist it, you know it is true: *the individual is death*. You might shrink back from this statement. You might assert that what drove the Germans into the hands of Hitler was not individualism but its opposite. Not so. In the heart of every Nazi, every SS member, every ordinary German *Mitläufer* was a lust for power and a desire to aggrandize themselves, to inflate the self—socially, culturally, politically, economically, sexually, and of course psychologically. The Nazi self was an expansionist self. Each self, each Nazi, believed in the illusion that it could expand to the size of the entire state: the self as state, the fundamental fascist delusion. This fascist delusion, however, is not limited to the Hitler regime. It is the delusion at the heart of all states, all nationalism. The aggrandized self, expansive, seeking to become the totality, seeking to push out its borders, to subsume within the sphere of self that which lies beyond its borders. It is no wonder that God, in the book of Daniel, at the moment of the end of time, hurls the rock that crushes the state. The state is the primary enemy of God, the state is the primary vehicle for evil in the world before the end of history—before the end of the historical world, our world.

She wrote:

Let's gaze into the future to see what will happen to these massive constructs and compressions of human evil in the form of the states of this world. Out of the ashes of war, two great states have risen above the others. One state, based on the principles of communism, is blocking the flow of individualist desire in the economic realm among the masses, while allowing for unchecked fulfillment of desire and accumulation among the elite. Where does the desire flow if not toward self-aggrandizement? The answer is that it is rerouted away from the economic realm into the state apparatuses. In other words, the desire, the energy, flows into the institutions of power: the secret political police, the army, the prison system. It is easy to see into the future of such a state. This state will develop the most widespread and brutal system of terror the world has ever seen. This state might be communist, but it is built on the very foundation of its antagonist—individualist capitalism. It knows no equality. It cannot, even in its wildest imagination, dream of true peace, because it is a system, by structure and definition, always at war with itself. Night after night, this system convulses with violence and destruction until the people can no longer endure their state, the state built from their own desires. This state will collapse, but the collapse will not bring into existence anything better. The violence and terror that have been previously concentrated in the mechanisms of the state will explode into the wider social realm, threatening its very survival. Society will turn on itself in spasms of violence, until, on the brink of utter breakdown, it will start to redirect this energy back into the structures of the state. The state will rise again, absorbing this energy, growing from it, expanding, until, finally, it has reconstituted itself, bringing an end to chaos, opening another chapter of state terror. If we look even further into the future, we see cycle after cycle of this—concentration, disintegration, fragmentation, re-concentration, and so on, time and again, on and on, evil building on evil, evil always increasing with no way out. Or one way out. The way is this: *a permanent revolution of the spirit.* This is another way of saying the coming of the eschaton, the end of time, the end of history.

Before we get there, I'll turn to the other of the two great state powers, the western power. This state will become the most dominant state in the history of the world, far exceeding the power of its eastern rival. This is a complex state, but not, as you might imagine, less destructive. On the one hand, the future of this state is one of war, though not war on the same scale as the wars of the previous thirty years. These wars will be sideshows and safety valves; they will allow for the excess violence built up in society to escape without being released inside the state's borders. On the other hand, the vast majority of violence will remain contained within these borders. The violence is of many types. It is the violence of racism—the structures of power built to enforce a racial terror through vigilantism, police brutality, and legal, economic, and political oppression. This is the violence of the policeman, that symbol of how state power reaches its hands into the heart of our communities, gun poised on hip. Jails rise around us. As soon as they are built, they fill up with convicts. The court system, the prison system, the roaming army of policemen—the components of legalized terror. To racial violence, to police violence, to the violence of the "legal" system, we need to add environmental violence. This state, far more than any state in the history of the world, will channel its collective desire toward the worldwide plundering of natural resources. That so much of the people's wealth will come at the expense of the earth will take decades to be fully clear. When people realize this is the case, catastrophe will be at hand. Yet, this people, even staring directly into the face of catastrophe, will continue to act out of the desire for more—empowerment through accumulation. It will fulfill its lust for violence by unceasing violence against nature. You might think that legal violence, racial violence, war, and the spoliation of nature would be enough to satisfy the lust for power, the individualist striving for more, for expansion. How wrong this is! This is but a small fraction of the total amount of social violence in the western power. The largest share of collective violence is channeled into the twin engines of the capitalist system: the office and the home, work and family. It is here, in the relationships of work, in the relationships of domesticity, that the great share of social violence is taking place. Capitalism depends on it. In the workplace, violence fills the spaces between the rungs of the hierarchy. It is the energy necessary to keep one person above another. One person dominates another, who turns to dominate the person below him, and so on down the line. Each person takes pleasure in his small amount of power. Each person is debased and humiliated by his subordination. The spaces between these people seethe with energy, energy producing evil as its nefarious byproduct: the evil of the individual spirit of the imperious self. The family, by which I mean the household, is created in the context of the workplace, its domestic mirror. As such, the greater a person is dominated at work, the more this person needs to dominate at home. At home, all men, peasant or worker, are king. The patriarch plays the role of monarch—the home a tyrannical domain. And home is also where the monarch's treasury can be found. It is the place of accumulation. This place is owned. More and more, "the home" is becoming a possession. But the ownership is a phantom. It is the "ownership" of debt, since the means to acquire the space have been borrowed from the banks and the state. Even so, the space, this home, this often shoddily constructed dwelling, becomes the screen on which grandiose longings are projected, hopes and dreams never to be fulfilled. Nonetheless, capital flows in. It searches to catalyze these dreams like a peyote vision. The majority of these hopes cannot be sustained by the adults—reality, weak as it is in the family domicile, is still too powerful to allow it. Instead, these hopes and dreams are invested in the central patriarchal possession, the children. In every suburban youth baseball game, the Yankees face off against the Dodgers. In every screeching school recital, a performance of future virtuosos. In every mathematical test, the glimmers of an Einstein. Disappointment, however, produces harsh responses directed from the patriarch against the others in the family, the wife, the kids— blows from the hand, deprivations, public and private humiliation, assertions of control. Schools take up the task where parents leave off, though without any of the parental idealism. Instead, schools don't want Einstein, they want technocrats, bureaucrats, future clerks, solid middling "experts" who play by the rules. These are bodies and minds that will fill the spaces of future work, the reproduction and expansion of servitude. If the relationship between parents and children contains part of the violence of the family, the relationship between the spouses holds the other part. Spouses in the system of western capitalism are at war with each other, despite Hollywood illusions of love, despite thinking they are on the same team. The war is acted out in the domestic economy of each household, primarily in the sphere of sexual relations. Murder, rape, and physical and emotional abuse infest the nation's households. What will happen to this nation? To its people? One might think the people would choose at some point to try to escape the evil, but no, the evil is the precise thing they see as good. The individualistic striving, the lust for material accumulation, the lust for technological mastery of the natural world, the joy in plundering the earth to fill space between the walls of one's personal castle with things, the desire both to be humiliated and to be the executor of humiliation, to be dominator and dominated, to project illusions of grandeur into the future—all of this will grow unchecked until the world can no longer bear it, until the surface of the world itself will crack, until the rock from heaven hurtles down on this kingdom, on each individual kingdom of one, and all is turned to dust.

She wrote:

The revolution is not in the first instance political. It doesn't, it can't, begin with the overthrow of the state. This is the lesson we learned from Russia in 1917—the revolution against the state brought another state into existence. This is what we saw in Germany in 1933. When a state is destroyed, a more powerful state rises in its place. This is the sorry fate of political revolutions that begin and end with politics. The revolution cannot begin on the level of the economy either. Revolutions on the social level will shift the energy of exploitation into other channels, other flows, but they do nothing to dissipate this energy. The Russian Revolution, for example, shifted the energy of economic exploitation from the landed class to the state apparatus, and these apparatuses turned into instruments of violence. Economic and social revolution, when it leads the way, results in convulsions of extreme violence, usually directed against the weakest in society: minorities, outsiders, dissidents. In most cases, political and economic revolution come together—and the results are always the same: the re-creation of the structures of oppression backed by violence. Neither political nor economic revolution can achieve fundamental societal change. Neither has any chance of achieving a true state of freedom—anarchy.

She wrote:

Anarchy is not a matter of political or economic revolution. You might find this hard to believe, but anarchy is beyond politics, beyond economic relations. From its position on the outside, anarchy cannot tolerate politics; it rejects economic systems that promote competition, accumulation, and exploitation of people and nature. The emancipatory agent of anarchy is found in the human spirit. Anarchy is nothing but this: *permanent revolution of the spirit.*

She wrote:

If the revolution in politics and economics is based on maximizing benefit for oneself or one's group—economic class, nation, ethnicity—the revolution of the spirit moves in the opposite direction: it begins with the overthrow of selfhood, the fracturing, collapse, and ultimate disappearance of the notion of the self. This is followed by a continuous struggle against its reconstitution. This fracturing and emptying of the self prevents the spirit from taking on external definitions and unmakes the self's individualistic notion of being. This unmaking takes place on all levels: names become shards of a unified language of creation; bodies become expressions of the primal material of chaos; souls become flows of the shared energy that binds existence together, flowing in and out of beings, animating life. It is only by cracking the shells of our subjectivities that we will be able to escape these prisons and hear the divine word, feel the essence of the primal chaos, feel the unordering of the world, access the energy of the life force. This state of being—shared language, extension of chaos, flow of existential force—this is the state of being of true freedom, the state of being beyond the mundane order of history. This is ahistorical existence, the existence outside time. And this existence can only come about through the permanent revolution of the spirit. Anarchy is a call for the end of time. Anarchy is the state of undifferentiation, the state of primal or primordial chaos, of the swirling mass that precedes singularity. The revolution of the spirit will start in the following way: one person will escape the bounds of selfhood and release a spark of energy into the world. This spark or pulse of energy will strike another, cracking that other's shell, allowing for that second subject's spirit to escape its prison and to dwell in the realm beyond the self. In this way, the revolution of the spirit will grow, will become universal. At the same time, counterforces will struggle to suppress this movement. These forces will work to reconstitute the self, to contain its energy back inside its bounds. This is evil—the differentiating, individualizing force. The spirit of anarchy is the recognition of the self as nonself, as the flow of a shared spiritual energy. Anarchy is the nonexistence of self, the knowledge that in each spirit exists all possible spirit, in each subject, all subjects, and only through the existence of all subjects can one particular subject know its essential being. Evil grows in the heart of the individuated subject. This evil grows larger until it consumes the world. Goodness emanates from anarchy, the spirit emancipated from the shell of selfhood. Anarchy is the free force of energy—the freedom to roam, mix, disappear, to be anything and all things at once, to be formless, shapeless, both bodily and bodiless, to be real and metaphorical at the same time. Both states—the anarchic and the individuated—are leading to an end. The end of anarchy is timelessness, the state of the divine. The end of individuation is death—death both individual and total, death in the realm of time, death while history spins on and on.

FEBRUARY 8 (MORNING)

More snow. Endless snow. The heat in the room has vanished with the night, though it's still night, despite the coming of morning. Dawn doesn't break here, it creeps forward, hardly moving. How did I end up here? This is the question that comes to me the moment I open my eyes into this three-quarter darkness, which is the closest it gets in Z. to daytime. I was in Prague. I boarded a bus in what now seems like a somnambulant state. I made my way to my seat, sat down, and fell in and out of sleep as images came and went, as if projected onto the backs of my eyelids with intermittently interrupted reels of film, the projector spinning and clicking in the background of consciousness. When I arrive in Špindlerův Mlýn, those dark, silent bodies head in the opposite direction. Is this memory? What are these partial, flimsy projections? Are they anything more than plays of light? Light caught on strips of plastic, animated by more light passing through them. Light on light, a world of flicker and shadow: flicker and shadow, the substance of the village of Z.

Death, Esther Bird wrote, *while history spins on and on.* It didn't take long for me to realize (I would say "learn," but I never learned it) that there was likely no campaign to take Julia down. There was no hit man named Naphtali, no commission set up by the University of Rome to investigate the evidentiary basis of her research. Julia had conjured an elaborate web of conspiracy. The most persuasive evidence for the idea that Julia believed her story was her high level of distress. She was clearly shaken, nervous, anxious—destabilized in every way. On the other hand, she was as clearheaded as always, able to explain the most esoteric, mystical notions, the most abstract, difficult concepts. The way she read aloud from the Rodrigan texts—whether in Hebrew, German, Latin, or English—stirred me, jolted me, provoked in me a burning desire, a desire for her, to be sure, but also one for a greater, better, more beautiful world. In those moments, with that language coming from her lips, Julia became that world, a play of light and color, which was the key to the opening of those heavenly gates; and they would open and beckon me toward the eternal dwelling, a kind of love, a kind of intoxication, the end and the beginning of being, the force of life flowing in and out of the body, condensing it, pulling it apart, reordering each and every cell.

One thing was clear: Julia was in crisis. Julia's life was pulling apart, opening up a chasm of longing, or delusion. She had come to me in this state, and I was the worst possible harbor for her in the midst of this crisis. I had returned to Prague, even though Prague was the last place I should have gone to. It was in Prague where everything fell apart, though perhaps everything had already fallen apart and it was only there that I noticed it, or cared, or felt it, or understood it, however partially I understood it. But I didn't understand it—for example, I could point to the seemingly simple question that began my preface to *Blue, Red, Gray*: *Who is Jan Horák?* There is no answer to this question. Why? Because the answer is a paradox: Horák both is and isn't.

Could the same be said about Julia's Naphtali, that he both is and isn't? I can't be sure. At times, I'd wonder if this was my last chance—my last chance for a life-in-time, a feeling of presence, and a future, a future beyond the layers of this onion—text-in-text-in-text-in-text, like a Russian doll. Infinite regression into nothingness, though it is nothingness as the animating force of creation, a single word from which all language emanates. A single word from this statement: *Let there be light*. But which one of these words is the primary one? The commending *let*? The empty *there*—the word of void? The word of existence itself: *be*? Or the word of vision, vision in its expansive, expanding sense—*light*? I would lie next to her, touching her, feeling her skin against mine, her breath on me, the graze of her toes and fingertips, her nipples, the heat of her sex. I would repeat those words. Let. There. Be. Light. Out of the chaos, out of the void, creation.

For some reason, or for reasons having to do with the non-existent investigation, Julia wouldn't leave the apartment during the day. By the time it got dark, she would be stir-crazy and ready to get out of there. She'd pull on her high leather boots, zip them up over her calves, button up her woolen coat, fix her scarf, and leave as quickly as she could. She'd want me to go with her. I had little desire to do this, but most of the time I succumbed to her pressure and followed her into the frigid night.

On one such night, we walked down to the river, followed it for a distance and then crossed over to the other side. It was midevening. The streets were still full of cars, the sidewalks with people in work attire making their way home or to meet friends in a restaurant or pub. They were young people mostly, younger than me and Julia, though at the same time I felt myself young, inexperienced, naïve. The sight of people in their twenties and thirties dressed up in suits always provoked this feeling, this sense that I'd failed to acquire basic skills, that decisions I'd made had led me in the wrong direction, that life had passed me by on a parallel and inaccessible path. At the same time, there is nothing more pathetic than a young man—especially a young man—in a suit and tie, hair neatly cut, carrying some sort of briefcase or urban bag, wearing polished (and pointy) leather shoes, a wide-faced watch, cashmere scarf, and a woolen overcoat, making his way through the city streets. It doesn't matter which city—Prague, New York, Berlin, Paris, Madrid, the basic idea is the same: a young man willingly submitting to a system that is bound to crush him. It is a profound and total submission. Certainly, there are rewards for this submission. Money is the most obvious one. Confidence is another, though it is necessarily a superficial confidence, because a crushed and submissive person cannot have true confidence. There is "freedom," too, for this man, however misunderstood. Despite this, the horrible notion always strikes me that this man, this well-groomed, suit- and cashmere- and leather-wearing pawn, this debased and humiliated entity, has it, on the whole, better than I do. Why? Because he has at least the feeling of stability, even if it is a stability designed by the most visionless architect. And he has a future, even if this future is predictable, insipid, and boring. And he has happiness, even if this happiness is constructed and implanted in his head by countless marketing teams and soulless data-crunching algorithms.

Julia and I continued through the narrow streets in Malá

Strana. She was walking quickly, seemed to know where she was going, though she didn't tell me, and we barely exchanged a word as we went. As we turned uphill, I had the thought that we were heading toward the Strahov Monastery, that she had discovered another way into the cellar, where those materials were stored in airtight crates, which probably weren't really airtight. Before long, still a good distance from Strahov, Julia turned into a small pub.

The only free table was in a small alcove by the door. We took it and each ordered a beer and a shot of whiskey. A young woman dressed in an outfit that seemed half medieval folk dress and half shoddy Prague casino costume brought us the drinks. I could tell Julia liked the pastiche, and she gave herself over to a guarded half smile. I took a few sips of beer and a taste of the cheap whiskey.

"You don't remember, do you?" she said.

"Remember what?"

"The time we were here, that night."

I looked around. It was a pub like hundreds of others in Prague—a kind of cavernous space that evoked a pseudo-Gothic history, a shabby, unconvincing periodization, one designed to lure in a tired tourist, who, after a beer or two, wouldn't care about anything other than the next round.

"I don't remember," I said, "I can't think of any good reason I'd have come to this place. And I don't know why we're here now."

"It's really not that bad."

"Sure," I said. I had no urge to argue with Julia or to discuss the merits of the pub in any significant detail. There was a fake candle on the table, a pale bulb set in a small, opaque cup. The light from it gave Julia's skin a strange, artificial look. Simulation, I thought, that's what this place was, nothing but surface, surfaces paper-thin, nearly transparent.

"This is where it all began," she said. "You'd come from Strahov. I hadn't seen you in days. You'd called me the night before, telling me to meet you here. You'd found something in the crates, that's what you told me. You were going to get it out the next day and bring it for me. And you did. You took it, stole it, the first piece on Cain, the first trace of Rodriganism in Prague. You slid it across the table. I could see the anxiety playing on your face as you passed it to me in the envelope, a look of fear, a look of expectation in your eyes. I opened the envelope and removed the vellum sheet. I could hardly believe it. I could hardly believe love could be this powerful—that desire could shape reality as it had at that moment. Don't you remember now, Sy, how your body pitched forward, how it met mine at a perfect angle? And the fear—the fear that your 'Horák' would collapse under the weight of two bodies becoming one? It would have collapsed, there's no doubt about it. What a fragile, delicate work 'Horák' was, what a vaporous thing, light, brittle, dissolving into air, thinner even than the pale erasure of words under those words—that story—a story seen by casting light through the back of vellum sheets while probing the front with a magnifying glass. It should have been lost, it should have vanished forever—and yet, as we sat here, it came back to life, reborn through the commingling of our desire. Then we drank to everything imaginable: to Rodriganism, to Cain, to Isaac Mondschein, and even to Jan Horák—shot after shot until we stumbled out of here. We made our way to Letna and fucked under a tree—now you must remember. In the hazy days that followed, the story emerged slowly from beneath those other words. It was a miracle, Sy, wasn't it? Wasn't it part of one of those impossibilities that come with wild, total belief? It was a belief flowing between us. It filled the lacunae in the texts, created a whole out of the jumble of fragments. Some days later, I was sitting at your desk in your apartment. You were out working on Horák. I was starting to get a handle on those barely visible marks and could hardly believe what I was reading. It was written in Hebrew, which slowly emerged from the Latin and reasserted itself. There she is. She. Cain. This Cain is a woman. She's the daughter of Adam and Eve, not the son. She's the sister of Abel."

Why did Julia bring me back there? Of course, I remembered it. I recognized it instantly. It was one of those unforgettable scenes of one's life, around which whole epochs of one's existence orbit, swirl in and out of this focal point, a point that can't be graphed on any axis, a point beyond space, beyond time, exploding beyond or outside known dimensions. The Z. point. The end point. The destination.

We drank the beers and the shots of whiskey. Julia went to the bar to order another round. She fell into conversation with the bartender, a guy in his late twenties or early thirties, skilled in the art of flirtation, or seduction. I didn't want to watch it, to see how easy it could be for Julia to slip away from me, even if she had no intention of slipping away. I had no idea what her intentions were. She appeared again in Prague. She had the book in her hand. She came into my apartment, took off her clothes, and made love to me. She needed documents. But what else? What lay beyond them?

Adam and Eve had a child, a daughter, and they called her Cain. To her parents, she was the most beautiful creature in the world, seemed to embody the purest form of nature. It was as if, they mused, she had been sent directly to Eve's womb by the breath of God. From the day she was born, Adam and Eve lavished her with attention. As they raised her, they taught her every skill they could imagine, how to work the soil, how and when to plant the seed, how to tend to the flocks, how to prepare the food, to make clothing, to build vessels, dig for water, press oil, and how, finally, to pay homage to the Lord. Cain learned everything easily, quickly; she was hardly a teenager when she surpassed her parents with her ability to grow and shepherd. And she far surpassed them in the intensity with which she dedicated herself to God. When Cain was still a young woman, her parents had a second child, a boy, and they called him Abel. Adam and Eve wanted to celebrate the birth of Abel. They told Cain to go into the field and to choose a beast to sacrifice to God in honor of Abel's birth. Cain went into the field, surveyed the flock, but couldn't choose one. She had never killed an animal before. When called on by her parents to make a sacrifice to God, she had always brought fruits of the field to the altar. She knew that the arrival of Abel was something special, an occasion for the choicest lamb. And yet, she couldn't bring herself to lift and bind one, to carry it to the altar, to drain it of its blood as she had seen her father Adam do many times before on those somber days of devotion when the family would cease work, abstain from eating and drinking, and beg for God's attention and blessing. Adam and Eve were distraught when she returned to the camp without the lamb. They sensed that God was looking, that Cain's failure to bring the lamb would seem like a lack of gratefulness for the gift of a child. Abel moved about on Eve's breast, fussing, taking the nipple and expelling it, refusing to eat. Could it be, Eve thought, that Cain's actions would cause God's wrath to turn on her brother? Adam, sensing Eve's nervousness, rushed into the field, grabbed the first lamb he came upon and ran over to the altar. He called to Cain for her to bring his blade of bone. On the handle of this blade, Adam had carved an intricate design of vines and leaves. Cain remained standing there, unmoved. Adam called to her again—bring the blade. He pointed to it hanging in a leather sheath by the opening of the tent. Cain just stood there looking at her father as he knelt at the altar, struggling to control the unbound lamb, which fought to free itself from his tightening grasp. Cain was frozen. Adam called to her again, this time in anger—a voice she had never heard before, a voice of terror and violence. Abel, her baby brother, started to wail. Eve shouted to her to bring her father the knife before God saw what was happening and stanched the flow of her milk forever, condemning Abel to starvation and death. Still, she couldn't break free—couldn't take the knife, couldn't bring it to her father. Finally, Adam couldn't stand it any longer. He tucked the lamb under his arm, ran to the tent, and took the knife. He raced back to the altar, called out in humble devotion to God, and cut the lamb open, allowing its blood to be swallowed up by the dry, dusty earth. When this was done, Adam came back to the tent. His hands were red with the lamb's blood. He took a torch from the fire, went back to the altar, and lit a pile of sticks. For some minutes, he let it burn, until the sticks had turned into a glowing pile of coals. He placed the lamb's body on the coals and prayed as the smoke from the burning flesh rose high into the cloudless sky. Surely, Adam and Eve thought, this would please the Lord. As the lamb burned, little Abel stopped his fussing, took his mother's breast into his mouth, and began to suck. God had heard Adam's call.

From one day to the next, the love, dedication, and attention Adam and Eve had lavished on their daughter Cain was given to her brother Abel. Abel was God's child now, Cain the disobedient sibling. Why, Cain wondered, had she frozen in the tent when Adam called out for his blade of bone? Why had she stared at the fire Adam had lit at the altar with such a vacant look? Her parents whispered to each other in the darkness after they thought she had fallen asleep: evil had somehow come into her body, evil from some unknown source, and now it was hiding in her blood. Perhaps, they mused, it had come through her nostrils in the form of mountain air. She could have encountered it when she took the flocks to the high pastures in the summer—alone in the hills that surround the valley. This is why, they thought, she would return late at night, why she led the flocks back into the valley under the cover of darkness, claiming she was coming late because she had discovered streams beyond the hills with the sweetest water. She had stayed as long as she could because the animals couldn't be budged from drinking. The withdrawn love might have bothered Cain, she might have suffered, but if she was in pain and if she did suffer, she kept it to herself. She continued to plant the fields as her brother Abel grew, to prune and care for the fruit trees, to tend to the flocks, to bring the flocks over the hills to those distant streams of sweetness, despite the objections of Adam and Eve. Though she would bring the best of her stalks, the highest and strongest, to burn at God's altar, Adam would always block her way, telling her to come only with the choicest lamb. Cain refused to bring the lamb, to shed its blood, to burn its flesh. More than that. When Adam would bring the lamb to sacrifice, she would remain in the tent, her eyes cast into the depths of the fire that always burned there, her gaze, her being, consumed by the flames.

Years passed and Abel grew into a strong young man. Though Adam and Eve knew how much Cain loved the animals, loved leading the flocks, though they knew about the great care she gave to every beast, treating them when they were sick, watering them with the sweet water of those distant streams, delivering their young, they gave the job of tending the flocks to Abel. Every night of the new moon, it was Abel who would take the choicest lamb and sacrifice it to God at the altar. Abel would spill the blood. Abel would burn the body and let the savory smoke rise to the nostrils of the Lord. Cain was despondent from losing her flock, yet she accepted her parents' decision. She spent countless days teaching Abel everything about caring for the animals. She loved Abel. He was a sensitive boy, maybe slightly weak, certainly weaker than she was, but tender, loving, and good. When he was ready, she passed her shepherd's staff to him and retreated into the fields and orchards, where she would spend her days.

One day, years later, Abel came to her in the orchard. She was by a pomegranate tree, filling a basket with fruit. Abel approached, and she offered him a pomegranate. He split it open and started to pick out the seeds. Juices dripped down his hands and arms. Cain also broke open a fruit and began to eat, her fingers red and sticky with juice. Abel asked about the orchard—and Cain told him that with every passing year the trees gave more fruit—figs and dates, pomegranates and lemons. The nut trees were also fruitful, the olives were plump, the grapes emerged in seemingly endless bunches. Abel told her about the flocks. They, too, were thriving, growing in number faster than ever before. It seems, he said in his usual quiet, innocent manner, that God has finally forgiven their parents for their transgression in Eden, allowing Eden itself to spill out beyond its gates and into this very valley, becoming the whole earth. Cain objected. It wasn't God's blessing that brought them this bounty, it was simply His lack of wrath. The bounty was the product of their labor—Abel's, hers, that of Adam and Eve. Even if this was the case, Abel persisted, God still provided the waters from the heavens and the earth, the bubbling streams, the ample rainfall. He provided the sun and the heat of the sun—making everything grow around them.

Cain demurred. She didn't want to think of the Lord at that moment, to think of His bloodlust, his rage against her parents for eating the forbidden fruit, a rage that nearly killed her mother while giving birth to Abel, a rage that found its way into her father's heart, turning Adam from a gentle, playful man into a melancholy tyrant, prone to sudden and violence explosions of anger, that turned him into the ruler of his family, a God on earth. She wanted to think of other things, like the sweet taste of the pomegranate seeds, the texture of the walnut shell, the green, vibrant fig leaves. There was too much beauty in this orchard to spend a moment contemplating the Lord.

Abel broke into her thoughts. "Sister," he said, "it's time we brought another child into this world. Even if you don't want to admit it, the abundance around you is part of God's blessing. Now we must be fruitful ourselves."

Abel's words shocked her. She knew what this would mean from sharing the tent with her parents. It would mean Abel's body entering hers. It would mean the dangers of childbirth, multiple childbirths, the pain, the suffering, followed by having her brother Abel lord over her until her death.

"A sister," she told him, "should not have a brother's child."

"When," he said in a strident tone she'd never heard from him before, "has the Lord decreed it?"

"The Lord has not decreed it," Cain said, "it is what I declare now."

"Then mankind will come to an end," Abel said. "Our parents are old and weak. They will die soon, and we will follow in their path—it is the only path. This means we must have a child. This is the Lord's will. Sister, you know it's true."

"The Lord has told us," Cain said to her brother, "that we are the first people on the earth, yet He knows that beyond these hills and across the great rivers and seas, there are others. You need to find these people to have children with them and not with me. In this way, you will spread your seed across the earth, and perhaps I will spread mine."

"No," Abel shouted. He was angry now. God would not permit it. God would not permit her to have an outsider's child.

"It is forbidden," he said, "to lie with strangers. It is against the will of the Lord."

"Who are you to speak for the Lord?" Cain said to him. "And even if this is the will of the Lord, I don't care. I'm your elder—and you, brother, have no claim over me."

"And Adam, your father?"

"He, too, has no rule over me."

"Then you have truly forsaken God," Abel said as he moved in and placed his hands on her shoulders. His touch was gentle, light, but she didn't like it, didn't want his leathery hands on her skin, didn't want his body close, above her. She shifted, and his arms fell to his sides. "It has been decreed," he said softly, slowly, "decreed by the Lord, by our father Adam, that you will have my child."

Before she could react, Abel thrust out his long, strong arms and pushed her to the ground. Her head struck against a surfaced root of the pomegranate tree, her vision blurred, tears came into her eyes. Abel leapt on top of her. With one hand, he began to pry her legs open, with the other pinning her chest to the ground. One of her arms remained free. She reached behind her. She felt Abel's shepherd's staff there. It was the staff she had given him when he had taken over the flock. She had carved the staff from the hardest wood—a petrified wood as hard at stone. She grasped it now and swung it wildly as Abel sought to enter her. The staff's bulbous handle cracked against his head. Abel's body fell onto her with all of its weight. She pushed him off, jumped up, and turned him over. Blood rushed from the wound on his head; blood oozed from his nose. She quickly ripped a strip of fabric from her tunic to bind him, but it was too late. His body convulsed, his movements ceased.

Cain put her hand to his mouth. His breath was gone. Abel, her brother, was dead. She fell onto him, her head pressed against his chest. She banged on him with her fists, trying to bring him back to life. Blood mixed into her hair—his blood. She looked down at her hands—blood and bloodred pomegranate juice. She rose in panic. She didn't know which way to turn. Ahead of her, beyond the orchards and the fields, was the camp. Her parents were there—her mother now preparing the evening meal, her father the daily sacrifice to God. Her parents, Adam and Eve, had agreed with Abel's plan, more likely it was their plan. It seemed doubtful that Abel, innocent as he was, meek and submissive as he had always been, would have had the vision and courage to carry out such an idea on his own. She would have to face them, to explain to them what had happened, to tell them what she had done. Cain turned away from the camp and gazed out at the distant horizon, across the undulating landscape that led into the vast, endless beyond. She began to walk toward it, first slowly, hesitantly, considering whether she should turn back and face her parents, face their grief, their anger. Yes, she thought, she had to go back, she had to see them, even if it meant her own death. As she turned and started back toward the camp a whirling storm approached her. It was a twisting, swirling mass of wind and dust. A voice boomed out of it. It was the Lord. He spoke to Cain, asking her what had happened to her brother. She told the Lord about the scene in the orchard, about Abel's attack on her, her defense, about striking him with the bulbous end of the staff.

The Lord bellowed with anger: "You have forsaken me! It was I, your Lord, King of the Universe, who sent your brother Abel to you. It was My will that you would bring his child into the world to continue the project of creation. But I can see you are full of evil, that evil dwells inside you; it is the lingering trace of the forbidden fruit, consumed against My will by your mother, Eve."

"If it was Your will that Abel come to me in the orchard," Cain responded, "then You are the evil one, and You are Abel's true murderer—his blood is on Your hands."

Cain turned away from God. Just as she did, the Lord struck out from the storm in anger, burning a mark on the back of Cain's neck with His fingertip. In fury, the Lord shouted, "You, Cain, shall leave here and never return. You are condemned to wander the earth forever. You are cursed. You will be hated wherever you go. But all will see the mark on your neck and know it is My mark. They will hate you, but they will not kill you. Instead, you will be despised, you will be a pariah among the peoples of the world." Cain turned her back on the camp, on her parents, on her life's work in the orchards and fields. She walked toward the far-off horizon, a horizon now nothing more than a black line against the setting sun.

Julia returned to the table while I was lost in these thoughts. She started to tell me something about the bartender. He's from Riga, she said, and came to Prague to study at the film academy. He's making a short film, she told me, about an Italian tourist, about her age, who has come to Prague to view the collection of paintings at the Anežský Klášter. It's amazing, the bartender told Julia, because he's been going to the museum every day, hoping to see a woman who would fit his vision—a real body that would lend inspiration for his script. For months, he's been doing this, going there, spending his time either in classes, at the museum, or working at the bar. When he's in class or at the bar, he's dreaming or her—daydreaming of this fictional her, and now, he told Julia—and she was telling me—he's found her at last. Julia was his muse.

I didn't want to listen to any of this. I tried to tune it out. I felt a nervousness start to tremble inside me, an envy or an anger or a hatred. I didn't want to hear how this young, handsome guy from Riga was seducing Julia, even if she was fully aware and in control of the seduction. She didn't care. She never cared about it. Whether she was seducing or being seduced, she didn't care. I could never tell what role I was in with her, whether I was moth or flame, and it didn't matter much one way or the other. Both—moth and flame—led to the same moment, immolation. Burning.

I open the stove in the pub and add a few pieces of wood. What was the essential thing about that night with Julia? Was there an essential thing? A thing beyond the hopelessly tangled knot of thoughts and feelings? It could be that the thing is memory—memory of the scene under the trees in Letna Park. Or, no, not memory but hope—hope that the door, which was opened that night, could be closed, or could lead to a corridor, which would lead to another door, which would open into a previously unknowable space. Corridors. Doors. Rooms— nightmare visions of the gentlemen's inn, its doors, its rooms, its corridors leading deeper down into the darkness. Words. Scraps of paper. Papers torn apart and reassembled. Files. Files reorganized not once but countless times. The Momus Report. The Keter file. The Cain responsa.

Entropy—that's it! Life pulling apart and decomposing. Paper clips rusting and breaking into pieces, papers falling and scattering on the floor, words written over words, erased words visible only when backlit and viewed through a magnifying glass. Existence as palimpsest—a story as a crosscut through layers of time.

It was a cool night. We lay on the grass. We were clothed by the shadows of moonlit leaves, gray branches woven on our skin. "Take a look," she said, as she pulled her hair up. On the back of her neck was a black mark. It was halfway down toward her shoulders, a little off-center to the left. The spot, not quite a perfect circle, was about an inch in diameter, the color as black as oil. I reached out and ran my fingertips across it, slowly, gently.

"Is it a tattoo?" I asked. No, she said, she's had it since she was born. "It's part of me," she said. "Then," I said, "you've been marked by God." I pressed my lips against the spot. A shiver ran from her body into mine. I covered us with my jacket, and we moved in and out of sleep—and somewhere between consciousness and unconsciousness I asked Julia if the mark meant she was condemned to wander, if it meant she wouldn't stay with me. Yes, she said, that was what it meant.

"I found out today," Julia said after she'd told me about her conversation with the film student, "that I've been fired from the university. The investigative committee concluded I've committed what they call intellectual fraud. There's nothing more we can do, Sy. My career is ruined. That's why I wanted to end it where it began—in this place. The story is over. Let's drink to the end."

FEBRUARY 8 (NIGHT)

It was already dark by the time I made it back to the gentlemen's inn. A heavy wooden door held together by two iron slats led down a narrow stone staircase into the cellar, much like the stairs in the Strahov Monastery. I was frightened, frightened of ghosts, which is another way of saying spirits, or memories, memories of old fears, old hauntings, intrusions, exposures, bodies, selfhood—a spirit left outside in the wintry air, a homeless spirit, a spirit blown away by a frigid wind. "The story is over," she said. *No.* I moved my lips silently. *No.* I reached out and put my hand on the back of her neck, running my fingertips over God's mark, the burn of His fingertip. *No.* A refusal. A total refusal. No. No. I felt like a child, a childish refusal to deal with reality, a parent's reality, a reality as fragile as the glass that held my shot of whiskey. I picked it up and let it fall to the floor. It smashed. The bartender, the filmmaker from Riga, let out groan and reached under the bar for a hand broom and dustpan.

I shone my flashlight around the cellar. The ceiling was low, and I had to bend my head to move through the space. The walls were close together. Musty. Airless. I focused on my breath to suppress a suffocating feeling, to keep myself steady, moving forward, moving toward the door at the far end of the corridor. I reached it, opened it. It was dark inside, darker than dark, a darkness folding into a kind of endless darkness, one of those holes in the universe. I stepped from the hallway into the room. I could feel the chill from it, from the well or pit of emptiness somewhere beyond or below me. An icy emptiness—my body pitching forward into it.

The beam of my flashlight transformed the gaping hole into an ordinary maids' quarters. Beds were stacked three high. There was hardly space between them for an adult human body. The top bed of the stack couldn't have been more than eighteen inches below the ceiling. There were three stacks of three— nine beds packed into this closet-size space. The nine trunks for clothes and bedding took up nearly all of the remaining floor area. The only space remaining, besides the impossibly narrow pathways between the beds, was about four square feet in a corner opposite the door. I started to open the trunks, to go through them, though by the time I was on the fourth one, I noticed that the beam of my flashlight was starting to fade. It was still okay, it would last for a few more days, I thought, but I'd have to use it sparingly—I needed enough light to get out of here, though it occurred to me that I had no idea where this "here" was—the maids' quarters, the gentlemen's inn, the village of Z., Prague, Europe, my body—life? Then I thought: it doesn't matter, these places are the same, one linked to another on the great chain of being—and to leave the maids' quarters would be like leaving life behind. For what? To fall back into the regressive infinity of the past? To fall forward into the time beyond history? I didn't know. No clue. Didn't even want a clue. Didn't want an idea. Rather, I was searching for a feeling, an emotional spark, searching through those trunks. For what? For the journals of Sidney Keter? For *The Book of Moonlight*? For the fate of the landsurveyor? My hand slipped to the bottom of the seventh trunk. I felt something other than fabrics and lace. It was paper. I threw the plain gowns and scratchy woolens out of the way and saw a dark-green folder. I took it out. It was a thin file with no more than a dozen pages inside. On the front was a handwritten label, on which was written: *Department X.*

The story contained in these pages is written in a naïve, innocent manner, the manner of a child, or, more accurately, a blend of a child and an adult, a disturbing hybrid. It's called "Night of Fire." The story begins in the chambermaids' room. There are nine of them, and their "leader" is a girl named Pepi. She's telling the other girls her plan: the maids are going to light the gentlemen's inn on fire. And that's not all, she tells them. At the same time that they light the inn on fire from nine different points, others around the village will do the same in the church, in the schoolhouse, in the inn by the bridge, at the house of the council chairman, at the house of the head of the volunteer fire brigade, and so on. Beyond that, the houses of the master artisans will be attacked, she says; the cobbler, the baker, the master tanner all will be lit up at the exact same time. Don't worry, she tells the others; the "movement," as she calls it, has already disabled the new fire engine given to the village by the castle authorities. The volunteer fire brigade will be helpless. As the village burns, panic and chaos will allow the group of arsonists and saboteurs to gather. They will meet on the road and together storm the castle. They will breach the castle's gates (Pepi has a plan for this, too) and then fan out into every last corner of the structure. When the signal is given, says Pepi, in the form of a piercing whistle, which will resound through castle and village alike, every member of the movement will light the castle on fire, burning it to the ground. After escaping to the castle's courtyard, the members will watch the castle burn. Then they will march back to the village. There, they will gather around the smoldering embers and ash of the symbols of village power—the inns, the church, the hated schoolhouse— and a woman, the visionary, the prophetess of the movement, will read aloud a proclamation about a new order, an order in which every chambermaid and peasant can live in freedom and with dignity. The prophetess's name is Amalia, the same Amalia disgraced by the old authority—the same Amalia driven into her home, tortured by the failing health of her family, by their abject poverty. Poverty and failing health had pushed her parents toward the grave. Next to Amalia, on either side of her, will be her siblings—her brother Barnabas, her sister Olga. And in front of them, Pepi explains, all of us. In this moment, she says, we will have moved out of the shadows—from basements and cellars and stables and barns and silos and storage rooms, from our dark, cramped corners, into the light of day, from mere creatures into human beings! The time approaches, Pepi tells them, for what will forever be called "the night of fire"—a night of justice, a night when evil and tyranny burn. It is almost here, she tells the other eight chambermaids, the night is almost upon us. It will not come gradually, but all at once—suddenly we will light our torches, suddenly and without warning the doors and walls and beams and roofs will be devoured by flames. Yes, she says, the fire is approaching—you can feel it as a wave of energy, it is a current gathering force in one place, here, in the basement of the gentlemen's inn, in the chambermaids' room, in the heart of each chambermaid. The night of fire, she tells them, will be a combustion of our hearts, each heart will burn but the fire will not consume it.

Stigma—a mark—the mark of Cain. The burning fingertip—striking out, wandering, burning, flashlight fading, jars of pickled mushrooms floating through my brain in rivulets of alpha-amanitin, the poisoning of the mind, the poisoning of the story, a story for which there is no cure, a story fated to die, a death before its ending, a story with no end or a story with only an end, the poisoning of history, time—time dying—history dying, coughing up blood in a tubercular cough, uncurable, unable to eat, unable to keep hydrated, a poisoned history desiccating—skin pulling taut, innards hardening into rock, poisoned, history petrifying, and with one smash it will be turned to dust, dust to dust, then nothing, then the beauty of nothing, meaning the beauty of all there is—then redemption and cure and health and life. I need to sleep. I cannot keep my eyes open any longer. I cannot write another word today.

FEBRUARY 9 (MORNING)

I wake up with this question churning in my mind: is the emptiness here, in the village of Z., absence or presence? Is it the absence of life, or is it the presence of the nothingness from which life emerges? When I was at the clinic, Dr. Hruška told me I needed, "more than anything else, to draw boundaries" between myself and others. Selfhood, he told me, is defined as much by what is beyond the self as it is by what the self contains. If everything flows freely in and out of the self, he said, it is as if there is no self. A nation, he said, is defined by its border, the page by its edge. Without borders and edges, he said, what would we call one thing or another? And what are we left with, he asked, if we can't distinguish between things?

"Freedom," I told him. He tried to maintain his poise, but I saw his face twitch as a frown came over it. I saw the furrow of his brow as he must have realized he'd made no progress with me. He was stuck, he had reached a therapeutic dead end. He took out his notebook and spent the following few minutes writing something down. Writing me down. Writing me.

FEBRUARY 9 (NIGHT)

Keter wrote about the Barnabas family in his journals, about the "castle stories" Amalia's sister Olga recorded in her diary. It was the day after the volunteer firemen's festival in the village, Keter wrote. The castle authorities had given the village a new engine, a gleaming, perfect machine. Everyone who attended the festival was in awe of it—with its ladders and hoses and crankshafts. Nearly the whole village turned out for the festival, not just to see the new machine, and not just to honor the service of the volunteer fire brigade. This day was the oldest of village traditions; it was the primary communal celebration of the year. The villagers came in their finest clothes, even if most of the garments were barely more than peasant's attire. Still, if a woman or girl had even an inch or two of lace, she would find a way to fix it to a collar, sleeve, or hemline. Well-to-do families, like the Barnabas family was at the time, would appear nearly transformed. Olga came in embroidered silks, Amalia drowning in lace, Barnabas wearing a tight-fitting "city" suit made of shiny material. This particular festival was important to the Barnabas family because this was the day Barnabas's father was made the chief of the volunteer fire brigade, a high honor in the village, higher even, some said, than the council chairman. The council chairman himself seemed to recognize this and personally led the ceremony that transferred the chief's badge from the previous chief, a man named Gross, to the official volunteer fire brigade jacket of Barnabas's father. This was a moment of total pride for the whole family, so much so that Gardena, the landlady of the inn by the bridge, came to their house, which was at that time one of the biggest in the village and in the center of the village by the church, to lend Amalia her garnet necklace. It was a lucky charm, Gardena said, sure to attract the attention of a future husband. Amalia took it with pleasure, thanked the landlady profusely, and clasped it over her high lace collar, making her look, Gardena told her, "like the daughter of an aristocrat, maybe the daughter of the count himself." Or maybe, Olga mused, it was an unnatural combination of aristocrat and common villager. Perhaps it was this combination, rarely seen, Olga considered, that caused the subsequent trouble by sending the castle official Sortini into a dizzied state of confusion. In any case, the day went perfectly. Barnabas's father had stood there proudly as the council chairman pinned on his chief's badge and gave him an official certificate from the castle authorities recognizing his appointment. The council chairman delivered what everyone considered to be a nice speech, praising the outgoing chief, lauding the new one, emphasizing the work Barnabas's father had done to train the village men and boys in fire-safety procedures. In addition, the council chairman stressed Barnabas's father's stature in the village, the central role he played in bringing the magnificent new machine to Z. It could be that the trouble that ensued after the festival could be traced to the council chairman's speech—Olga certainly thought so, according to the Keter journals. Why? It was really quite simple, Olga said. The council chairman had praised Gross and Barnabas's father, but he had completely (and some say inexplicably) ignored Sortini, the attending castle official, who was in charge of everything related to the fire brigade, including the new engine, even if Sortini himself, if asked, would have said that this, as all else, fell under the ultimate authority of Klamm. The ignoring of Sortini and the praising of Barnabas's father was a major error on the part of the council chairman—or, seen another way, according to Olga, it was brilliant move to destroy her father. It was hard to know, Olga said, which side the council chairman was on. In any case, the party lasted well into the night. The band played the village songs. The people danced, drank beer. Everyone seemed joyful and alive, especially Amalia, who in her lace and garnets seemed somehow above the others, beyond them in her ecstasy, certainly beyond them in her beauty. Sortini, the high official, stood apart from the crowd during the festival. It was rare that a high castle official appeared in the village, and this might have been the first time Sortini did so. He held back, didn't talk to anyone, and no one could tell whether he listened to the others talk, if he even saw the people there, or whether he was lost in his own tangled web of thoughts about official matters, official duties, which were rumored to be massive in scope. Apart from the council chairman in his official speech, everyone at the festival personally thanked Sortini, praised him, especially for the magnificent machine. At one point, when the band launched into a particularly boisterous song, Amalia even had the boldness to invite Sortini to come with her to the dance floor. She made a deep bow in front of him, displaying her considerable charm. Sortini didn't seem to notice this—but he must have noticed, Olga thought—and only reacted with a slight twitch of his head, which caused his official castle hat to slip a bit to the left side. Amalia bowed a second time and turned and walked back to join the dancing. There, amid the others, she moved with utter grace, swooping and twirling among the crowd of villagers. It was clear, Olga said, that Sortini was watching her intensely, studying every gesture, movement, every part of her body in motion. It was unclear whether Sortini stayed that night at the gentlemen's inn in the village or if he returned to the castle immediately after the festival. If he did stay at the inn, it would have been a momentous event, the powerful official's first overnight stay in the village—at least his first public stay. In any case, early the next morning, there was a knock at the Barnabas family window. Olga heard it—it woke her up—and came out of the bedroom she shared with her sister to find Amalia standing at the open window with her nightgown flowing behind her in the gentle draft. Through the open window, Olga saw a castle messenger hand a note to Amalia. The messenger waited there as Amalia opened the letter and began to read it. It was a short note, no more than a quarter of a page. Amalia paused when she came to the end. Then her whole body started to shake with a tremor that Olga came to understand as the physical manifestation of repulsion, and this repulsion quickly transformed into a raw, instinctual anger. She tore the note.

She tore it as if she were ripping apart the entire world. She stepped to the window and threw the pieces into the messenger's face. When Amalia turned around, Olga could see her lips were slightly parted, her eyes wide. By this time, the messenger understood that nothing more would be coming from Amalia. There would be no reply for him to take back to Sortini, no reply to his demand for Amalia to come to him and to do with him those unspeakable vulgarities. Still the messenger hesitated a little longer—and one can understand this, Olga said, because never in the collective memory of the village had a single demand by a castle official been refused. When the messenger was finally gone, Olga asked Amalia about the letter. Amalia wouldn't say what had been written there. Instead, she said, in almost a whisper, that it was the vilest, most disgusting, humiliating thing she could ever imagine. Her refusal of Sortini's request, Olga could tell, drew on her instinct for survival, and the letter itself, Olga maintained, was an invitation to death. Another type of death awaited Amalia—and the whole Barnabas family. In the coming days and weeks, as word of her refusal spread throughout the village, one person after another cut ties with them. Amalia's father, the master cobbler, lost his clients. They were taken by his former apprentice, Brunswick. Amalia's father was stripped of his new position as head of the volunteer fire brigade—the council chairman himself came to the house to pull the badge from Barnabas's father's official fireman's coat and to repossess the official certificate from the castle that hung on the wall in the Barnabas family living room. One by one, the family's friends were lost—all on the pretext, unstated, of course, that Amalia offended the castle authorities so egregiously that when punishment finally came, it would be total. But punishment from the castle never came, as week after week, month after month, the family sunk deeper into poverty, into disgrace. For their poor mother, it was too much, and it drove her toward mental and physical breakdown. After a while, she could barely walk, barely speak, couldn't feed herself. Her father was hardly any better. He sat for hours each day in his wooden rocker, mumbling about his lost badge, about the chairman removing the certificate he'd painstakingly framed on the very night he had received it at the festival, hanging it in pride of place near the ceramic oven for his family and guests to see. Their father rocked in his chair, mumbled, and stared into the empty spot where the frame had been, until, that is, the family lost the house and was forced to move. In view of the entire village, the Barnabas family carried their last remaining possessions, meager and worthless as they were, from their large house (the Brunswick family moved in that same afternoon) to a cramped, drafty hovel a few streets away. Barnabas and Olga would stay up late into the night trying to figure out what the castle's punishment might be, when it would come, what they could do to mitigate it, what they could do to make things right, to get things back to the way they were before. Eventually, Barnabas even went to work for the castle in the capacity, so it seemed, of personal village messenger for Klamm, though he never met Klamm, and didn't know for sure if the few messages he was given to deliver were actually official castle business. It wasn't clear if the messages were unofficial castle business, or the official private business of the officials, or unofficial private business, or some other category Barnabas hadn't

yet imagined. His trips to the castle often ended with him being denied entry to the castle's sprawling domain. Other times,
he was permitted to enter, but then had to wait for hours in
some drafty antechamber. If, by chance, he was permitted to
enter what seemed like an official castle office, the scenes he
witnessed there were nothing short of bewildering—papers everywhere, people (whether they were officials or not wasn't
clear) peering down into large books, the contents of which
were hidden from view by wooden screens. Beyond these
rooms—did such spaces exist beyond these rooms? They did,
but rarely could Barnabas peer into this beyond, and when he
did, it was just enough for him to see that beyond these rooms
were other rooms with other spaces beyond them. Still, Barnabas could come home and tell Olga about everything he'd experienced at the castle, and they would dissect each detail, follow every thought, however outlandish. Now and then, Amalia
would appear during these nighttime sessions and reproach
them for telling "castle stories," stories, she said, that were
nothing more than children's fairy tales.

Stigmatized, humiliated, degraded—Amalia was the most
despised person in the village, but the aggression from her
neighbors didn't penetrate her. It seemed to bounce off her.
Day by day, her power seemed to grow. Each day the castle
took no action, each day she moved through the streets with
her head held high—her beauty unfurling, growing, casting
its shadows on the ugliness around her. There were whispers,
whispers passing in the darkness of the chambermaids' quarters
at night, whispers among the peasant women working out in
the potato fields, whispers among the seamstresses and wid-

ows, that Amalia had stood up to the castle and she had won. Sortini had not returned to the village. Why? Because, they thought, he didn't dare to appear. He did not dare to appear in front of her—her, a woman who wasn't a high official, wasn't a village secretary, wasn't even a messenger for the castle. It was whispered that when a village secretary or a messenger would see Amalia coming, he would bolt inside and lock the door, trembling until she passed. It was whispered that village secretaries now refused to be seen in the village by day, in fear of Amalia. It was whispered, finally, that Amalia was the one who would free them from castle tyranny. Amalia was their savior. But when? How low must she fall before she rises? The people wanted to see the sign, the sign that would tell them the time had come, the time to tear the whole thing down, to tear the world down, to let it burn. Then one day a stranger arrived in the village. He claimed to be a landsurveyor and said his name was K. On the back of his neck was the mark of Cain.

FEBRUARY 10 (MORNING)

I walked into the Anežský Klášter. I was alone. It was during the day, and Julia didn't leave the apartment during the day. For some reason, I couldn't shake the idea of Julia starring in the bartender's film about an Italian woman in her forties coming to Prague to view the collection of medieval art. It would have to be a film of raw texture, I thought, with long shots of works at the Anežský Klášter, shots of the woman's gaze, her stillness, her languid movements as she glides from painting to painting, an obsessional piece, a surreal piece. Magnifying detail, like wrinkles on skin, and cracks in the surface of the paint, and the dark walls, and the arched ceilings. There would be other visitors, perhaps blurred, moving in and out of view. Ghosts—invaders from the future into the medieval world, a world defined by its flatness, its color, a world of symbols, books, flowers, fruit, birds, bread falling from the sky like rain. I paused in front of a painting of Jesus. He stands on a coffin. A soldier in the left-hand corner of the foreground looks up at him. Jesus is thin. He's wearing a red-and-green robe, which is open at the chest to reveal the bloody gash. Blood drips from it—fresh. His feet are delicate, tender, birdlike. They seem to be moving forward, stepping down from the coffin toward the viewer. Moving toward an encounter with the viewer—with me. In his left hand, he holds a staff with a golden cross on top, the icon of his crucifixion. A golden halo encircles his head, glowing like the sun against the bloodred sky, providing a link between Jesus and the golden stars in the firmament. Could this be it, the painting that captures the imagination of the Italian woman who's come to Prague to view the collection at the Anežský Klášter? Could this be it—the subject of a film by a young man from Riga who's come to Prague to learn his craft? Or another: Mary wearing a crown surrounded by gold, Mary in the heavenly realm, in the kingdom of God, presided over by God the Father. Jesus on the Mount of Olives. I passed by these. They weren't quite right. Nothing was quite right until I encountered the one painting it had to be, the only painting Julia could have stood in front of for hours, the only painting in the Anežský Klášter that could be the subject of the bartender's student film, the painting of Mary of Egypt. The colors in the painting were muted compared to the others, earthy, brown—

the brown of bread—chalky whites, ruddy background, a back-drop of stars, it was the desert at night. Mary's hair flowed down and covered her entire body in a gnarly pelt. My eyes trained on her delicate feet, which gave the whole body a weightless feel, a look of floating in space, a desert space, a desolate space. She cradled three loaves of bread in her hands. Like my jars of preserved berries, fruits, and vegetables, they were the means of her survival. Each day a crumb for Mary of Egypt, and a crumb, seeded with the spirit of God, became a whole meal. Julia gazed at her, gazed through my eyes at her, my imagination, which was filtered through a camera lens pointed by a film student from Riga. Mary of Egypt—driven by desire. It was a ferocious desire that propelled her on her journey to Jerusalem at the time of the Great Feasts. She went there for desire—not for faith—because only among the thousands of other pilgrims could she fulfill her insatiable lust. She was a woman of the body, totally, wholly, fully body—and among the pilgrims she sought to quench her urges in a whirl-wind of fucking and orgies. After days of constant physical satisfaction, Mary felt the impulse to enter the Church of the Holy Sepulchre. She made her way to the entrance, but as she got set to pass through the door an invisible force blocked her way. In this moment, she knew the truth: to gain entrance and approach the divine essence of Jesus Christ she would need to choose between the body and the spirit, and if she chose the spirit, it meant a total renunciation of her physical desires, her lust, her incredible bodily passion, a passion she thought must surpass that of any other human being. The idea to give up this pleasure, a feeling of her whole physical being awakened to ecstasy, was nearly impossible to imagine. And yet, she knew it must be done. In the choice between the body and the spirit, there could only be spirit. Tears flowed down her cheeks as she stood at the entrance to the church. With each tear, she willed away part of her lust, shedding it, or burying it deep inside herself. She touched the invisible wall that prevented her from entering the church. As the tears fell, the wall began to crack. It cracked in a hundred places, one crack for each tear. She pressed her palm against it and the wall shattered, falling around her in invisible shards. She entered the space. She was alone at this early hour. She reached the relic of the true cross and got down on her knees. She gazed at the pale reddish-brown stain of Jesus's blood on the pinewood. She knew if she wanted to live in the realm of the spirit, she would need to repent. She would need to abandon the cities and towns. She would need to go far away from people and live as a hermit. She left the church and made her way to the Jordan River to see the monks at the monastery of John the Baptist. There, she was absolved of her sins and received the Holy Communion. The monks gave her three loaves of bread, and Mary left the monastery to go into the desert to live her life of solitude. Soon, her clothes became tatters. Her hair grew wild. She had no shelter and slept each frigid night by burying her body in the sand. What did Julia think when she gazed at this painting? Did she think she could renounce it all? Did she think she could renounce the world? Her body? Every pleasure in touch, taste, smell? In order to attain a state in which she was light enough to walk across water, as Mary of Egypt had done? Could passion really be quelled, destroyed? Mary's passion? Julia's? I looked at Mary of Egypt, sister of Nebuchadnezzar, the Babylonian king—the human-as-animal, human-as-beast, the beast of God. I gazed at the painting, and there was Amalia. She was looking out the window at me with the raw force of life in her eyes, a power, if released, that would have devoured the village of Z. Devoured the pathetic Sortini, who would never have had the guts to face her even if Amalia had obeyed the summons. The summons, it occurred to me, was nothing but a self-summons, a summoning to the theater of his own debasement. That's why he couldn't attend the theater, that's why the instant he dispatched the messenger he had to flee back behind the castle walls, that's why he needed, once there, to retreat into the castle's inner chambers, so that there, he, Sortini, could nail himself to his own cross, which was nothing more than two entirely ordinary planks of wood fastened together. There was only death. No possibility of resurrection. None. Amalia had the power to shatter invisible walls with the press of her palms, with the force of her spirit, spirit twirling in the loop of time. This has to be the moment when K. (Kain/Cain) began his journey. He left Prague on a sleigh drawn by two horses. He was bound for Berlin but ended up instead in the mountain resort town of Spindelmühle. This was the "becoming-real" of a lucid dream, a dream of Mary of Egypt's body, a body conveyed by spirit, glowing, pulsing with the energy of pure faith in Jesus Christ. In the many years that passed in this dream, Mary of Egypt should have died a thousand deaths—thousands of times, she should have died of starvation, thirst, hypothermia, thousands of times burnt by the sun's merciless heat. Then one day a man appeared in the desert. He was standing above her as she woke. At first, she thought she was imagining it. She shrunk back away from him, afraid to be touched. The man told her that word was spreading around the towns lining the periphery of the desert about a woman in the desert who had become a living spirit, a spirit pure enough to ascend to heaven when she desired and then to return to earth. The idea that there was a being who could bridge heaven and earth, who could walk with both humans and angels, the man said, was starting to result in strange practices among the people. People, he said, were starting to worship this being, this woman, who was said to be as light as air. In some churches, the people were taking down the crosses, replacing them with stacks of three loaves of bread, because it was said that this desert woman had lived for thousands of years on this precise amount of food—three loaves of bread lasting an eternity. The three loaves of bread, the people said, symbolized eternity and immortality, a combination that transcended the spiritual power of Jesus Christ. Something needed to be done about this, he told her. But what? Why, he asked, would this woman want to eclipse Jesus Christ in the minds of the people? Mary didn't believe him. She could feel Jesus's spirit, the spirit of goodness, moving around her, through her, into her soul. Then she felt the truth: this man was evil. He had come into the desert to kill her. He sought to rid the desert and the world of her spirit. Goodness would be overrun. The unrighteous would rule the earth. Julia's cheeks flushed—yes—I can see them now. The film student's camera closes in on her as her pulse quickens, as she imagines the man's hand rising up with that long blade—as she imagines the knife thrusting into her stomach, then out, then into her breast, then out, then into her neck. Julia's breath quickens. Mary fell to the sand. Everything was dark, everything vanished into the desert night until the pale beam of the rising moon washed over the landscape. Am I in love with Julia? Or is it the longing for another life, a life caught neatly in the camera frame? Mary of Egypt's body was found by a lion some weeks later. It hadn't decomposed. In death, she had become incorruptible. The lion pawed at the ground. He dug a pit and gently pushed Mary's body with his muzzle. The body rolled over and fell down to the bottom. Her eyes were open, as if she were still alive and could gaze up at the powerful animal above her. Or it could be that she looked past the lion, past its golden skin, and into the heavens. The lion pushed the pile of dirt into the hole, burying Mary.

FEBRUARY 10 (NIGHT)

The stranger K. came from the Italian front. He had survived the Battle of the Piave River, where tens of thousands of others had died in the most worthless, meaningless way. He made his way north on his own, separated from his regiment, a regiment that was, in any case, mostly dead. The war had weakened K. He had two wounds from the battle, both of which were now infected, one on his foot from stepping on a jagged scrap of metal, the other on his arm when a fragment of wood from an exploded tree lodged itself in his bicep. Neither puncture was serious, relatively speaking, but exposure to sweat and dirt had inflamed them. By the time K. arrived in Merano, he could barely walk, barely lift his throbbing arm. The infection had spread into his blood. He was feverish and delusional. He had a few valuable items he had gathered along his way with the army, including an Ottoman candelabra, pure silver, which he traded for lodging and care in a Merano hotel. The innkeeper had seen his frightening state and called a doctor, who came and dressed the wounds. Still, it was unclear for days if K. would survive, whether his body had the inner strength to fight off the infection. A woman from the town, the daughter-in-law of the innkeeper's brother, attended to him between the doctor's visits. She changed the bandages on the wounds, washed them out, fed him the strong broth the inn's cook had prepared. When he was finally better, K. packed up his things and left Merano at the break of dawn without saying goodbye to anyone, including M., the young woman who had nursed him back to health. He continued to Vienna. On the outskirts of the city, he joined a group of Romani around an open fire. It was pure impulse that caused him to throw his identity papers into the flames, erasing himself from civilized existence. There was a forger in Vienna named Osterhase. He was a man the color of gray ash. Over the years, he had mastered the process of constructing nearly every official document from Moscow to Lisbon, from Rome to London. Who, Osterhase asked the stranger, did he want to be? The stranger looked into Osterhase's eyes for a long time, then he said to him: "My name is Kain."

Osterhase laughed. "You are asking me," he said, "to do the impossible. I can make you into anyone," he added, "but I don't deal in ghosts, in the already dead, and I don't deal in myths and fables. Some forgers might try it, but if they do, their days are numbered, the police will be onto them soon enough. If you really want to turn into Kain, though why anyone would want to be that damned figure is beyond me, you'll have more luck somewhere else." The stranger held out a few gold coins and said again he would take papers with the name Kain.

"You must know," Osterhase said to him as he took the coins from the stranger's hand, "that borders are now vanishing, new states are emerging, who knows how long they'll last. To which state," Osterhase asked, "does this Kain belong?" The stranger told him it didn't matter—that Osterhase should give him the papers that would best allow him to keep moving. He had no plans to set down roots, to stay still. The following day, he returned to Osterhase's workshop and picked up his documents. He gave Osterhase an extra gold coin for his quick and perfect work and turned to leave. Before he got to the door, Osterhase asked him about the mark on the back of his neck. That mark, Kain said, was the scar left by the touch of the fingertip of God.

Kain continued north, first to Prague, then to Berlin. In Berlin, he found a room in a boardinghouse on Auguststrasse and work as a janitor in the orphanage across the street. Kain becoming Keter, Sidney Keter, the *keter* of the tree of life, the crown of the *sephirot*, the most hidden of all hidden things. Invisible. Colorless. Beyond human comprehension. The stirrings of creation—the *ein sof*, the unending, infinite, the negation of all that is. Nothingness—or nothing but *the desire for being*. The highest state of being in the world: compassion. I am my brother's keeper. More than that: I am my brother Abel, my brother Abel is me. We are one being, joined by the force of life. In the evenings and throughout the nights, at a small table in his room in the boardinghouse, after his long, hard work in the orphan-age was done, Kain Keter began to write a history of the world. It was the story of the unfolding of time, beginning with the expulsion from the Garden of Eden and ending in the future with the coming of the divine kingdom on earth—*tikkun*—the assemblage of everything that had been blown apart. What was the force, he wondered, that shattered the original harmony, a harmony preceding creation itself? It was nothing other than the rage of the Lord. Kain Keter. Keter Kain. Night after night, he sat at the small table on an old wooden chair. There was a window into the courtyard, which, when opened during the oppressively hot summer months, let in a variety of smells: soap from the laundry, sweat, onions. And sounds—slamming doors, men shouting at wives, mothers and fathers shouting at their children, children crying out in terror, children at play. He was determined that his story would cover everything. He wouldn't be satisfied by anything less. It had to include everything from everywhere, for how else, he wondered, could there be a real reckoning, how else will the messianic force understand what took place on the earth in its absence, these thousands of years bereft of spirit, a period by its very nature limited, confined, finite, as opposed to the infinite, the endlessness before and af-ter time? This everything, the world within time, he thought, this was history. He wrote: *In the beginning, a wind swept over the face of the deep.* God emerged and spoke the first words in the secret code of creation: *Vayomer elohim yehi or vayehi or.* It was a type of automatic writing, a Sufi's chant, a speaking in tongues, Muhammad's recitations—and with every moment of such beauty a pulse of ecstasy coursed through Kain Keter, and with every moment of evil, a pulse of despair. He felt the birth of everyone in history as if it was the birth of his own child, every death as if it were the death of his own parent. At times, the pleasure and pain of writing this universal history was too much for his frail body, and he would let out rapturous or chilling screams, often attracting the attention and concern of neighbors in the house. More than once, the young man who lived next door, Isaac Mondschein, would crack open Kain Keter's door in the middle of the night after one of these wails, only to see the man sitting hunched over his small table, a look of terror on his face, his body bathed in a pale moonlight that streamed in through the window. It was a text, Mondschein thought, that could only be written in darkness, or, he would correct himself, a text written only by the light of the moon. To himself, he started to call Kain Keter's project *The Book of Moonlight*. When the final period falls at the end of the last sentence of the book, Kain Keter told Mondschein one day, it will mean the end has come, history will cease, infinity will return. What we think permanent will decompose, what we possess will disappear, all that is known will lose its meaning, the invisible will become visible, harmony will be restored. This, he said, is the power of the final dot, the final mark at the end of the story, the end which is itself the only possible true beginning.

I open a jar of canned cherries, spooning them out into my month, careful not to swallow the pits. I say softly to myself, as I write this, the sounds of the words tumbling around: the village lay deep in snow . . . nothing could be seen . . . nothing to indicate the presence . . . nothing . . . presence of a castle . . . fog and darkness . . . nothing fog and darkness . . . fog and darkness castle was there nothing . . . presence darkness castle fog surrounded indicated there nothing . . . he looked up . . . up into the apparent emptiness . . . nothing presence emptiness apparent indicate surround darkness fog . . . fog and darkness . . . fog and darkness. The jar of cherries is empty. A question comes to me, a question with a clear yet impossible answer: How could a person arrive at the clinic Zelená Hora? *How did I arrive there?* No trains go there, no roads lead there. No bus stops there. The wooden bridge over which one must pass to cross the stream has rotted and collapsed.

FEBRUARY 11 (MORNING)

Dr. Hruška told me to write it down. Tell the story, he said, from the beginning to the end. If you write it down, he said, we can read it together in our daily sessions. We can find those gaps, he said, those holes, contradictions—those (he didn't say this last one) lies. Or, he said, we can locate where you veer off target, the point where you take the detour. This might be when the memory came to me of the night when I first met Daniel Cohen at a party in Kreuzberg, when he took me to the house on Grunewaldstrasse to meet the chemist Dr. Kaesbohrer. Kaesbohrer had been trying for decades to cure a very specific malady—the feeling of two antagonistic mazelike structures existing at the same time in a single being, structures hostile toward each other and irreconcilable. After discovering the theoretical projection of the malady in the form of a mathematical equation, he began to experiment with an appropriate chemical response, the creation of an antidote, a drug. Through a long process of trial and error, he told me and Cohen, he had discovered it. The result was a cloudy yellow liquid that could, as he said, "blend the structures," thus solving the impossibility of the maze, not by finding an "exit," but by guaranteeing its infinity, the existence of layer upon layer, gaps that lead to deeper regions of the maze, openings that circle back to previous levels. Objects, he said, could move along pathways, slipping from one system to the other—and back again—like, I guess, the writer Daniel Cohen slipping from Berlin to Zelená Hora and then to Sladkovsky's bar in Prague. Or Milena—from Berlin to the Hotel des Bains on the Lido in Venice, passing through the labyrinth of my past and future translations of works by the German novelist Anton Grassfeld, and from there into Cohen's imagination, and mine.

Write it down! What was Dr. Hruška wanting of me other than a kind of self-death? And this trip to Z.—a resurrection? I could never have written it down. And because I couldn't write it down, I had to flee. There was only one way out of Zelená Hora, and that path led through Daniel Cohen, through his manuscript, via Milena, to the Hotel des Bains. At the Hotel des Bains, I found an endless series of doors, which led into lost spaces, rooms with forgotten scenes unfolding, scenes waiting for an audience, for a person to open the door—for a spectator, who, as soon as he or she passes the threshold, becomes a participant. They are scenes of imagination, scenes flowing from my pen, trapped between papery walls—yellowed by the passing of time. An example: a girl named Diya is there, the daughter of a woman from Senegal, perhaps my daughter, an offspring of my mind, or the daughter of the German writer

Anton Grassfeld—she is his character, my translation of her—or perhaps she is my character embedded in his work—or neither. She is a character broken free of me, a character who has escaped Grassfeld, and she's here, in this in-between zone, to exist without the dominance of an author. I open another door and Esther Bird is there. She is reading to me. They are stories about Jacob's ladder. She tells me stories of a child named Amos who died when he was two years old. Amos is the son of my former lover, Ida Fields. And he is my son. Ida Fields is my only lover—a lover who has now multiplied and divided, each fragment of Ida becoming another: Pepi, Julia. And others, more spectral, distant, ungraspable entities: Milena, Mila. There is a performance artist named Fo. The branches from Ida lead around the world: Warsaw, Tehran, Amsterdam, Berlin, Venice, Prague. All of this contained in that potion, a potion made from the resin of a Siberian cedar, which had been struck by a shard of Soviet artillery fire during the Second World War. The wounded cedar, from which comes a wounded history, and the narrative it contains—punctured, wounded, oozing a life force, which is to say, emanating the breath of God.

Here I am! That's how Abraham responds to God's calling on him to sacrifice Isaac, his son. Here I am! Yes, here I am, and I am writing it down. Not for Hruška—not for his "case study," not for his ordered notes with dates and times and roman numerals, rather I'm writing toward the end, toward the disintegration of myself, toward the end or the disintegration of the universe. The eschaton of the final period (.), a blow, a strike powerful enough to destroy the world. Bang. Ha! My brother Henry would shake his head, would shake his head at the "utter nonsense" of the idea that a single period could blow up the world, making room for a world to come, a world yet to be marked, a clean, empty world, a world with no language—a world in silence.

The snow is falling outside the windows of the pub. It is so heavy that it seems like someone is playing tricks on me by dumping bags of feathers from the rooftop. A theater set—the village of Z. A play with a single character named Sy Kirschbaum, a play set in the pub of an abandoned village inn in a desolate valley that has somehow escaped the gaze of history, where time has stopped, where the end has already come but nobody noticed. It could be that such a play was written by my best childhood friend, the husband of Ida Fields, Gabe Slatky, a playwright, who years ago wrote a work called *Snowfall*, and it could be that this *Snowfall* peeled itself off the page and materialized itself here, a real-life stage, an epic theater, a theater of life. Write it down, Hruška told me, and that's what I'm doing, even if it is too late to write it down. All of it. I'm writing it all down, but I can't find the thread, only a set of characters, a cast: Ida Fields, Gabe Slatky, Grassfeld, Fo, Daniel Cohen, Pepi. And there is a road in the story. It leads out of the village into the forest and eventually bends toward the castle hill. Snowflakes turning into feathers, fields into roads, hills into castles—the psychedelic transmogrifications of a mind poisoned by jar after jar of century-old blueberry preserves.

FEBRUARY II (NIGHT)

Hruška told me to write it down, but what's written down can be analyzed and dissected. Unlike speech, words on paper can't be lost in the air. They can be erased or crossed out, erased, like that story of Cain, the daughter of Adam and Eve. Nearly vanished marks, but still there. I've been stuck inside the pub all day. I'm running low on wood—will need to pull the cart over to the schoolhouse shed tomorrow to restock, assuming the cart can make it through the newly fallen snow. There must be two or three feet of fresh snow by now. It's incredible how much snow falls in this valley—this valley of nowhere.

FEBRUARY 12 (MORNING)

Nahum Griggs is a character in Martin Dellman's unfinished novel *The Man Who Disappeared*. It's set in 1985, the year Dellman wrote it, the year he died. In the novel, Griggs arrives unannounced at the lakeside cabin of a writer, the novel's narrator. The narrator is named Martin Dellman. Griggs and Dellman had both been members of New York's Village Anarchist Society in the late 1960s, with Griggs one of the founders of the Black Anarchist Reading Circle. Dellman has lived in the cabin as a recluse since his wife passed away. When his wife was alive, they would summer in the cabin. Now he lives there year round. He almost never has guests other than the boy who paddles to the writer's dock in his canoe every other day during the summer. When the boy arrives, the writer invites him up to the cabin for a bowl of ice cream. The boy is shy—he's awkward, nervous, keeps fussing and pulling on his clothes, adjusting his socks, his bathing suit, his T-shirt. Not comfortable in his own skin, Dellman thinks, not comfortable in his own mind, a mind that might not yet even be a mind, one seemingly imprisoned by walls of convention, a mind that hasn't considered a single thought beyond the most ordinary, and yet it could be that at some point in the future, it is a mind that will soar high above the lake, the mind of an eagle, a mind behind the red eye of the loon. The boy, Sy, comes to the lake with his parents and older brother Henry at the end of June, leaves the lake at the end of the summer to go back to school. Sy's father, Walter, is a professor of American literature, his mother, Fran, a social worker. Summer scenes—two boys paddling by in a canoe, two boys fishing. Fran at the end of the dock lying on a beach chair in her bikini. Fran swimming by in her goggles and orange swimming cap just after the break of dawn. Dellman at his desk. Dellman drinking whiskey in one of the Adirondack chairs on the porch. It's winter when Griggs arrives. Summer is a memory now, preserved in spikes of heat that come from the fire in the Franklin stove.

Griggs comes out of the forest. His clothes are ripped, and the jacket has lost most of its filling—lumped and saggy, it could hardly provide protection against the bitter northern cold. On top of that, Griggs is burning with fever. He makes it to Dellman's porch and collapses. Dellman hears the thump of Griggs's body hitting the wooden boards from his office. Not expecting guests, he grabs his baseball bat and goes downstairs to investigate. When he sees the body on the porch through the window, his first thought is that a man has been struck by a stray hunter's bullet and has managed to make it to the cabin, following the path of chimney smoke. Dellman opens the door, expecting to see blood all over the place. He bends over the man, looks into his face—a face both dark and pale. Despite having not seen him in decades, Dellman knows right away that this man is Nahum Griggs. Griggs's beard is longer than it had been back then and is now speckled with gray. His face is thinner, his cheeks sunken in, hair receded. Griggs is wearing a pair of black leather boots laced up to the middle of his calves. They have copper eyelets, some of which have fallen off. Dellman manages to get Griggs to his feet, to shuffle him inside, and to lay him down on the sofa. The whole time Griggs barely seems to notice, is barely alive—and if it isn't for the sweating and the shivering, Dellman might mistake this living body for a corpse. When Griggs is stretched out on the sofa, Dellman peels off his wet socks. Griggs's feet are as cold as ice. Then Dellman works to strip off the tattered jacket, the wet sweater underneath it, the black jeans. Once this is done, he can take in the full measure of the ravages of time, the emaciation, the scars. At least, Dellman thinks, there are no open wounds, nothing broken, and besides the fever and the potential frostbite, nothing that seems threatening or dangerous, except, perhaps, for the sorry feet. Dellman covers Griggs with a wool blanket, throws more logs into the fire, and returns to his office to wait for Griggs to wake up.

There is no question of focusing now, of getting back to his story—those stories that rise out of the misty lake and the territory surrounding it, a territory that is at once ordinary, bucolic, domesticated, and, at times, wild. He takes a thin paperback book from the shelf, blows a layer of dust from the top. He hasn't opened this particular book since he moved his library from his West Village studio into this office at the college many years ago. He can picture it—Griggs handing the book to him during his, Griggs's, last meeting of the society, before he was sent to the Vietnam War. Griggs would be sent, of course, Dellman thought, and, he, of course, would not be sent. He was a couple of years too old—and had just weeks before this meeting of the society received an appointment as a writer-in-residence at a college upstate. His first novel was forthcoming. He had everything he wanted. He even had the primary thing he desired without knowing he desired it—to be ordinary, to be comfortable, to be middle-class, set, stable, to feel that life was predictable, to feel mastery over his existence. How different this yearning was from the philosophy of Nahum Griggs—Griggs, who wrote the text he now holds in his hand, a book called *Becoming Powerless*. It's a curious book, he recalls, part radical political manifesto, part memoir, part fiction, and part poetry. Part thoughts on war. On *the* war. On war in general. On the state of Civil Rights, race relations, literature, art, film. Dellman gazes down at the cover, black letters on a yellow background, no image, the book's title in a typewriter font, underneath it, same font, Nahum Griggs. On the back, only a single quote: *I will put my teaching into their innermost being and inscribe it upon their hearts—Jeremiah 31:33.*

When the whole of the Black radical movement was turned toward organization and mobilization, toward empowerment, Griggs moved in the opposite direction. A quiet, shy young man—he was not a fighter, not a shouter, certainly not a preacher. But he was a radical—a radical, Dellman thinks, in the truest sense. That's precisely why they—*they*—had to get him out of the city, out of the country, and into the jungle to fight their useless war. Why has he come here? Why the cabin—and how could he possibly have found his way through the dense woods with no map, no car, carrying nothing but an old, faded backpack?

It is nighttime when Griggs wakes up. At first, he seems confused, but after a glass of water and a piece of bread, he starts to calm down. Dellman notices he isn't shivering anymore, isn't sweating through his underclothes. Griggs's fever, Dellman thinks, must have broken while he slept. Though it takes him noticeable effort, Griggs sits up on the sofa. He looks down at his body, registering, Dellman thinks, the lack of clothing—shoes, socks, pants, and sweater are gone. Dellman tells him he was soaked when he arrived, freezing. Griggs lets out something that seems like a burst of laughter, but Dellman isn't sure. "I must have been quite a sight," Griggs says. "I can barely remember it."

"Are you ill?" Dellman asks. "There's a country doctor out here in the winter. I'm happy to call him. He's come to check on me a few times. It takes a while for him to get here, but it's not a problem."

"No," Griggs says. "What day is it? What's the date?"

"It's the twenty-eighth of December," Dellman tells him.

"The meeting is on the thirty-first, New Year's Eve. She told me to meet her at your cabin on the lake. She said she'd come after dark. She told me to be here. She told me not to be late."

"Who are you talking about?"

"The woman with the long gray hair. Short. Pale."

"I don't remember," Dellman says. "What's her name?"

"Esther Bird." Griggs says. "She was the editor of the newspaper *Freedom* back in the '40s. Then she disappeared.

Everyone thought she'd been murdered. In the winter of '69, she appeared again in the city, started to come to meetings of the Black Anarchist Reading Circle. She was one of the few white people there. I caught up with her after her third or fourth meeting. We had a couple of drinks at Benson's. She told me about the anarchist scene in the '30s and during the war, people pushing angles from free love to bombing the Empire State Building. This is when, she said, she met a man named Keter, called himself Kain Keter, or Keter Kain, or Sidney Keter, or Isaac Mondschein. The feds had a file on him. They showed it to me after I got back from the war. They told me they'd been wrestling with the case for decades, and they'd recently determined—this was '71 or '72—that a key piece was missing from the file, a paper from '52, which, they said, had another, smaller, older paper attached to it with a paper clip, and that this other smaller, older paper contained what they called 'an answer to a question that was no question,' in other words, they said, it contained the key to the lock, the solution to the puzzle, the location of the truth. The beginning of the hunt for Keter was the reason Esther Bird had to make a run for it in the first place, to get out of the city in '46. It took her over twenty years to outrun the hunters, or to dodge them. She could never really outrun them, she said, because she always had to be looking over her shoulder, expecting someone to bury a knife in her back at any moment. She could only stay in the city for a couple of months, she told me, because if she stayed any longer, they'd track her down, and if they tracked her down, they'd track him down, and if they found *him*—Kain, Keter, Mondschein—the whole web, the entire movement, small and weak as it was, would be torn apart. She'd come back to the city to find new life for the movement. She was going around to the groups, most of which, she said, were full of kids without a clue. For them, it was an excuse to smoke grass and play folk music—they had no serious ideas. Except, she said, for a guy named Martin Dellman. He was the real deal, though on the edge of being a bourgeois sellout. She didn't say it like that, but that's what she meant. But even after he sold out, she said, which was inevitable, he'd still have, deeper down, the spirit of real anarchism moving through him. Eventually, she said, it would push him away from society. He'll become a hermit, she said. She told me she'd seen the type before. She was right. Here you are, alone in the exact place she said you'd be. We met a bunch of times while she was in the city. You'd never believe the energy that radiated from her—a damn strike of lightning. Being with her felt like being smacked in the face with the truth. It was the truth of a better world, a glimmering future of peace, equality, and selflessness, the inversion of values, the disintegration of narratives and identities, the fading of borders and hierarchies, power diffusing into the ground, the air, into oceans and rivers, washed clean. There is no place for that type of truth in our world. The people hunting her started to close in. One day a note appeared on the table where we held our meetings: *Migration time. E.B.* Migration time was right. I was headed to Vietnam. You'd think growing up as a Black boy in the city would have prepared me for something, showed me how deep the human disaster could go, but it was nothing compared to that place. Not sure I can use the word 'war' for it. It was an orgy of murderous violence and debasement of every kind. You'd think that whatever kind of man would fall into such a place wouldn't make it out, or would somehow make it out but would be completely disfigured. Morally disfigured. I'm talking about the soul. My soul was ripped to shreds over there. I somehow managed to sew it back together into a misshapen thing. And this was lucky, lucky to have been able to collect the shreds, tatters, fragments, pieces of my soul in order to put it back together and have it whole. For many years, though, I couldn't see how incredibly lucky I was—and it wasn't only that I'd collected the pieces. I slowly realized that while my soul had been ripped apart, the damage hadn't reached the whole way down. It hadn't touched the soul core. The core of my soul was intact. It became stronger, even as the soul itself became weaker. These wounds started to draw the total power, the total force of my entire body, down toward them to bind them up. Do you know what I mean, Dellman? If not, it doesn't matter, the important thing for us now is that it was Esther Bird who taught me the process of soul care even before my soul had been torn apart. How did she do this? She had found a first wound, nothing more than a tiny cut, a prick, before I went to Vietnam. She traced it, located it, touched it. It was the first night we met at Benson's. It was a joy and a trauma when she found it—when she, in a sense, guided my fingertips to the spot. The irony was that when I got back from the war and tried to tell my VA psychiatrist, Dr. Vallabene, about Esther Bird, he told me that this 'so-called Esther Bird' was just a manifestation of a psychotic break. He tried to put me on pills, but I refused to take them. I told him to his face that he'd gotten the whole thing wrong—and you can imagine how this white doctor, this Harvard graduate, reacted when this Black kid back from the war started lecturing him on right and wrong. I thought about getting into my core ideas with Vallabene, but that would have been a mistake. Vallabene's job was to control me, to channel whatever force was left in me after taking those pills in a useful, productive direction—productive for them, not me. I shut down. Refused to talk to him. Vallabene took this as a further sign of psychosis. Told me to check into a clinic, the VA would pay for it. He said it would be a way for me to eventually be 'reintegrated into the mainstream.' My silence, more than anything else, unsettled Vallabene, sent him spiraling down diagnostic rabbit holes. It was as if my lack of answers called everything, especially his diagnoses, into question. I might as well have grabbed his Harvard diploma from the wall and smashed it on the corner of his desk. Eventually, Vallabene had enough. He referred me to a colleague, Dr. Buergel. Buergel, unlike the hulking Vallabene, was a small man, thin, black hair, glasses, delicate features, feminine. At first, I thought I could trust him—some combination of his look and his gentle manner soothed me. He didn't push pills on me. He listened to me talk about my soul wounds, my soul care, Esther Bird, and he wrote down notes, looked like he understood what I was saying. For a while, I thought he wanted to believe me, to believe in a deeper truth, to tap into a kind of force that was unbound, maybe to reconsider the very meaning of mental health. But it turned out that Buergel was an agent of dark forces. It was really messed up. It was Buergel who first showed me the Keter file. It was Buergel who told me he'd been wrestling with Kain-Keter-Mondschein for decades—and it was Buergel who was tracing the flight of Esther Bird. Once he revealed this, I knew I had to lie low—or vanish. I mean fully off the map. I had no cabin in the woods, Dellman, I had no money. I couldn't take government money because it meant they could locate me. It meant living as a dead man. I became a ghost. Haunted the world without being seen, without speaking. Just *being*. There were times when someone would recognize me on the streets, maybe someone from the meetings, from the circle, but if they tried to talk to me—usually they didn't—I'd get the hell out of there, fast. There were many plants in the movement, you know about that, Dellman, enemies sent to infiltrate, to get 'information,' to pass notes along to other men, men with briefcases. Remember Lenny Jones? It turned out he was deep in with the feds, would take pictures of my notebook pages while I was taking a piss at Benson's. Jones knew his stuff, that's for sure—better than most. He knew Kropotkin from Bakunin, Proudhon from Marx. All of it—he was smooth, smart. I wouldn't have expected him for a second until I saw it in another file Buergel showed me, my file, as thick as a dictionary, thicker than Keter's. Black, anarchist, radical—there was enough in the file to lock me away for a long time if they wanted to, they said. If they couldn't sedate me with pills, it was time for prison. There were plenty of unsolved crimes they could haul me in for, and before I vanished and became a ghost, I was interrogated for everything imaginable: prostitution, sodomy, drugs. These were warning shots, they were just for them to let me know they were waiting for me to make a mistake, waiting for me to make connections, to restart the movement, reform the circle, to contact Esther Bird. Man, there were probably more people in the FBI who read my book than in the Village and the Haight combined. By '75, I had to vanish, I had to fade into the shadows, and in New York, you know, there's an endless play of shadows crisscrossing this way and that. It was a perfect time to become a ghost in America. The economy was going bad, the whole system was starting to crack. For the last ten years, I've been watching it, writing it—the rise of fear and brutality, the way the rich have grown richer as the poor have struggled to survive, watching and writing as the idea of poverty has been criminalized in the American mind. The core brutality of life pushed out of view, as more and more of life becomes mere representation of life. In this representation, the injustice dissolves, and what we don't see doesn't exist. But a ghost sees everything. When there is silence, we think there is no noise, but a ghost hears even what's concealed beneath this silence—those cries, those chilling and haunting echoes, those reverberations. All men are created equal—that's the original lie. There is no original sin, there is only an original lie, a lie upon which all others are based. The lie that Adam and Eve would die if they ate the forbidden fruit. The punishment for knowledge: eternal submission to the tyranny of the Lord. No equality after that point, only submission, only hierarchy, both of which confront the opposite, truth. And what is truth other than the existence of a time and space beyond submission, before submission—a truth as wide and expansive as an ocean before the emergence of land, a borderless oceanic space that merged with the watery air above it. There is a figure called *Hundun*, the primal being of chaos. But they wouldn't leave Hundun in peace. Holes were drilled into its body, creating out of that which was undifferentiated things distinct, divided, fixed. At the same time, we have this element, this energy, called truth. In the beginning it was joined with Hundun and animated everything, was part of everything. Now it's a barely perceptible glimmer—or not even that. It's like an ember, an ember covered in white dust. It's still hot, still has energy, but it's concealed, and it can only be activated by a flow rushing over it, coming into contact with it: wind, breath. The combination of energy and breath results in flame. A first flame thrown by the last living ember, that is the state of truth these days. But Dellman, you know what I'm going to say—I'm going to tell you that in this weak, delicate flame there is the potential for a fire that could consume the entire world. The terror starts and forces me underground. I vanish. I start living as a ghost, haunting the city. Out of the people in the Black Anarchist Reading Circle, some ended up in jail, many killed or maimed in the war, but most found their way into normal life, absorbed by the masses walking down the streets to work. This is how the movement ended. It was punished by the police. It was demonized by the media. It was written out of the schoolbooks. It was pulled from the gallery and museum walls; it was shredded by the publishing companies. A ghost covered in dust and sackcloth. *My word is like fire, like a hammer that shatters rock.* My ghostly thoughts, my ghostly whispers. My words come pouring out of the ghostly spirit: they engulf, they shatter. *I see nothing but fire.* I see nothing but fragments of stone. What I touch doesn't burn. What I touch doesn't break. My spirit passes through things. I am nothing in this world. There I am, amid rain and smoke, looking down into the dark water.

My body longs to plunge into it, to dive toward the bottom, a bottom that can never be reached. *A wind from God swept over the surface of the deep.* This wind wraps its cool fingers around our arms, drags us up and into those distant, higher spaces. Not now! Not now! I shout—or would have shouted, if such a spectral form could shout. Then I understand it: the time of iniquity is not past or future, it is present. It is not beginning or ending. It is unrelenting, enduring—without beginning, without end. At the same time, it is a phase in the totality of life, one preceding the coming of the great evil, an evil that would push existence to the edge of the abyss. A man by the name of Barnabas appeared one day a few months ago. I'm not sure how he crossed the threshold between that life and this life. He had a letter for me. I took it, unfolded it, and saw it was from her. I hadn't heard anything from her for over fifteen years. The letter was short. It said only one thing. I should come to your cabin on the lake. She would meet me there, here, on New Year's Eve."

Griggs falls silent. He sinks back into the sofa, takes his cup from the table, and drinks. Dellman doesn't say anything, doesn't know what he could say. The idea that a woman named Esther Bird should appear at his cabin is unbelievable. What Griggs said is clearly delusional, but it also strikes Dellman as fundamentally correct: the way in which American society had deteriorated, rotted out, the election of Reagan to a second term—the actor, the charlatan, who speaks about cities on hills and at the same time assaults the poor, inflames racial violence, ravages the environment. Dellman had moved permanently to the cabin in part because he couldn't take it anymore, couldn't take turning on the television and seeing the old man with his innocent smile talking about values and morality. This is Reagan's America, and Griggs is the ultimate enemy, the ultimate outsider. Dellman, for his part, could vanish without becoming a ghost. He could move to the lake, write, drink whiskey, mourn his wife, mourn his lack of children, lament his loneliness, sit on his porch in a weathered Adirondack chair, ignore the world around him, and once or twice a year drive to the nearest post office to mail a stack of pages to his editor in New York. Once upon a time, his name had probably also been on lists in secret files, and maybe there was even a small, thin file with his name on it somewhere in the archives, but then his stories started to appear in the *Paris Review* and the *New Yorker*. He got the job as a permanent writer-in-residence, he won some minor awards, bought a house in the town upstate and inherited his parents' apartment on Central Park and the cabin on the lake up north. Griggs went to Vietnam, Dellman went upstate. This was 1970, fifteen years ago. In all this time, it hadn't occurred to Dellman to think about what happened to others in the movement, that is, others not like him, university-educated white males with their options open. He knew about some of the members, he thinks, they became lawyers, one served a term or two in Congress, another, Marvin Miller, is a sociologist at the New School. Summer camp, Dellman thinks, nostalgia, memory—that's what the movement has become for him, sweet, innocent, airy. He hasn't thought of Griggs, even though a copy of *Becoming Powerless* sits on his bookshelf close to where he spends his days writing. He has no access to Griggs, Dellman thinks, no access to his truth, and it isn't because he's barred from it, it's because he ignores it, it is because he writes his way around it. Dellman's world is made up of material, materiality—the opposite of the ghostly. Everything in his life is utterly material, he thinks, pens and paper, whiskey and Adirondack chairs.

Then they wait. Or, better, they also wait. They cook, they eat, they take walks in the woods. They talk late into the night. They sleep. Nahum Griggs waits for Esther Bird to come. Martin Dellman waits for something else, he doesn't know precisely what, a sign, an expression that could determine how to understand what's going on, to understand Griggs, to grasp the precise nature of Griggs's mental state. *My word is like fire*, Dellman repeats to himself throughout these days of waiting, *like a hammer that shatters rock.* The bigger circles of the movement, Dellman recalls, had mostly people like him—young white men in college or just graduated, many working on doctoral degrees, novelists, poets, philosophers, artists. Everyone was on the edge, Dellman muses, the edge of falling into those endless urban spaces—spaces both abandoned and full, spaces pulsing with images, with flickering illusions of better lives and impossible futures based on mythical histories. Their target was "power"—power in every form. The power of the boss, the power of institutions, the power of the state and its war machine, the power of police terror, the power of the corporate media to control one's thoughts. The draft had fractured the movement, pulled some into the maw of combat, others fled the city for unknown places, others protested and went to jail, most, like him, filtered into regular life. Some years later, when he was at a writers' conference, he had introduced himself to a younger poet, flirtatiously, he'd thought at the time, as a "former anarchist." Now he had a hard time knowing what he'd meant. The young woman gave him a perplexed look. Former. Anarchist. He met his future wife, Livia, during his first year as the college's permanent writer-in-residence. This was the best year of his life, he often said, the year he published what he considered his best novel, *Shadowscapes*, the year he met and married Livia—the year Griggs went to war. The year the anarchist circles in the city unraveled, became a jumble of curving lines, lines moving into two directions, one direction for him, one for Griggs. And now, it seems to Dellman, those ends have finally come together again, have met, have reformed the circle, now that Griggs has found him in the cabin in anticipation of the arrival of Esther Bird. Reconstituting what he thought was the irretrievable past. Livia, his wife, was thirty years old when she died. That was ten years ago—1975. Then six years after that, at the end of the summer of 1981, Dellman resigned from his position at the college, packed his car, and drove north to the cabin on the lake. If Griggs were a ghost, Dellman thinks as he lies awake in the darkness, maybe he could make contact with Livia, maybe Griggs could coax her back toward this life, away from the realm of the dead. Griggs on this side of the border, haunting the world—haunting him, Dellman, while Livia is on the other, lost among the millions of shades. And Esther Bird? It could be that she is also a ghost, that she would appear at the lake as the head of a legion of the dead. A resurrection—is this what Griggs is waiting for? Resurrection as redemption, redemption as revolution? New Year's Eve approaches. Dellman grows more anxious. Griggs continues to tell him stories. He describes the daily confrontation with violence, hunger, cold, fear—but also the other side: joy, love. Did I die in Vietnam? Griggs asks one evening. Of course I died, Griggs says, I died the moment I stepped foot there. In order to live again, Griggs says, I had to leave my body behind, cast it off like a snail's shell. What happened to him in Vietnam? Dellman wonders. Maybe he slipped off the edge, slipped back into the space of chaos. What has happened to me here? Dellman continues. Could it be that I've been searching for Livia this whole time, searching for memories, for a shared consciousness that straddles the line between life and death? To live with one foot on either side, if it meant to live with her. Griggs's madness is creeping in, he thinks, working its way into his mind, seizing hold of his body. There is nothing to do but to give over to it, he tells himself during these sleepless nights, to give over to it while waiting for the coming of Esther Bird. The problem with his theory, Dellman thinks, is that Griggs isn't crazy. The problem is that Griggs sees everything clearly, if one defines "everything" as it should be defined, that is, if one defines it as the reverse side of what we normally perceive as "real."

"The crows assert," Griggs says as the time creeps closer to the midnight hour on New Year's Eve, "that a single crow could destroy the heavens. But the guardians of heaven see the crow's flight, they trace its trajectory. They are ready to swat the crow from the sky as soon as it comes close to heaven's gates. What is the way inside those gates? How would you, a novelist, write the scene? Imagine the sentries at the gates, fiery swords in hand. When these sentries swing their swords, they never miss their target. All previous attacks have been dispatched with ease. Nothing can make it through. It is utterly impossible for something to make its way by the sentries. And yet, Dellman, let's assume—or simply imagine, that this crow, as it approaches heaven, becomes a bird spirit and, because it is now spirit, it somehow evades the fiery blades of those swords and makes it into the domain of God. This is the paradox, Dellman, of impossibility and, not the possible, the actual. Write a story that is both ongoing and already over, write a story with two irreconcilable endings, one that contains both the death of spirit and the triumph of spirit, the extinguishing of flame and the raging of the free conflagration, a conflagration of love powerful enough to burn the world—*the word is fire, time is the hammer that shatters rock*—a story constructed with words of fire, words that burn, words that shatter. To read is to shatter, to shatter is to begin the process of rebuilding, to burn is to lay the foundation to grow again. This is *becoming powerless*, the powerlessness of the bird spirit soaring through the air, having left behind the body of the crow. This is a being that has left behind being, a presence that has become absence. It races through time, it is faster than time, it races until the end point of time, then it dips, then it swerves and curls and is suddenly heading in the opposite direction, bringing the future back into the now, and in this way, when the sentries' swords cut through the air, the bird spirit is there and not there, because the present through which the swords cut is already the past."

A cold day. Clouds roll in late in the evening. No stars, no moon can be seen. Snow starts to fall. Shortly before the midnight hour, Griggs rises to his feet and puts on his jacket and boots. He saw a flash of blue-green light, he tells Dellman, it came from the middle of the frozen lake. It must be the sign of her arrival. A flash of blue-green light, the arrival of Esther Bird. She is bringing the new scriptures. It is a work that has survived forever in the creases of history and just beyond the borders of power. It is called *The Book of Moonlight*. When it is revealed, she once told him at Benson's, it will sprinkle down from the sky in a shower of blue-green light—blue-green light, the color of the breath of God. Griggs leaves the house faster than Dellman can lace up his boots. He vanishes into the darkness. Dellman shouts to him: Wait, stay, hold on, but there isn't time. Griggs is gone. He's gone onto the frozen lake. The lake ice isn't firm, Dellman shouts into the darkness, it has only frozen over a few days ago. The ice won't hold, Dellman shouts again, you'll fall through, you'll chase the blue-green light not to the gates of heaven, not following the bird spirit, but into icy oblivion.

FEBRUARY 12 (NIGHT)

Nineveh, the great power in the east, a lion among lambs. The end is coming for the lion, it will be cut down as all lions before it. Who will act as the emissary to the Ninevites, who will tell them justice will prevail? The source of injustice dwells in the great temple, a being awash in blood from the Ninevites' sacrifices, drunk from their endless offerings of wine. Cain, daughter of Adam and Eve, arrives in Nineveh. God has banished her from the land of her family. Evil—that's what Cain felt when she confronted the divine presence while standing over Abel's bloody body, and it is the same evil she feels again each time she enters the thousands of cities in which she has lived during her wanderings. It is the evil she feels now, as she passes through Nineveh's gates and comes into the market square, eying the temple in the distance. Night will fall and last forever, she thinks, the sun will be blotted out, cold and darkness will cover this land, limitless cold, endless darkness, as day after day Nineveh suffers, until its end comes, until evil finds another place to dwell, until I wander there.

FEBRUARY 13 (MORNING)
No light breaks in the village today. The sun doesn't rise, the darkness doesn't end, the cold only deepens here, here, the valley of the Ninevites, here, the village of Z. Flashes of memory, flashes of a deeper past. I know it is time to leave the inn by the bridge, to leave the village. I go down to the larder and bring up as many jars of preserves as I can carry in my backpack. This means that clothes and other things must be left behind.

FEBRUARY 13 (NIGHT)
I took the road into the woods again, but because of the extreme cold the snow was harder, the walking easier. This old carriage route was in sorry shape—trees and bushes encroached from both sides, at points choking it off completely. The contrast between this growth and the death or stasis that reigns in the village was jarring. The way was long, incomprehensibly long given the apparent proximity of the castle and the low rise of the hill it sits upon. At one point, a mile or two out of town, the road seemed to bend in the direction of the castle, it was the beginning of a steady curve that would end, must end, at the castle's gate. I kept walking, despite the cold, a cold that

gradually crept under my clothes and over my skin, tingling and burning me with its icy touch. I was about to turn around when I saw something up ahead in front of me in the dim light of my fading flashlight. It was a stone pedestal of what had previously been, I thought, a garden wall. Beyond the pedestal was a small stone hut, which sat at the edge of a sizable clearing. A wooden sign was fastened to the wall above the door and under the roof: *Bertuch's Garden*. So this had been the home of the castle's vegetable dealer, I thought, the man who threw blankets to Amalia's father as he stood each day on the side of the road begging forgiveness for his daughter's transgression as the carriages conveying the gentlemen to and from the castle rushed by him at top speeds.

Bertuch's door was unlocked. I went inside. Though I could see from the outside that the house was small, I was still surprised by the cramped interior. There was a rickety bed made of wooden planks in the corner covered by a straw mattress. Next to the wood stove were two pairs of boots of irregular shape, the sole of the left boot in both pairs raised half an inch or so above the other. In addition, the left boots were at least an inch smaller than the right ones, indicating a fairly substantial variance between the gardener's two feet. Other possessions, meager as they were, were scattered around the place, stacks of worn-out blankets, a pair of coarse woolen pants inelegantly patched, a woolen shirt, some sorry pairs of socks, and canvas sacks containing what appeared to be shriveled remains of onion. The stone walls had no decorations. The space had nowhere to cook—no equipment for everyday life. It could be, I thought, that Bertuch took his meals in one of the village inns, or at the castle. There was a leather-bound ledger on a small table. It contained simple entries like "onions three" or "carrots two" or "beets one." The entries were organized by date—day then month—without indication of the year, one year simply rolling into the next. Along the back wall there was a small door that opened into a wooden box. I flashed my light into it and saw that it was about a quarter full of firewood. I closed it and turned back to the room. I gazed back through the open front door and into the darkness. The line came to me: *This final, tiniest, vanishing, even nonexistent hope is your only hope.*

I sat down at the table. The chair wobbled, despite the weight I must have lost since arriving in the village. My arms and legs felt as thin as sticks—my clothing sagged. The cold ripped through me like never before. I went to sleep and woke up in this village, in the village of Z. The bus ride, the long hike from Špindlerův Mlýn—nothing but dreams. There was no reversing it, I thought, no slipping back through the oneiric tunnel. I turned one page after another of Bertuch's ledger, surprised by the neat script, the order, the rigorous approach to recordkeeping, spanning not years but decades—a whole life of onions three and carrots two and beets one and on and on and on. Toward the back of the ledger were some blank pages. I ripped out a few and took a pen from my jacket pocket. I wrote to the only person I could write to from this position on the other side of a dream, my brother Henry.

Dear Henry,
I have found my way to the village of Z. There's no point trying to locate it on a map. You won't be able

to find it. Z. is one of those unmapped places, just the sort of place you don't believe exists. I know it's hard for you to accept that there are limits to humans' collective ability to grasp, comprehend, and determine things and events. For you, the human being is a heroic species. He climbs the highest mountain peaks, builds structures that rise to towering heights. He invents. He cures. He overcomes every problem through a combination of the exercise of his rational mind—his intellect—and his will to power. But there is no such being here in the village of Z. In fact, the only person here is your brother. I am alone, alone in this valley, otherwise a desert of life. Today, I discovered the house that once belonged to the gardener and vegetable dealer Bertuch. The house is close to the castle's gate, though I haven't made it as far as the castle. I'm writing this from Bertuch's table, from a page ripped from his ledger, a ledger that records every deal for vegetables Bertuch made in the village and at the castle for decades. Another way of putting it: I am writing to you from the edge of the village, from the space between the village and the castle's gate—in other words between one world and another. We don't think we'll ever arrive at such a boundary, but suddenly it's there. What do we do then, Henry? We hesitate. Or I hesitate. You never hesitate. On the other hand, you must hesitate. It's our basic condition, yours as well as mine, and maybe it's only my perspective on your life that reveals a constant forward motion.

Maybe it's a product of my desire—it could be that I need your motion, your propulsion, to compensate for my stillness. I need your iron will to compensate for my powerlessness. Ghost stories—I came here chasing them, running from them. Do you remember New Year's Eve 1985? Do you remember our father rushing from the house around midnight? The phone rang— that jarring ring of our pale-blue rotary phone fixed to the kitchen wall. Our father answered. It was Martin Dellman. "Dellman called," he said to our mother, and then he was gone from the house. We heard the car door open and shut and then the car crunching over the cold dirt driveway. The headlights vanished behind a wall of trees. Have you thought of that moment since that night, Henry—the becoming-ghost of Martin Dellman? One time, the following summer, I paddled our canoe over to Dellman's dock. I hitched it up, got out, and walked up the path to the porch, where he always sat during his breaks from writing. For a moment, I could have sworn that Dellman was where he'd always been—in his Adirondack chair, glass of whiskey in his hand, looking out over the lake. I could hear his call: "Come on up, Sy, my boy, come on up for a bowl of ice cream." I went into Dellman's house that day. On the small table by the armchair in the living room, there was a copy of Nahum Griggs's *Becoming Powerless*. Tattered. Probably read one hundred times or more. It was printed on cheap paper. The binding glue had dried out. Pages were on the verge of falling out. I opened it. Saw Dellman's marginalia filling the empty space around the printed text, at times written hastily over the print itself. In all fraternal relationships, Henry, there is a Cain and there is an Abel. The problem is that it's impossible to tell one from the other—because Abel is the airy spirit of Cain, and Cain is Abel's shadow. It follows that we must, at one and the same time, remain fixed at home among our family and wander the world as a person condemned to eternal restlessness and solitude. Does Cain love the spirit of Abel, which dwells within him? Does Abel love the murderous Cain in his soul? It could be that our intensity finds its source there—in the presence of our internal otherness, the being-in-our-being that threatens our selfhood with complete obliteration. You weren't there that day in the late summer when Dellman's brother arrived from the city.

"You must be the little Kirschbaum boy," he said to me when he came over to talk to our father. "I'm Paul," he said, "my brother often wrote about you in his letters. I'll have to make copies for you. There are some wonderful descriptions." I felt nervous, anxious, felt the swelling of tears in my eyes, felt the pain of missing Dellman, the pain of loss, a pain I hadn't realized I was carrying within me. Maybe Paul sensed something, because he said, "You should come by the house and take something of Martin's, something to remember him by. Martin left his unpublished papers to your father. It'll be enough to keep your father busy for the next decade. Either that or he'll end up burning them in the stove. I'm glad Martin didn't leave them to me. I don't think I'd be able to manage it. Your father's a good man. He did his best with my brother, always did his best for Martin." The next day, I went to Dellman's house. Paul was cleaning out the kitchen and told me to look around and to take what I wanted. I slowly passed through the living room, down the hallway, and found myself in Dellman's study. During all my years visiting him, I'd never been in there. Some of the books and notebooks and stacks of paper were already in boxes, but most of it wasn't packed. There were hardback editions of his novels. We had them in our cabin, too, signed by Dellman, dedicated to our mother and father—or to the "Kirschbaum family." I went over to the desk. An old metallic green Smith Corona sat there with a blank sheet of paper loaded into it. There was a stack of typed pages next to it. A glance through them revealed the central subject of the manuscript, a character named Nahum Griggs. All of this would go to my father, and he would see that it found its way to where it belonged, the folders of the university archive. Then I realized I knew exactly what I wanted. I turned from the office and made my way back to the kitchen. Paul looked on as I opened the second drawer from the top next to the refrigerator and pulled out Dellman's ice cream scoop. I studied it, Henry, its semispherical head, its long, elegant neck, the mechanism, including a wonderful spring, that caused the blade to slice the ice cream out of the head, and that most pleasing canary-yellow wooden handle, which always reminded me of summer squash. Last year, when I was home with our father, I remembered this scene and thought, after a long time, about Paul Dellman, about what Paul Dellman had said about our father. I told this to him, but our father was in one of his moods. He was sitting under a dim light in the reclining chair in his office at home. I asked him about Dellman's papers. He closed his eyes, Henry, and I could tell he didn't want to think about it. What happened at that moment beneath our father's closed eyelids? An old man's memories flickering against the screen like the grainy filmstrip of a home movie. I don't know why, but I pressed him. Where are the papers now? Did you give them to the university? He was silent for a minute, then he said no, they weren't in the archive, they were still at our cabin, boxed up and stored in the crawl space under the roof. He never got to them, he said, he could never bring himself to open the boxes, to rip off the tape, to unseal them. When I heard this, Henry, I knew I had to go out there. If our father couldn't open those boxes, it had to be me. These boxes were not meant for a man of progress, like yourself. They were full of things that lacked definition, meaning, value—the scribblings, useless, unpublished, of a sick man. A waste of time—I can hear those words coming from your mouth as you judge things on your spectrum of success and failure.

Should I condemn you for this? For reflecting the values that swirl around you, those same values that resulted in your apparent happiness, your wealth? If we place all of that—family, wealth, reputation—on one side of the scales and the ghostly form of Nahum Griggs on the other, which way would the scales tilt? There is a kind of justice here, Henry, though not the type which can be sought in the courts of law where you practice. Law—we need to locate the place where this word falls apart, where it fractures into its mystical fragments. I'm writing to you from the edge of the castle, the castle on the hill above the village of Z. I've traced many threads to this place, including memories—both real and imagined—of Martin Dellman. These threads have been bound together into a single volume, a book, which, at its heart, contains the story of two brothers, one brother is named Cain and the other brother is named Abel. Or, no, it is a story of a ladder that appears on earth and stretches to the gates of heaven. Or it is a story about transformation—a character becoming someone else, an act of "renaming," a renaming powerful enough to bend the vector of fate. There's only one possible name for this book, the words of which sprinkle down on us in blue-green light. It's the glow of the moon, Henry, that palest of light—a light which defies description while infusing us with an undeniable energy, an energy that drives us toward the precipice—an edge of what one might call "madness," a madness that requires of us one last step.

Life as we know it depends on this decision: Should we take the step or not? Should we test the depths of the chasm in front of us or just stand where we are, gazing down into the darkness, imagining the bottom? In those boxes of Dellman's papers in the crawlspace in the cabin I discovered a fragment about a young man from a small town near Kyiv. His name is Isaac Mondschein. He goes to Berlin after the First World War and ends up in Nervenklinik in the 1930s. He is the author of a book, a book, he says (or believes), that is written in blue-green light, the ink of God. He calls it *The Book of Moonlight*. On the banks of the Landwehrkanal, a voice rings out. The beginning—the call, the cry of existence. It's dark and foggy. Passersby find his body. They bind up his wound. Ten minutes more and it would have been over. Life is rushing out. Death swoops down like an eagle. Death doesn't manage to get the body, but it rips out a chunk of his spirit. It takes this piece of spirit with it as it retreats back toward the heavens. There, beyond the castle's gate, the fragment of spirit is hidden inside a vanished world, in the ruins of a vanished life. To get this piece back, to become whole again, means putting everything at risk, Henry—the risk that there is no end, the risk that there is nothing like "wholeness" either in this life or beyond. I'm writing to you from Bertuch's garden, the last stop before the castle. Despite how close I must be to the castle I cannot see it. Darkness conceals everything. The cold is forbidding. Tomorrow, as dawn breaks, I hope to enter the castle and, with luck, find what I am searching for, what I must find in order to return.

Your brother,
Sy

I make a fire in the stove and now sit by it eating from a large jar of pickled mushrooms. I imagine those gates, the entrance to the castle. The gates must be there in front of me, but they are veiled by darkness. It's time to continue into this unknown zone. At first light, I will pass through the castle's gates, assuming "first light" ever comes.

FEBRUARY 14 (MORNING)

A faint, purple light arrives at daybreak. I couldn't have anticipated just how much I would want to stay here in Bertuch's garden house—how much I would long to return to the inn by the bridge. What I despised yesterday, I need today. What yesterday seemed desolate, today appears full of life. My life. My breath, an existence such as I have made it. It is an existence without answers. Answers are not part of existence. There are no answers here. The answers lie beyond, beyond existence.

FEBRUARY 14 (NIGHT)

The road continued uphill past Bertuch's garden. From a distance, at points when the road curved, it seemed to come to an abrupt halt, dead-ending into the dense forest. When I'd reach the precise spot where the road vanished, it would suddenly reappear, heading upward and away. Had I not utterly abandoned myself to the climb, had I not been intent on persevering regardless of what was in front of me, I would have turned back each time I was seemingly blocked by one of those walls of trees. I could hardly believe my eyes, in fact I didn't believe it at first, when I made one final turn and the outlines of the castle's western wall rose in the distance. I quickly advanced, fearing that this fata morgana would dissolve as improbably as it had found its form.

To my surprise, the castle's gates were open, their iron flaps swinging back and forth in the strong mountain wind. Although it had been calm until past Bertuch's garden, up at the castle the wind blew in powerful gusts, bending the short trees, which appeared as row after row of supplicants—those souls who've come to Count Westwest to beg for mercy, like Barnabas's father, like me.

The castle is similar in appearance to the village, the central difference being that here the stone buildings are pressed together tightly, separated not by streets but by impossibly narrow alleyways, some barely wide enough for a single person to pass through without turning to the side. Nor are these alleys straight. To the contrary, they bend around curves in the stonework, run headlong into walls, fork in all possible directions. Upon entering this system of passages, one's bearings are lost— and there is no telling whether one progresses deeper into the structure or whether one skirts endlessly along its outer wall. As I moved through these alleyways, I eventually encountered a series of small doors. They were locked, many without handles, set to open, apparently, only from the inside or not at all. I tried pushing on them, hoping they would have been weakened by the passing of time, no luck, if, indeed, luck had anything to do it. I thought back to the night on Grunewaldstrasse with Daniel Cohen, how the chemist Kaesbohrer described the relationship between those two inherently antagonistic mazelike systems, each twisting around the other, each intertwined inextricably with the other, and yet each never meeting the other, never touching, and thus producing by this eternal proximity an ever-increasing tension, an energy. It was this relationship that Kaesbohrer sought to understand, to solve for through his mathematical equation, an equation complex and flexible enough not only to map the systems themselves but to account for the space between them. Between systems. Between lives. Could this be what Kaesbohrer had in mind, these exterior passageways (if they were exterior) of Z.'s castle, running, presumably, in parallel with those passageways in the interior of the structure, never touching, linked by doors that were not doors, doors that were doors but never opened, never had the possibility of opening? At the time, in Kaesbohrer's basement laboratory, I felt that there was something terrifying about this idea, and I recalled the feeling of terror I felt as I uncorked the vial of cloudy yellow liquid Kaesbohrer had given me, the feeling right before I poured it down my throat. I had every reason to be terrified. This was the beginning of a decades-long trip that eventually brought me here, here to the physical manifestation of the equation on Kaesbohrer's wall, an equation worked out by a man who'd spent nearly seventy years living underground, a man haunted by an undefinable sound coming through the earth from the southwest at a distance, he believed, of between twenty and two hundred meters.

What would happen if a person slipped from one side of the equation to the other, from one system to its antagonist, its opposite, or, as Kaesbohrer would say, its counterfactual? After hours of walking, perhaps covering the same ground over and over, perhaps never stepping foot in the same alley twice, I saw a small door that had given way and half fallen back into the darkness of the castle's interior. I wondered if Kaesbohrer's formula accounted for such events as this—erosion caused by years of snow and ice, heat, wind, warping, rot. Did the formula take into consideration acts of God? Slippage, rupture, mystery—maybe even miracle—all of this contained in the most elusive variable in Kaesbohrer's equation, the so-called "general unknown," or the *allgemeine Unbegreiflichkeit*, the unknown to the general power, the U^a.

I stepped through the narrow door, pushing aside the remains of the wooden slats and metal supports. I turned on my flashlight and pointed it first in one direction, then in the other. I could see that I was in a narrow corridor with stone walls on either side leading up to an arched ceiling—a low ceiling, no more than a foot above my head. The question of which way to go stilled me at first. This decision seemed to me both decisive and at the same time not to matter a bit, as one could imagine that both directions would wind up at the same place. I turned to the right, made my way slowly as the hallway bent, first gradually, then at sharper angles. There were no windows along the hall, no doors leading either further into the interior or back outside into the alley. At last, the hallway ended, and I entered a vestibule with a small domed ceiling which must have been at least twice as high as the one in the passageway.

At the other end of the vestibule, there was a large door leading out of the space, above which, in gilded letters, was written: Department X. I walked across the vestibule, pressed the door handle, and the door unlatched. I stepped inside the room and shined my light around. The bulb seemed to be weaker than before, and I started to worry, not knowing how I could manage without it. How could I confront this darkness, both inside this place and beyond it, a darkness that consumed the village, that barely lifted even at the noon hour—if there was a noon hour here? There is a breaking of dawn, though even this is not always sure. There is an expansive night, which, at times when the sky is clear, is lit by the moon and stars. If there is a noon hour, it is a joke, serving only to emphasize its opposite, midnight, though it could be that even "midnight" is illusory, because midnight means one day passing to the next. Does one day pass to the next here in such a sequential, logical order? Not at all—one day melts into another, and that another day casts back into the previous one, or it suddenly leaps forward into a third.

The room was divided into two parts. There was a kind of gallery, which was set off from the other part by a set of low wooden rails. Chairs were placed close together, forming what seemed to be a kind of waiting area. On the other side of the rails, there were three high desks that faced the gallery. Each desk had a stool behind it. From this vantage point, the person sitting on the stool at the desk could look over whatever materials he had on the desk and at the same time could look out over the collection of petitioners in the gallery. Behind the desks, on the opposite wall from the entrance, there were two large stoves decorated with jade-colored tiles. There was a stack of wood, too, a lucky break for me, and a box of beeswax candles. I noticed that on each desk there were two holders for candles, which showed themselves primarily by the residue of wax gathered there. I took two of the candles and lit them with matches I'd brought with me. Then I lit one of the stoves. I undid the straps of my backpack and unrolled the three eider-down blankets I took from the inn by the bridge, laying them next to the stove. A fine camping spot for the night.

FEBRUARY 15 (MORNING?)

The lack of windows in this room makes it impossible to tell what time it is—even whether it is morning or night. I could retrace my steps to the caved-in door along the passageway, but I hardly see the point. It doesn't matter much to me whether it's morning, afternoon, or somehow already evening. Today's awakening has reminded me of my awakening in the Hotel des Bains, where I fell asleep to the sound of Esther Bird's storytelling. This was after I got Cohen's manuscript back, after I had met Milena in the hotel's "imperial" dining room—another abandoned space, like the village of Z.

When I arrived at the clinic in Zelená Hora, I asked Dr. Hruška, during our first session, how it could be that Milena was also a guest there. It seemed improbable, maybe impossible, that she would have ended up in the same place at the same time as I did, close to twenty years since we had last seen each other.

"If you are here," Dr. Hruška responded, "how could it be that she wouldn't be here?" And to the question of why her daily meeting fell directly after mine, Dr. Hruška simply said,

"How could it be otherwise?" Weeks later, I had the memory of the night on Grunewaldstrasse with Daniel Cohen, at the time still an unnamed character, and the chemist Kaesbohrer—a memory that ended with the drinking of the chemist's antidote, his cloudy yellow liquid. This is when Dr. Hruška's case study of me began to come apart at the seams—or that's what I had thought, or wanted, or needed, or that's what I desired. But Dr. Hruška wasn't done, far from it. It could be he hadn't started, and what I took for a "coming apart at the seams" was really a preliminary stage in a more advanced organizational strategy.

When I entered the castle, I suspected I would be confronted with memories of Ida Fields, and now here she is. Ida Fields, the actor, a creator of theater both on and off the stage, breathing life into Gabe Slatky's plays, her husband, my best friend, a volcanic constellation. Ida found her way to Berlin. It was wintertime, another February like this one, cold, austere, sky hanging low. We wandered along the canal in Kreuzberg, eventually over to Urbanstrasse, where Ida spotted a sign for a theater called *Der Blaue Punkt*. We entered through the doors on the street and followed the signs into the building's courtyard. The theater's entrance was off to the left. We went inside. At first, nobody else was there. A poster hung on the wall with the program of performances. That night, the theater was doing a piece called *Songbirds*, written and directed by Rosa Fuchsbein. Ida wanted to go. I didn't care either way. I would have done anything Ida wanted during those days she was in Berlin. I wanted to be with her, close to her, to live in the penumbra of the possibility of making love to her on those cold, dark mornings, those cold, dark nights. Since the performance didn't start for hours, we went around the corner and had a drink.

When we returned to the theater, we found the scene transformed. The previously empty space was now full, people waiting in line for tickets, others drinking beer, talking, leaning against walls, smoking. Ida and I got in line for tickets. Ida seemed excited, gave me expectant looks, had a kind of dazzled expression playing on her lips. After we got the tickets, Ida went to get us beers at the bar, and I made my way through the space in search of the coat check. I found it across the room, gave the young, bearded man there my blue wool coat and Ida's checkered one, and took the claim slip. When I turned around, I almost bumped into the woman who was next in line, Milena, though I wouldn't know the name Milena until later. In the brief moment when we almost collided, she moving toward the desk, me away from it, two moments existed in one. There was the moment when I saw her. This lasted for a few seconds. And there was the moment when I *encountered* her, absorbed her, communicated with her through our shared gaze. Words formed, then fell apart. They rose like mountains and then collapsed into giant heaps of dust—strength, vulnerability, fragility, boundlessness, soaring, risking, terrified, clashes of opposites sitting on the edges of the possible, the very edge that is falling apart, disintegrating. All of this in seconds, maybe less, seconds stretching to their limits, stretching beyond their "present" to the now, to the here, here and now between the castle's walls. She moved by me. I saw Ida across the space, holding a bottle of beer in each hand, looking around for me. I raised my hand to catch her eye. She saw me, came over, handed me a bottle.

She grasped my free hand, and we went into the performance space to find our seats.

I watched as Milena entered a few minutes later. People came over to talk to her, some hurried, some relaxed, some touching her gentle shoulders, shoulders covered by coarse deep-blue silk—a dress that hung from her body like willow branches. Ida saw me looking across the space. "Do you know her?" she asked.

"Who?"

"Her," Ida said, without additional specification.

"No," I said.

A man sitting on the other side of Ida interjected, "That's Milena. She's a costume designer—and the new director of the theater. And the woman beside her with the curly hair, that's the playwright Rosa Fuchsbein." The man then introduced himself to us. His name was Tijl. He was thin, had short black hair, wore thin gold-rimmed glasses, spoke with an accent I couldn't place.

"Do you come here often?" Ida asked. He was there at least a few times a week, he said; his girlfriend or partner, a woman named Fo, was preforming a series of shows in the space, a series that had been going on for nearly a year already. I looked back to Milena. She had moved a few steps to the left. She was staring at the stage—a look of unbreakable intensity. The lights fell. In the darkness, I could see four people come on-stage carrying props, setting up the scene. They were the actors, four women, four "songbirds," each wearing a different color of robe, robes stitched together by her, by her fingers, her touch. The touch of flesh on silk.

I caught sight of her again after the show. Ida wanted to stay at the theater's bar for another drink. I didn't want to stay but didn't want Ida to know I wanted to go—that I needed to get away from Milena, to stop whatever was happening to me from happening—to break the force pulling me toward her, toward Milena and away from Ida Fields. It was a shock. For the past seven or eight years, since meeting Ida, not a single day went by that I thought anything could break her hold on me. Now, suddenly, there was a life beyond Ida—and this life "beyond" meant a life of freedom, of possibility. Beyond her. Beyond my desire for her—beyond the seemingly unquenchable passion, which, after these unbearable years, was now being fulfilled, and yet even as it was being fulfilled, it remained impossible, limited, set to expire.

"Isn't it true," Hruška asked me in one session late in the summer, "that Daniel Cohen was there in the theater when you first met Milena?"

I didn't see the point of this question. "Yes, it's true," I said.

Milena made her way through the crowd gathered around the bar. She paused to exchange greetings with people, to feel those hands and fingers on her arms, shoulders, to receive hugs, kisses. There he was, by the window. She found Cohen there. He was leaning against the glass. He had a beer in one hand. His jacket was draped over his other arm. It was loud in the space. I could barely hear what Ida was saying to Tijl, and the two were standing right next to me. Cohen seemed relaxed as Milena laid her hands on his shoulders. He straightened up, ran a couple of fingers over her cheek. He kissed her—that scratchy black beard rubbing into her smooth, round cheeks.

They fussed with each other for a few minutes, rubbing and tugging, before Milena pulled back and said something that made him laugh. He took a drink from his beer, then she took the bottle from him and turned back toward the crowd, eventually moving over to where Rosa Fuchsbein was standing. Ida turned to me at that point and asked me a question—something simple like "what's going on?" or "are you okay?" or "what are you thinking about?" or "what are you doing?" I can't remember what I said to her. Maybe I told her to get on the next airplane and go home, to go back to Gabe, her husband. Maybe she responded and said she was leaving the next day— maybe she'd already said this earlier in the evening, before the play, when we were sitting at a nearby bar. Maybe I told her I was going to Prague, that I'd been hired to translate a novel by Jan Horák from Czech to English, from a language I didn't know. Maybe she told me I was lying, being a coward, maybe I told her I wasn't standing where she thought I was, that I was actually across the room, that I'd grown a thick black beard, changed my name, that I'd met her, Milena, the night I went down into the basement of that building on Grunewaldstrasse, waking up hours later in a pile of ash, the burnt remains of a fire that devoured a ladder stretching from earth to heaven, Jacob's ladder, which emerged as the moonlight cut through a gap in the clouds, a ladder, which I, like Jacob, refused to climb. Did I leave the theater with Ida? This is what Hruška asked me when I told him the story—when I told him the story of becoming Daniel Cohen. It was a preposterous question, a question with two opposing yet still fundamentally true answers: yes and no. I stood at the window of my room at the clinic Zelená Hora on that spring evening, looking out over the garden. There was she, removing a pebble from her shoe. It was delusional, I've said before, to think I could pry her away from Cohen. But the truth is: it wasn't delusional. It was inevitable—but not that I could pry her away. She was never with Cohen. It was a mistake, an error. The error was Cohen. He was an error, one created in the space between me and Milena one night after a performance at *Der Blaue Punkt*.

Julia came home from one of her walks. I was working at my desk. It must have been one or two in the morning. I hadn't heard her come in and didn't know she was there until she put her cold hands on my shoulders underneath the T-shirt, startling me, causing my mechanical pencil to leave a wide, curving mark on the page. Julia never wore gloves when she went out at night, even when I reminded her.

"What are you writing?" she asked. I told her I was composing a series of lectures, fictional lectures, given to a fictional group of students at a fictional college in a fictional course called Introduction to Literature. She asked what the purpose of this was. I didn't want to answer this question, but said I'd come to realize that I was searching for something, that even though I'd come close to it before, I hadn't grasped it, attained it—I hadn't discovered it. She wanted to read it, but the thought of her reading those words unsettled me, especially since she'd just come inside from the cold winter night. She was coming back from who knows where. But I couldn't prevent her—maybe I wanted her to read it. I got up and let her sit down over the notebook. She leaned forward, bent over the pages, the barely legible scribbles. "You write like this intentionally," she said without looking up, "because you are afraid of your reader." I told her it wasn't intentional. It was just the way I wrote, the way I'd always written since I was a child. "That's the point," Julia said, "you've been hiding behind your scribbles for your entire life. Look. Here, for example. I can make out some proper names: Daniel Cohen. Milena. Berlin. These are little islands sitting in a sea of chicken scratch. You would've never made it out of an Italian kindergarten. There's still a sense of craft there, some basic sense of discipline, order, self-control." I nodded, didn't respond, couldn't disagree with anything she said. It was true that I lacked order, control, discipline, a sense of craft. This disorder and chaos had prevented me from seizing control of my life, of making a reasonable progression into adulthood, of forging a solid notion of who I am. At the same time, I thought, if I had had a solid notion—or, really, any notion—of selfhood, how would it have been possible to complete *Blue, Red, Gray*? It would have been impossible, precisely because the novel's completion required an obliteration of self, a disintegration of the I. "Where is Daniel Cohen now?" she asked, still bent over the notebook, tracing words with her index finger. I said I had no idea. "Shouldn't you know it?" she pressed.

"How could I know it?"

"When did you last see him?"

"At Sladkovsky's. He told me about his dreams. He prophesized the end of days."

"He's sick," she said.

"He's fading away," I told her, "he's an abandoned character."

"No," Julia said, "he's not fading away. It's the opposite. He's just now starting to emerge from the background. Cohen won't tolerate being abandoned at Sladkovsky's. You might have cast him into the lions' den, but he knows how to tame those wild beasts."

"Nobody can tame the lions," I said, "it was God who that tamed them."

"Or the author, the author who had the will to write to the end point—the courage to see the whole story through. That was our mistake, Sy. We left Cain in the wilderness. We didn't bring him home. We didn't write it to the end. There's something different with Cohen. It struck me right away when I arrived back in Prague. If Cain has no ending, Cohen has no beginning. He appears at a party. He takes you to the house on Grunewaldstrasse. He is at the theater. He strokes Milena's cheek. He's at the clinic. You meet him in the clinic's library. He's working on a manuscript called 'Guests at the Hotel des Bains.' She steals it. You chase her down. You are with Cohen at Sladkovsky's, returning the manuscript to him, one now full of her marginalia. This is supposed to be the end of Cohen, his encounter with her marginalia, the writing of her story over his story, Milena becoming the book's author, replacing him. But Cohen resists. He won't be erased like that. He pushes his way back in—and the question that hovers between the two of you that night at Sladkovsky's is whether he wants an ending or a beginning, a past or a future." This was too much for me. I reached over Julia's shoulder and slammed the notebook shut. Cohen's past, Cohen's future—years in Berlin, years in Prague, months at Zelená Hora, the affair with Milena (his affair), the night on Grunewaldstrasse with the chemist—it all came together in a swirling, morphing composition, unstable, unfinished. Here I was, with Julia, in that overheated small apartment in the center of Prague, a stone's throw from the hordes of tourists passing over the Charles Bridge, gazing up at the astronomical clock in Old Town Square, wandering by the statue of Jan Hus, unaware that this was a man who went up in flames. Here I was, and here she was, and Daniel Cohen, I said to her, had been killed by a lion, and when the Babylonian king went to the lions' den and called out for Daniel Cohen, Daniel Cohen did not answer. The Lord had not intervened. The lions' mouths had not been closed; the lions had not been stilled by Daniel Cohen's touch—they had consumed him. They tore apart his flesh. They crushed his bones in their mighty jaws.

"Then his ghost has returned from Babylon," Julia said. "I saw him tonight walking along the river. He's carrying those secret words with him, words sealed in a book that can only be opened at the end of time. I stood on one side of the river and he on the other. I called out to him, 'How long do we have left?' He lifted his arms above his head and shouted, 'Time, times, and half a time.' He paused, then added, 'When the breaking of the power of the holy people comes to an end, then shall all these things be fulfilled.'" Daniel Cohen as shadow, Daniel Cohen as ghost, Daniel Cohen as prophet. Long ago, he led me down the stairs of a building on Grunewaldstrasse, shattering my boundaries, breaking apart my life, setting me on multiple, divergent trajectories—splitting me into fragments. Julia rose from the desk and moved across the room to stand in front of me. She pulled off her wool sweater, then her T-shirt, then she undid her bra. She unbuttoned and pulled down her jeans. She took off her underwear. "Now I am nothing but body," she said.

We were lying in bed after making love. I said to her, "I've always wondered why your name is spelled with a *j* and not in the Italian way with a *g*."

"This question proves you know nothing about me."

"Tell me."

"It's too late at night, Sy. Too late in life. You should have asked this question years ago."

"Please, Julia. I'm wide awake. I'm ready to hear it."

"You're wide awake," she said, "you're always claiming to be wide awake. That's why I knew you'd be awake when I arrived here. You'd be sitting at that desk, scribbling your illegible words. Maybe you were sitting at the desk that night waiting for this story—the story of the *j* in Julia. It's the key piece in your work, the piece that ties one part to the next, but you can't think of it, can't figure it out—and that's why you're stuck, and that's why you have me knock on the door, appearing in Prague after these many years to help you solve this puzzle. I'll tell you. My mother, Natalia, came from Venice. She named me Julia with a *j* after my mother's mother, who was Giulia with a *g*. Giulia, my grandmother, was imprisoned during the Second World War and died in a transit camp. My mother and her brother were hidden by friends of the family, a family originally from Spain, though they'd been in Venice for two generations. They would pretend to be fully Italian, but at home would speak Spanish. At home, they were against the war, against the fascists—and my mother and her brother learned to speak Spanish in their house. When the war ended, they waited for my grandfather to return from the mountains, but he never came back. Nobody knows what happened to him. My mother was still young when her mother was sent away, five or six years old. In this sense, it's easy, the *j* in Julia comes from the Spanish, a tribute to that Spanish family, and a symbol of the trauma inflicted on her by the nation of Italy, by the Italian language. When she was older, she would never call herself Italian, even though she lived her whole life in Italy—and when it came time to name her only child, me, she refused to give me an Italian name. This is the surface explanation, but it goes deeper. My mother was a poet. You might wonder how a woman who rejected her own language, Italian, could be a poet in that very language. Not only that—she wrote tender, subtle Italian. Not sentimental, but musical, lyrical. When she was a child, living with the Spanish family, she had a poetry teacher, a former friend of her father's, named Amos Negri. Negri was a figure on the margins. He had taught at the university for years but was pushed out by the fascists. After that, he earned his living by tutoring in a variety of subjects—Latin, Hebrew, mathematics, poetry, and philosophy. He worked on poetry with my mother, introducing her to works in Hebrew, especially the medieval poetry from Spain and southern France. He had known my mother's grandparents and could trace her family's history back to the Jewish ghetto in Modena, back, perhaps, to the arrival in the early sixteenth century of a couple from Girona, my ancestors Jacob and Julia Rodriga. Negri had discovered one of Julia's poems in the Modena archives; it was called 'Cain's Arrival.' At their final lesson, he gave the original copy of the poem to my mother. When my mother shared this poem with me, the whole Rodrigan world opened. It was the beginning of those powerful countercurrents that would bind us together, you and me, Sy.

As Negri told it, Jacob and Julia eventually fled the ghetto in Modena for the north. They were on their way to Prague, perhaps their destination, perhaps a stop on a longer journey. Nobody knows. My mother's poetry contains the breath of these mystical yearnings, the power of that radical thinking. But in Italy, she said, there was no soil for these roots. There was nothing but stone, concrete—Italy's greatest ideas had been spent in the past, its beauty was caged in history. The name Julia, for my mother, was an attempt to break through these walls, to break through these concrete-and-stone foundations. It was a search for soil to plant new roots, a poetic gesture amid ordinary language, one that might disrupt but that had no chance of breaking through. It couldn't break though because no poetry could break through. Nothing could overcome that brutal time. You might wonder how a practical man like my father could relate to these things. He was a businessman. He came from a long line of bankers. At first glance, there appears to be nothing spiritual about this man. How could my mother have fallen in love with him? It is often the case that beneath the surface of a man like my father is a swirling mass of disordered thoughts, ideas, impulses—impulses that can't be reconciled with the world as it is but can't be processed or rejected or expelled from the person. They are pushed down into the center of the soul, where they form layers, one on top of the next, compressed by the pressure of various forces—social conformity, professionalism, manners, expectations. Then comes the puncture—the puncture that taps into this sweet underground flow and results in a rising. My mother was this puncture—and the force of this puncture and the energy it released defined my childhood. I grew up amid the vibrance of this spring. When I was thirteen, it had run dry. The family was in crisis. My mother died. My father was devastated. I needed to trace it back to the deeper source. Luna Negri—that was my mother's pseudonym. You can guess the meaning of Luna Negri—the black moon. It might mean the new moon, and you know that the new moon is only the reverse of the full moon, and so the black moon is both full and empty, it is all and nothing, it is simultaneous presence and absence. I had to follow the path of Jacob and Julia Rodriga to the north. It was exactly ten years after my mother's death. When I arrived here in Prague, I felt like a stranger, not because I was a young woman coming from the university in Rome, but because I was now an adherent to a faith nobody shared, a faith in ghosts, the ghost of Jacob Rodriga, the ghost of Julia Rodriga, the ghost of the tutor Amos Negri, the ghost of my mother, the poet Luna Negri, and others—the ghost of my grandfather, a partisan fighter lost in the mountains, and my grandmother, who died in transit from one lost place to another, a death in the in-between. Ghosts moving from Spain through France and into Italy—or from Spain to Portugal and from Lisbon by ship to Venice. Or by another route—the city of Girona to Barcelona, Barcelona to Amsterdam, Amsterdam to Venice, Venice to Prague. I started to write a history of these ghosts. Then I met you and I started to wonder whether you were just a necessary part of my story, a person carried into it by my imagination, a person created to fulfill my desire, my desire for hidden documents, secret documents, lost documents, which you found for me. My desire for the central source, a key to the puzzle, my desire for *The Book of Moonlight*, which you wrote for me."

"After you left Prague and started to fade from my memory," I told Julia, "I began to think of you as part of Horák's novel, as a kind of peripheral character, one of those characters that gets cut in the revision process, left in the notebook, never transformed from scribbles onto the printed page. But it was impossible to keep you there. You kept pushing your way in."

"It's both, Sy," she said; "you created me, and I created you—and these two fictions met in some other work, authored by neither of us, and neither of us know how this other work began or how it will end, or even what will happen on the very next page. We might have interpretations. Things have been foreshadowed, but nothing is sure. The only thing that's sure is you are here now, and I am here now. We are here together in this small room, on this particular page. We have no past, no future. Every word we speak is new, every touch we share is new, and when this sentence ends, there will be blankness, darkness, and we will dissolve into faint traces and echoes in someone else's imagination."

NIGHT

I call it night, but the truth is I don't know if it's the night of one day or the morning of another. I fell asleep—and it's impossible to tell if I slept for mere minutes or if it were many hours. It was chaotic sleep, fitful, exhausting. The result of this confusion is that I've now lost track of what day it is—the night of the fifteenth, the morning of the sixteenth? I don't know. I have fallen out of the calendar. I have fallen out of time.

How could the village of Z. have existed for decades beyond the reach of humankind? Is the answer simply that nobody bothered to search for it? And why? Because it didn't matter. It had nothing to offer, no value. Or was it that whenever a person came into position to see the village if only this person looked in its direction, the person instead looked the other way? In other words, was it an accident, a hiding in plain sight?

I opened a jar of blackberries and took a few bites, felt my stomach churn. I paced the room, ran my fingers over the surface of one of the desks. I moved my notebook there, felt the aura of those officials, who day in and day out read from their pages, or, it occurred to me, the officials were not reading from these books, but erasing, word by word, line by line, books full of sentences, paragraphs, and stories until only blankness and eraser residue remained, crumbles of rubber now turned to powdery dust. Blank book upon blank book, literary monoliths or megaliths—books into stone, words into dust. Yes, this must have been it. The officials' job was not to record life but to erase life. Was this the essence of castle power, the power to erase deaths, to erase births, to erase whole generations from the official ledgers? It could be that these same officials had attempted to erase the cobbler's daughter Amalia, but Amalia refused to be erased, because as soon as one Amalia was erased another Amalia would appear on another page, maybe even in another book altogether, and as soon as that one would be tracked down, yet another would appear. A sturdy wall must be erected, Hruška once said to me, between translator and author, between novel and history, between the inside of a story and what falls beyond. What to do, I asked Hruška, with scenes that exist in multiple places? For example, I said, let's say there was a scene in Daniel Cohen's Berlin apartment decades ago. Cohen is there alone. Milena rings the bell, comes inside. She is carrying an old-fashioned American Tourister suitcase, yellow. It's winter, or early spring, or late fall. I don't know exactly when it is, I said to Hruška, but it doesn't matter. Cohen asks her if she's going somewhere. She says no, then she places the suitcase down on the sofa. She opens it. Cohen sees it is full of the costumes she's designed for the theater. Dresses and robes and pants and shirts—some tight, others loose and flowing. I'm going to play every role for you, she says to him. I have many lives in this suitcase, she continues, many lives and many deaths. And only one life will survive to walk out of your apartment at the end of the performance, and this life will become my life, our life, your life. The question is how to figure out which one. Cohen stands there in silence as Milena undresses, as she puts on the first costume, pulls it over her naked body, as the performance begins. The first character, I told Hruška, is Nora from Ibsen's *A Doll's House*. Call me your little squirrel, she says to Cohen, your songbird. The costume is simple, a tight-fitting dress with red-and-white stripes, making Nora look like a candy cane. It's Christmas, the family gathers, the old man, the young woman, the sick husband, the caring wife, the children. Cohen is forced to play his role, the ailing Torwald, the hopeless bourgeois mired in debt—the debt taken from him by Nora—the male debt, which transforms her into a real person, a financial entity, a debtor, the truest member of capitalist society. She engages in a financial transaction—yes. She owes. She struggles to get back to even; this is the erotic desire of the middle class, to make it back to zero, a masturbatory zero, an orgiastic zero. But the other state is equally full of bourgeois eroticism—to be pressed down by debt, to be tyrannized by the minus sign, the masochistic fantasy of self-sacrifice, of failing to repay, of seeing the number owed grow instead of shrink, of rubbing up against the raw edge of criminality—because in its essence, all capitalism, all relations of debt, are legalized crime. Power of one party, the lending party, over the other, the borrowing party. The power to shape a life, the power to rob another of freedom and dignity. Why would Nora submit? Is it, as Nora thinks, a decision motivated by care, by love? This is the delusion. There is no love, no real love, in this servitude. Nora discovers this as she leaves the house, as she exits from Ibsen's play, a burning, a heap of ash. No, it is not for care or love, it is a way of aligning oneself with the great force of capital, to discover one's meaning or purpose as a tool of capital, as a conduit for its flow. The performance is over. Milena vanishes and reappears without the candy stripes. She's naked—her skin is both dark and pale, her body thin—very thin, too thin.

She reaches into the suitcase and pulls out a black dress. It had been worn by an actress at the Maxim Gorky Theater who played the part of Nelly Sachs in a piece based on her correspondence with the poet Paul Celan. The piece was done for one of Maxim Gorky's side stages. It had two actors, the woman who played Nelly Sachs and the man who played Celan. The entire thing consisted of a compilation of fragments— fragments of letters, fragments of poetry. The older Sachs, the young Celan—the play ended with a poem about their meeting at the Stork Hotel in Zurich. I was in the theater for the premier. I was there as Nelly Sachs said, as Milena repeats to

Daniel Cohen, "The day empties itself in the twilight . . . Sullied with dream." *Traumbesudelt. Rouse yourself; why do you sleep, O Lord?* It is your God, not mine, your faith, not mine.

Costumes and more costumes—fundamental changes, transformations, shifting atmospheres, the air between her and Daniel Cohen first thickening, then rarifying, brightness into cloud and fog, processes turning and twisting, the body becoming, overcoming, one character supplanting the next. She reaches into the suitcase again. It's a skintight black suit, the one worn by the actress who played Milena Jesenska in Rosa Fuchsbein's *Milena*. A voiceless voice, an echo of a voice, an echo of her voice in his voice—his letters overwriting hers, wrestling with hers. She sits at her desk in Vienna, responding to his torrent of anxiety. She feels the walls closing in around her, the walls of reaction and hate—the right wing rising, gathering confidence, searching for enemies, internal and external enemies, enemies like her, socialists, communists, anarchists, feminists, a woman who spreads her legs for Jews. She wrote hundreds of invisible letters to him, spoke to him in disappearing voices, a voice silenced forever in a place called Ravensbrück on the Schwedtsee. Red hair, black bodysuit that reached up the midway point of the actor's neck. How long did Milena keep that costume on? Hours? Days? Weeks? Did she ever take it off? A ghost, haunting the empty half of a correspondence. She could have taught him about death, about the process of decreation, the worship of inflicting pain, the tyranny contained in every tiny gradation of power, the life-and-death significance of seemingly ordinary categories and classifications—and the need to classify, to define, to organize.

He could understand this. But beneath it, there was something else, something he could only vaguely sense. It was an evil, an evil enflamed with power, an evil raging and racing toward the end—*an end*, Esther Bird writes, *while history spins on and on.* More costumes from the plays of Rosa Fuchsbein, from *Songbirds*, from *Nervenklinik*, which takes place in a walled-off space in Berlin's Charité Hospital, in a room with a mystical text written on its ceiling, a text, *The Book of Moonlight*, that becomes visible only in complete darkness and after the "reader" spends hours gazing up at it from the floor. Then Milena takes out costumes from Fo's solo performances, a series of shows that ended with a piece called *Silence*. Days, weeks, months— how long did these performances last for Daniel Cohen? Years?

Finally, there is one last garment in the suitcase. By now, the others are scattered around on the floor. This last costume is the only one she hadn't designed. It's a white dress made of silk and lace. She pulls it onto her body. Cohen feels a pang of nostalgia, as if he has seen this dress before. When he described the scene to me years later in Zelená Hora, I immediately knew what it was. This was the costume Ida Fields wore in the first play written by Gabe Slatky, a high school one-act play. Ida's character had been unnamed. She was preparing to give the eulogy at her brother's funeral, trying to make sense of the incomprehensible space between his life and death. This was the essence of the piece, maybe the essence of art. What else should art strive for? If something can be known, if it can be discovered, if it can be found, if it can be clearly spoken, it is not the true subject of art. How Gabe knew this at such a young age is beyond me. Or maybe he didn't know it, only felt it—an inkling of it.

Milena strips off the final costume. She starts to shake with fever. Her body is burning—and at the same time, when Cohen approaches her and puts his hands on her, he feels she's as cold as ice. He offers her a pair of gray sweatpants and a sweatshirt, but she refuses them. She climbs into his bed, still naked. She won't play the role associated with Cohen's gray sweatpants and a sweatshirt, she whispers, a role pulled from the pages of a novel about a man who finds a desperate woman on the Chamiso Platz one winter night and takes her in. It is the story of a nameless woman with the name of Mila—Mila from Milena. It is a story, she whispers, told by the two-in-one author-narrator: Daniel Cohen, and yes, by me, Sy Kirschbaum, his novel and mine. By the next morning, her fever has passed but the tremors remain, the tremors are stuck in her hands. She can't get rid of them. She can no longer draw, or cut fabric, or sew. To still those hands, this is not an issue of science or medicine—it is an issue of literature. It requires a journey into the unknown, the unbound, the landscape of dreams. It requires a journey to Zelená Hora. It requires a journey to the village of Z., it requires a journey to the deepest interior of the castle on the hill.

NIGHT

I wake up and light a couple of beeswax candles. There's a draft somewhere, which causes the flames to dance and sputter. As I sit here by the stove, I hear a faint noise coming from the distance, a kind of hum, or, no, a whistling sound, a piping, seemingly emanating from deeper inside the castle. This is it, I think, the sound of the swarm, the same noise Kaesbohrer heard in his basement in the building on Grunewaldstrasse, the one that was both the invisible antagonist—the precise antagonist—and the ultimate evil, which had been burrowing its way through the entire city of Berlin by way of a series of tunnels and bunkers while the world above was unaware. I wonder if this castle is not actually a castle but a formula, like Kaesbohrer's formula, the solution to which, to the castle that is, is simply zero. Zero. Nullity. Void. The end of time. It could be the formula, it occurs to me, for evil.

That stubborn counternarrative. It was a vision I'd had while coming out of the blackness after drinking Kaesbohrer's cloudy yellow liquid. It was a domestic scene, a husband, a wife, two kids; the father was a writer in the aftermath of a psychotic break. It was the story about a writer looking for his way out—out of the apartment, out of a life. He'd locked himself in his tiny office, a converted storage space off the kitchen. There he'd discovered a tunnel, which went either upward toward the rooftop and the open air or downward into the basement, into those labyrinthine spaces, an abandoned world of darkness existing below the surface of the streets. After the breakdown, Sasha, his wife, had taken the kids away. Maybe she was gone for good—maybe it was the end of life there, the end he'd been seeking, the elusive ending of every unfinished novel gathering dust on the shelves. The novel ends, he thought, with the end of the author. Even then it doesn't end.

The noise again—it jars me from these thoughts. Not memories, because these are not memories, and yet they are something like memory. It's the type of thought for which there is no word, maybe a concept: parallel memory, fictional memory, possible memory—or it could be that they are real memories after all, that the "everything else" beyond the counternarrative was its parallel, its fictional mirror.

NIGHT

I put about ten candles in my backpack and packed up my things, including rolling up the three eiderdowns. I left the room through the interior door by the stove. I moved through an empty chamber and into a smaller room. I stared at the wall and imagined looking out a small window through the gray mist at the valley below. What village have I stumbled into? Is there a castle here? Or: which castle have I wandered into, is there a village here? Keter found Momus in Prague in a large apartment near the castle's gardens. In his journals, Keter describes Momus's place as messy—clothes, dishes, newspapers, and books were scattered around. Wine bottles, mostly empty, and wineglasses sat on surfaces—side tables, counters, windowsills. The large man, Momus, wandered around the space in an untied robe. The place was cold, but Momus kept the windows open, afraid, he said, that ash from the coal dust generated by the stoves would fill his lungs. Momus shrugged when Keter pointed out that the outside air seemed no better. Momus had seen the mark of Cain, a mark that had traveled through centuries. By then, it had faded, becoming nearly imperceptible. But still there, a perfect circle, reflecting the perfection of God's fingertip, the same fingertip that had carved the law into stone, the law given to Moses on Sinai. It would be reasonable to assume, thought Momus, that if it were the same finger, then Cain's mark would have the same status as those profound decrees—that in some sense Cain's mark would also be law. Did the valley burn? Did it convulse? Was it devoured by the earth? Did plague break out here? Did conflict rise, pitting castle against village in one final confrontation, or villager against villager—the Brunswick faction against the faction led by Amalia, the daughter of the master cobbler? Or maybe poison seeped into the wells. No, Momus told Keter. It was vengeance, the righteous justification of the moral law, it was the pulling of evil back onto the side of good, which meant, Momus said, utter annihilation. Or, rather, it was one monster eating another, one evil being superseding the other—multi-headed eagles, beasts with sets of small wings and the jaws of a lion. People think this is a period of decadence, Momus said to Keter, but decadence is only the outer shell of anxiety, collective nervousness, the forebodings of doom, Eros directed not toward consummation but toward interruption. The first flickers of arousal. Its sublimation into drunkenness, gluttony, prostitution, fashion, national pride, everyday domination, domination of self, of family, the imaginary domination of people in far-flung parts of the world. You can see for yourself, Momus said to Keter, that my wine bottles are empty. I've had my fill. I've consumed every drop. I've fallen in and out of countless stupefied delusions since arriving here from the village of Z. There was no other way to try to discover what it meant, what explained the collective annihilation that was about to come to a story that ends in midsentence. Part of my training as an official, as Klamm's village secretary, was to develop a capacity to drink a lot of beer without getting too drunk, to outlast the last peasant at the pub. This is vital for a competent official, Momus said, it was his most important skill. The love of beauty, Momus said, is a form of drunkenness. Colored glass; mosaics; long, curving lines; botanical forms; bodies intermingling, merging, vanishing—the worship of the ephemeral, the whole world becoming ephemeral. This is the dance of death, said Momus, the abandonment of everything that holds the world together. And what are those things? In our drunkenness, amid our whirling dance into oblivion, we have forgotten what they could be. In our sobriety, Momus said, in our head-splitting sobriety, we lurch after the first thing that seems to make sense, even if it makes no sense, even if it is the exact opposite of sense. Life, Momus said to Keter, is a story that ends midsentence. Life, he said, is a story that has no ending. Life is the failure of story. Life is the impossibility of continuing a story that at the same time has no possibility of ending. Life is the story of a protagonist dropped off the page. Life, Momus said, is the time waiting for Cain to arrive. Life, he said, is the moment of Cain's arrival, one moment expanded into thousands of years, one moment with a beginning and an ending that come together in a perfect circle, the mark of Cain, the trace of God's fingertip on human flesh.

Cain wandered away from his family's land. He thought he heard a wailing in the distance, a piercing lamentation rising from his mother and father, who now most likely stood above the murdered, lifeless body of his brother Abel. The wall of fire having vanished, they would look out over the arid terrain and see only stillness. Cain was already far from home. It was dark and cold. Cain built a fire. Then he constructed a small altar, tried to mourn his brother through faith. He had no sacrifice to offer, tried instead to find a bridge to God through prayer, through a plunge into total devotion. He inhaled smoke from the myrrh resin he had added to the fire. His head felt light. The flames played shadow theater on his closed eyelids. He searched his soul for the breath of the Lord. Nothing was there. He had banished from himself the love of God. His discovery, the discovery of this void of love, cast Cain into despair—first his brother Abel had been taken from him, then he had been cut off from his mother and father, and now he was empty of the spirit of the Lord. What used to be fertile was now barren—what used to make sense, what connected him to truth, was now in disarray. Confusion reigned. That night, as he fell asleep and his dream opened, Cain fell into the unbound, disordered space with the sensation that he might never return to that other world. Here, in his dreams, the solidity of things broke down, time took great leaps forward only to stumble and fall back, to rise again and move not in straight lines but in a series of slanted vectors, curves, and spirals. This was a godless landscape, a realm melting at its edges into a kind of primordial chaos, eroding into the crashing waves of the watery deep. Cain stood up and walked to the edge of this vast ocean. Then, knowing the risks, sensing the presence of Leviathan, the guardian of the deep, he dove into the water, submerging himself below its churning, foaming, windswept surface. When he pushed his head back above the water, he saw that he was surrounded by ocean. The land—his consciousness, his selfhood—had disappeared. All that he had been, he felt, had washed away. If this were true, Cain thought, maybe God's mark had also been stripped off by the whirling water. He felt the back of his neck with his fingertips. He ran them along the rough patch of seared flesh, that perfect circle. The mark was still there, still aching from God's fiery touch. When he felt the spot, a shiver of pain shot through his body—all the way into his toes and fingertips. The pain threatened to pull Cain from the oceanic deep, back through the fracturing solidity of the dreamscape, returning him to consciousness. He had no desire to return, no yearning for the world of God's creation, the world ruled by God and his commands. The more he resisted the move back from the boundlessness of the oceanic deep to the world of reality, the more the pain on the back of his neck increased, becoming like a hot, burning needle that pieced his flesh. Deeper and deeper the needle plunged into his neck until Cain couldn't stand it any longer. The endless ocean vanished, and he found himself in a strange land next to the altar he had built. He looked around: nothing but darkness in every direction. He had a strange feeling inside himself, as if something fundamental had changed. It must be, he thought, that he had absorbed too much water, too much of the oceanic deep, and now its essence was within him, flowing through him, mixing with his blood. Through his veins, then, ran two fundamentally opposing substances. There was the life force, blood, the essence of creation, infused with the breath of God. And there were the brackish, raging waters of the deep, the spirit of disorder, of chaos, entropy—the power of uncreation.

Flashes of a vision came to him. There was no telling whether what Cain witnessed was actually happening at that moment or whether he had conjured it somehow or whether

God had filled his mind with the scene. His parents were there. They were standing over Abel's lifeless body. For a long time, Abel's body lay there on the ground as it had fallen. Adam and Eve stared at it. They did not know what to do with it, with this first corpse, this first human death. They wept as they called out to God to come, to take Abel back to the divine realm. Then they saw a raven alight on the ground next to Abel's body. It was carrying another of its kind in its claws. The raven set the dead bird down, hopped next to it, and began to scratch at the ground until it had made a small hole. It grasped the dead bird's body and placed it in the hole. Then it pushed the loose dirt back into the hole on top of the bird, burying it in the ground. Adam and Eve worked as the raven did. They dug a hole in the ground. They set Abel's body there and covered it with dirt. They marked the spot with a small pile of rocks. While they worked, the raven was soaring above them in wide circles. When they were done, the raven shot out toward the far horizon. Cain saw the bird as it passed above him.

When day broke, Cain carried on in the direction of the raven's flight. At the same time, Cain wasn't following the raven, he was wandering without direction, without aim; he wandered because his fate was to wander, to be a wanderer, a man without home, whose goal was simply to make it over the next hill, to make it to the next stream so he could drink. Cain traced paths that were not yet paths, lines that were not yet lines. Some say Cain wandered for hundreds of years; for centuries he was cocooned within himself, hearing only his thoughts, the beating of his heart, the pulse of his breath, and the sounds around him, wind, rain, the songs of birds. At times, he would exercise his voice and bellow into the vast, empty canyons, or he would send his voice over the surface of the river or sea like a dragonfly. He ate what he could find. He had been forbidden by God to plant seeds and to grow roots, and in any case he had lost his urge to cultivate the land. He wanted to leave the land as it was, to take only what it would give him, nothing more; and in his heart he refused the idea that what nature provided, the fruits from the trees, could have come from the treacherous, murderous God. Rather, he knew that as they rose out of the ground, their roots, their source, lay in the watery deep. He knew this because he carried the essence of the deep within him, and whenever he ate these fruits, this essence, this substance, would flow with more vigor, propelling him into ecstatic trances.

After his long wandering, Cain came over the ridge of a mountain range and saw a large group of buildings pressed close together. There were hundreds of them, maybe thousands, situated on the side of a wide bend in the river where the plain stretched out toward the east. The gathering of buildings was arranged around a large central structure, access to which required the ascent of a long, steep staircase. As Cain came down from the mountain ridge, he saw people working in the fields beyond the city's walls. Others were cutting chunks of stone that had been hewn above in the hills and hauled down by cart. Others were forging metal or pressing olives into oil or working to turn the skins of animals into leather. Apart from the workers, children and animals milled about outside the city walls. Cain saw that the only way in and out of the city was through a great gate, which was guarded by a regiment of soldiers with iron swords.

Cain went to the gate and tried to pass through to the city. Two of the guards immediately blocked his way. "Stranger," said one of the guards, "what brings you here? No foreigners are permitted to pass through these gates without permission of the king, his deputies, or the high priest."

"Then take me to the king and I will ask for permission," Cain said.

The guard seemed startled. "Take you to the king? How could I possibly do such a thing? I am a guard of the gate. A guard of the gate can't even enter the royal palace, let alone stand before the king. If I, captain of a regiment of guards of the gate, cannot enter the palace and stand before the king, how could you, a stranger, likely a vagabond, step foot on the marble hallway that leads, so it is said, to the royal chamber of gold and cedar?"

"Is the tower that I saw from the mountain ridge the royal palace?" Cain asked.

"Where have you come from?" The guard said to Cain. "It's as if you've fallen from the sky. Everyone knows that the tower is the temple of El. El dwells inside the temple's innermost chamber. It is El who has brought this city power, riches, and glory, who has chosen and blessed our king as he has defeated our enemies and expanded our domain. Our wheat grows plentifully, our fruit trees are fecund, our animals are fat, thanks to the blessed El."

"Then take me to the temple," Cain said, "and I will ask the high priest for permission to stay."

"To the temple!" A second guard broke in. "That is utter nonsense. Even the high priest can only enter the temple when permitted by El. The lower priests can enter when performing their rites. This happens once per day at designated times. The most holy elders in the city, if they can make the journey, are allowed to climb to the top of the stairs to lay offerings by the door. Otherwise, commoners can gather at the temple's base, nothing more. Even the king, the most powerful person in the city, can enter the temple only if he is invited and accompanied by the high priest, which happens three times per year on the most holy days. And to think, a stranger like yourself mounting those stairs and entering those holy chambers! El would respond with absolute fury. He would strike you down in an instant—and in his rage, he might raze the whole city to the ground."

Cain recognized it was hopeless. The guards would never allow him to pass. He turned away and went out into the fields. He moved through the sunken paths between the ripe fields of wheat. He reached out and felt their texture, admired their golden color, which in the low sun of the late afternoon was tinged with a pinkish hue. After a while, a horn sounded and around him the field laborers, sun-beaten and dusty from the day's work, lay down their tools and began to gather together on the road that led to the city. As their numbers grew, the noise began to swell, and Cain was surprised by how many people came out of the fields: men young and old, women, and children who barely reached to their parents' waists. Some women had babies tied to their backs with strips of cloth. Old women leaned on walking sticks or on the arms of their neighbors. Others moved about the crowd with barrels of water, pouring it into smaller clay vessels for the people to drink. The people's haggard state was not too distant from his, Cain thought, as he made his way over to blend in with the crowd. The peasants met Cain with suspicious glances but were either too tired or too timid to expel him. When the mass of people began to move toward the city's gate, Cain went with it, and in this way was carried past the guard and into the city.

It had been a long time since Cain had been with other people, and now he found himself surrounded by hundreds. Once inside the city, the crowd of laborers started to thin. People broke away and disappeared down different streets, some into buildings that lined the square. Cain followed one group to an alleyway so that he wouldn't attract attention by the gate. He was careful to avoid the eyes of the city dwellers who passed him by. The noises in the city, the smells, the endless number of movements and sounds, were disorienting. How, Cain wondered, could such a place come into being? How could all of this come from the life beyond the gates of Eden, from the womb of his mother Eve?

As night approached, the people began to disappear from the streets into their houses. Cain hadn't stepped foot in a built structure since he left his parents' camp. If he had required shelter to protect from storms or wild beasts, he would seek out a place in nature that would protect him—a grotto, or some branches woven together above the ground. Now he had no choice. The city's guard was roaming the streets. He stopped an old man and asked him where a stranger could find a place to spend the night. The old man looked at him with a bewildered expression. "You speak," the man said, "in a way I can understand but have never heard before."

"I'm not from here," said Cain.

"That is clear," said the man, "and in that case, you have no other choice but to go to the inn by the bridge. Be sure to ask the landlord and not his wife, the landlady, for a bed and food for the night."

Cain thanked him and turned to go, but then he felt the old man's hand on his arm. "Just one more thing, stranger," he said. "Be careful whom you talk to here. Everyone who hears you will know from your voice that you don't belong to the city or its hinterlands. They will know you are from somewhere far away, a place people here, including myself—and I was a merchant who traveled widely—can't even imagine, can't fathom. Because of this, you will be unfathomable to them, and because you will be unfathomable, they will hate you. This has been the way here since the beginning of the reign of the new king. It's only since the rise of the new king that we have guards at the city's gates. Before him, under the old king and all previous kings, people, even strangers from far away, could pass freely in and out of the walls. It is very surprising that you, the strangest of strangers, have managed to enter the city at all."

"Who is the king here? How did he come to power?" Cain asked.

"Please lower your voice," the old man said. "This is not something we can discuss in the streets. It is not something we can discuss anywhere, even in the privacy of one's room. I'll tell you this: the king washed the old king away in a river of blood—that's all there is to know. The old priesthood, too, was annihilated. The high priest of the temple of El now obeys the king, not El, despite what he says. The people live in terror of the wrath of El—but what they are really afraid of is the wrath of the king, the king who now considers himself a god, a god more powerful than El." The man was whispering now in Cain's ear. "Beware, stranger. Watch what you say—or better yet, say very little, or nothing at all. Most importantly, never mention the king or the high priest of the temple of El. Go straight to the inn by the bridge. Keep your head low. At daybreak, leave the city with the day laborers. Never return here. In this city, a tyrant rules—and the god El, humiliated and powerless, is forced to worship him."

Then the man was gone. It was as if he had receded into the stonework, or into thin air. Cain set off in the direction the man had pointed out to him. It wasn't long before he reached the riverbank and saw an inn for travelers, merchants, mostly, who had come to the city to trade. He made his way inside. Beyond the entryway, there was a large room full of men eating their evening meal. There was not a woman in the place besides the one who brought the men their food. Jugs of water and wine sat on the tables and were passed around for the guests to take long, messy drinks—the wine staining the men's beards a deep purple. Cain tried to keep his head low, as the old man had instructed him, now and then looking out for the landlord, whom he finally spotted coming out of the kitchen while shouting something back to the cook and directing the waitress with a movement of his arm.

The landlord was much younger than Cain had expected him to be, though in truth most of the men in the city and out in the fields seemed young to him—for Cain was much older than anyone in the world. The landlord moved over to the outer wall and opened a small window to let in some air. The room was hot, the air stagnant and malodorous from those bodies packed together. Cain took the chance to approach, moving quickly around the benches.

"Landlord," he said in a low voice, "I've heard that this is a place where a stranger can find a bed."

The landlord, startled, looked up at Cain. Some naïve expression played on his face. Still, the landlord could tell that his new guest was not an ordinary stranger. He had taken over the inn from his wife's uncle years before, and the inn had prospered under his management, though in truth the success was mainly due to the efforts of the landlady, his wife, who worked tirelessly in the kitchen with the cooks and even harder with the servants and chambermaids such that the inn quickly established a good reputation among the merchant class. Part of the inn's success was also because of the new king, who shut down many of the other inns in order to make sure he had an eye on foreigners arriving in the city. Each landlord, under the new rules, was only allowed to provide a bed for a guest if the guest could show an official letter of permission from the king to reside for a specific time in the city. Failure to adhere to the rules would mean losing the inn entirely, and if the illegal guest were somehow deemed an enemy of the state, the punishment for the innkeeper could be much worse, even, in extreme circumstances, death by public execution. The king's principal goal was to control trade and to tax merchants who came into the city to sell their goods—and all merchants who came to the city had to reside in one of only a handful of authorized inns. In other words, the landlord would be risking his entire business, and potentially his life, by allowing a man like Cain to sleep there even for a single night.

The landlord motioned for Cain to follow him from the dining room into a narrow hallway. At the end of the hallway, a staircase led to an upper floor. The landlord took Cain into one of the rooms.

"You can stay here for the night," the landlord said, "but you have to promise me you'll stay in this room from now until morning. Then, in the morning, you must leave the inn for good. You cannot be discovered here. There are sure to be spies for the king in the dining room. They are thrilled to report violations of the law, despite the free wine and meals we give them, despite the pleasures they enjoy here. Stay here. I'll send up food and drink."

A short time later, a young woman opened the door and set down a plate of food and a pitcher of water on the table in the room. Cain had, in the meantime, removed his robe and was bent over the water basin rinsing his body, scrubbing away the endless layers of dust. The woman looked on, then she said to Cain: "I don't recognize that mark on the back of your neck. It must belong to a people from far away. I see you haven't brought goods to trade or gold or silver to buy from others. I was watching you in the dining room. You've come a long way to Zion. Tell me, stranger, to which people do you belong? Which people mark themselves with such a mark on the back of their necks?"

Cain turned around to face her. "I have no people," he said, "and I've come a long way, but for no purpose. This mark was not made by a human hand. It is the mark of God."

The young woman approached Cain. "If it is truly the mark of God," she said, "I would like to touch it, to touch the same place touched by Him."

Cain moved toward her. He fell to his knees and arched his back. His hair, which had been tied up for the washing, came loose, covering his face in a shaggy mane. The young woman stepped forward, peered into the spot, a spot as black as night. It seemed to her for an instant that this spot was actually not a spot but a hole, a hole pulling her in by the force of its limitless depth. As she moved closer to it, she realized that the spot was not black after all. It was, rather, a combination of every color—yellows, reds, blues, greens, purples, white—every hue, every shade, composed in an impossible way that seemed at once with and without pattern, order, logic.

"This can only be the work of God," she whispered. "How lucky you are, stranger, to have been touched by the all-powerful El."

"I don't know El," Cain said to her. "The God who made this mark has no name. This is not a mark of luck or favor. It is the mark of eternal punishment. To carry this mark with me is the heaviest burden one can bear. No amount of wheat or water, even enough to feed and quench the thirst of this great city, can equal its weight. It is a weight that presses on the soul."

"Then how do you carry it? Your body is frail, your arms and legs as thin as snakes."

"I'll tell you how," Cain said. "Inside my soul, I have the essence of the deep. It is the substance of primordial chaos— and the mark of God floats on the surface of this substance as a ship, no matter how big, how heavy, can float on the surface of the sea without sinking."

The young woman reached out and touched the mark with the tips of her fingers. A surge of energy was suddenly present in the room—a wild and twisting surge that seemed to spin out of the mark, entering her hand and arm and then her entire body before circling back to him. The pleasure of the touch mixed with agony—for there was not only fathomless good contained in Cain's mark, there was also pure evil—and violence, and rage. There was love, but there was also fear and vengeance. And there was hope. And there was lust as savage as can possibly be imagined, an unimaginable lust set on devouring its object. She trembled as she held her fingers on his neck. She could not retract them, could not keep them on his skin.

The young woman's name was Lilit, and that night she and Cain had the same dream. In the dream, the mark on the back of Cain's neck opened as wide as the city's gates. Lilit walked through this portal into the multifarious blackness, a blackness that contained all color. She was naked, though the color itself wrapped around her and kept her body warm. Even though Cain was the bearer of the mark through which Lilit had passed, he was also inside it with her—also naked and dripping wet with color. They moved toward each other until their bodies met and intertwined. Their breath commingled, colors blending, striating, thinning, filling, moving in and out of blackness. They fell. It was a well—and it went as deep as they could imagine. At the bottom was a garden. They found themselves amid fruit trees in full bloom. It was a perfect circle of trees surrounding one central tree, a tree taller than the others and already bearing fruit. Neither of them had seen this particular fruit before. The fruit seemed to pulsate with an inner light—yellow, orange—a luminous fecundity ready to burst its skin. Cain and Lilit sensed that eating the fruit would obliterate the dream and cast them back into the yawning emptiness of sleep. Still, the allure of the fruit enticed them. They approached and each picked a piece. The fruit was as heavy as it looked, plump, soft to the touch. They tasted it at the same time, sucked and licked at its golden sugar. Juices ran down their mouths, embalming them in stickiness. By the time they had finished the whole piece, their blood was alive, hot, sweet, sticky—they fell into each other in a wild orgy of pleasure.

By then, it was nighttime in the garden. A cold wind started to blow. Cain and Lilit pulled themselves apart, felt their solitude again, felt their fear begin to grow, to expand, and it expanded such that it began to push back at the darkness, to push away the very dream in which they were. Then they woke up, each in different beds, in different rooms of the inn by the bridge. Lilit knew instantly that it had happened. She was pregnant with the stranger's child.

The next day, Cain wandered through the city. He saw large groups of people passing back and forth through the guarded gates, heading out into the fields beyond the walls, bringing finished goods in from the workshops. The elderly and the infirm and the mad remained behind in the city—mostly minding their own business, occasionally prodded to move along by the pointed end of a guard's spear. There were others, too, who stayed behind in the city. They wore lavish fabrics—purples, rich blues, yellows—and went around with retinues of servants. Many of these men came to the inn by the bridge to inspect the merchants' wares, to arrange purchases, to settle debts, mostly peacefully, but sometimes with shouts, threats, and violence.

Cain went to see the temple of El. All day long, the commoners in the city brought offerings for the god—animals, grain, fruits, oil, carvings of wood and stone, earthenware vessels, spices. The people would be met at the bottom of the stairs by members of the priesthood, who would then prepare packages for official carriers, also members of the priesthood, so that they could bring them up the stairs to the temple's doors. No commoners were allowed on the stairs except on designated days, when certain members of the community could climb the stairs and gaze through the open doors into the darkness of the interior. Under no circumstances were commoners allowed to pass through the doors and into the temple. Even many members of the priesthood had not reached high enough status for this. Cain brought no offering. Still, he wanted to get inside the temple to see if El was the same God who murdered his brother Abel and sent him on his endless, aimless journey. Cain approached the temple. He waited for a moment of relative calm and began to climb the stairs. By the time members of the priesthood at the base of the temple spotted him, he was already a good way up, too far away for them to catch him. When he reached the top, two priests in white robes came out to block his way, asking him what he wanted, why he dared to test fate by climbing those holy stairs.

"I have come to see the God that dwells here, the God El, who lives in this temple."

"It is against the king's law for any commoner to try to enter the temple," one said, "especially a stranger from a strange land. You must leave at once."

Cain stood there and gazed beyond the two priests through the temple's open door. Inside, Cain could see a room, and beyond the room was another, and so on for as far as the eye could see—room after room, doorway inside doorway, such that one's line of sight could continue into the deep recess. At the far end, perhaps in the very last room, Cain thought he saw a flicker of light, the palest glow of orange coming from deep within the space, a glow that seemed as distant as the far horizon.

"Does a fire burn in there," Cain asked, "or is it the flaming body of El?"

"The holy fire lights and heats El's inner sanctum. It cannot be extinguished, or the city would face El's wrath. This is what the high priest tells us. No others, not even the next highest priest, have been to the twelfth room."

"El lives there in the innermost sanctum?"

"He *dwells* there," the priest corrected Cain, "he receives the offerings there, from there he blesses the king and the high priest and cloaks the city with his grace. Now, stranger, you must go. It would be bad for both of us if you are found to have gazed inside the temple, a stranger, a stranger who speaks in a way both foreign and familiar, as if your language has come from deep in the past."

Cain took one last look inside the temple, then turned to go back down the stairs. The late-afternoon sun fell on his face.

"Hold up there, stranger," the priest called out. "What is that mark on the back of your neck?"

Cain turned back. "That is the fingerprint of God, the Nameless One."

Days passed. The landlord couldn't bring himself to expel Cain from the inn, especially when he learned that this stranger from another time and place carried the mark of an unfathomable God on the back of his neck. Each night, Cain would meet Lilit in the garden, and they would go together to the tree with the glowing orange fruit. They would pick one piece, taste its sugary flesh, and make love covered with its riotous juices. After these long, lustful embraces, they would plunge into one of those four rivers that forked away from a single, unseen source coming down from the highlands above. The rivers would wash away the sticky juices, invigorating their senses, and Lilit and Cain would take drinks of the purest water.

Cain walked through the city. Around him, old women sat on the stone streets and begged for food. Crippled or injured men from the fields and mines were there, some with wounds festering, bodies thinning, slowly dying for all to see. Would-be prophets stood on crates and addressed the crowds, speaking the language of righteousness and doom. These speakers could talk about most anything, it seemed to Cain, until the subject fell, as it always eventually did, to the king or the high priest, at which point the guards would emerge and move them along. Amid the general opulence of Zion, Cain saw suffering—starving children, women forced to sell their bodies for food and shelter. Everyone in Zion seemed to work so that the god El could be propitiated, so that the king's palace could grew bigger and more lavish, so that the members of the guard and the priesthood would want for nothing, especially the high priest, who would appear each week at the top of the temple's stairs in a bejeweled robe, resplendent in the eye of the sun. The members of the guard and priesthood were strong, healthy, powerful men, and they dominated the city in the name of the king and El. Cain observed the gluttony of the merchants at the inn by the bridge and the lasciviousness and violence of the guards, who filed in and out of the brothels day and night only to terrorize people in the streets in the name of their master. He saw the impiety of the priests, who cared more about polishing their gold and silver medallions than about faith.

Cain began to speak about these observations to others in the city—to Lilit in their shared dreams, to the landlord and his wife, despite their attempts to avoid or silence him, to the merchants at the inn, who simply laughed at his innocence and stupidity, to women begging in the streets, to the speakers on their crates, to orphans darting in and out of the alleyways in search of food (or anything else) to steal. How could it be, Cain asked, that such injustice was permitted, that the original goodness of creation could have turned into a world where the few dominated the many in the name of king and God? Cain's words started to spread through Zion. They moved from mouth to mouth, until it seemed that the entire city was buzzing with these questions.

One night, the king's guards raided the inn by the bridge. Six men entered Cain's room and arrested him. He was in the garden with Lilit when they broke through the door, emerging from the shadows of his consciousness. Lilit vanished from him, her body dissolving. The fruit and the fruit tree disappeared, and Cain fell out of the circle of trees and through a dark tunnel as blow after blow landed on his body. The guards bound his hands with rope and led him from the inn through the streets by torchlight to the base of the temple. They instructed him to climb.

When Cain reached the top of the stairs, a figure dressed in a long robe of many colors can out from inside the temple. "What is this?" the man said to the guards around him, or to nobody in particular. "This stranger doesn't fall to his knees or shield his eyes before the high priest of El?"

A man, who appeared higher in rank than the others, spoke up. "The stranger's name is Cain. He arrived in the city some weeks ago. He carries a mark on the back of his neck, which he claims comes from his God. He says this God is nameless, that He is the creator of all that is, all order in the world, he says his God formed plants, animals, and people. He says this nameless God created his parents, Adam and Eve, who, he claims, were the first people on the earth."

"Now I see with my own eyes this stranger, about whom so much has been said. Stranger," the high priest called out to Cain, "approach!"

Cain moved forward, gazing at the priest's luxurious silken robes, his bejeweled fingers and neck.

"Take off your robe," said the priest, "and show me the mark of your nameless God."

Cain turned his back, untied his robe, and let it fall to the ground. Naked, Cain got down on his knees and arched his back. His hair fell away, revealing the mark. The high priest stepped forward until he was standing over Cain's body. He looked at the spot. It was a kind of blackness, the priest saw in the torchlight, that while from a distance looked like pure blackness in fact contained a multitude of colors. It was a swirling, gyrating pool of layer upon layer of every color imaginable—beyond what was imaginable. There were greens so green they were no longer mere green but the very essence of greenness, a primary greenness that spread from the mark to the world in endless variegations, giving life to leaves and stalks, animating the whole of the natural world. And the brown of the mark was no mere brown but the color of the very dust and clay, which formed the basis for material existence—and no mere blue but an oceanic blue stretching deeper and deeper toward the abyssal depths of the darkest deep, and reds as pure as flame, which, once lit, could never be extinguished.

Awestruck, the high priest couldn't help but reach out to touch the mark on the back of Cain's neck. His long index finger pressed into Cain's skin. Cain felt a jolt of energy. The high priest seemed frozen, unable to pull his finger away. Cain closed his eyes. He found himself in a room. It was dark and cold; strong winds swirled around him. He was moving through one space into another and into another, going deeper into the interior of the temple of El. A fire burned in the distance, the flame of the ever-burning fire that warmed El's innermost sanctum, his dwelling place. Cain made his way to the fire and saw the high priest standing there amid the flames. His body was burning without it being consumed.

"In the holy presence of El, in the holy womb of the goddess Asherah, I offer you, Cain, as a sacrifice." The high priest sprung from the fire toward Cain with a long iron sword glowing red with heat. He swung at Cain, catching Cain's arm and leaving a deep gash. Blood poured out of the wound—blood mixed with some other substance unknown to the high priest, unknown even to the god El. It was the essence of the watery deep, and this essence poured out of Cain and cooled the high priest's sword. It extinguished the ever-burning fire. It flooded the inner sanctum, El's dwelling place. It didn't stop there. The watery essence rushed through the temple, bursting through walls, filling passageways, drowning everything within. When the waters overtook the high priest, a powerful winged creature appeared. It flung itself toward Cain with an intensity that Cain had never seen before, but right before the winged creature, the god El, reached him, it was consumed by the floodwaters, which by then had merged into a powerful current. The waters carried El to the temple's entrance and flung him from the temple's summit, sending him crashing to the ground, killing him instantly. The waters didn't overwhelm Cain. He moved with graceful strokes through the turbulence until he, too, reached the temple's doors. When he came outside, he saw that dawn had come and the sky had opened up. The water that poured forth from the temple in a powerful river was met by water falling from the sky and water emerging from the ground. Chaos reigned—its deluge washing Zion from the earth.

The high priest pulled back his finger. He stood there for a moment gazing at its tip, then he fainted and fell to the ground. Cain stood and faced the others: "Your high priest has seen a vision of the death of El and the destruction of Zion. He has felt the storm of chaos, which moves through my veins."

Cain turned and looked out at the city below him. Something was happening there. In the moonlight, he could see movement in the streets and alleyways. One after another, fires started to burn, smoke rose from the buildings. Crowds gathered in the city squares. Cain watched as the king's guard rushed to disperse the people. The masses quickly overwhelmed them. Cain looked to the other side of the city and saw that the main force of the king's guard had formed a defensive line around the palace. But it was no match for the crowds. They easily broke through and swept the guard away.

The high priest rose. Still shaken, he managed to utter to the others around him, "This stranger has brought chaos here. He must be killed, sacrificed to El, or we are doomed."

"This is not only chaos," Cain said to him, "it is justice. Your touch has unleashed this chaos, high priest, and by night's end the vision will be fulfilled. The king and the high priest of Zion will be dead. El will be drowned in the primordial ocean. The people of Zion will be free."

NIGHT

Humming sound—vibrations in the walls and floors, sonic pulsations around me. I moved deeper into the castle, through room after empty room. It was as if once I passed through a space, it vanished, dissolved in a haze, a dreamlike memory of the past. Space breaking down into its components: length, width, height, depth. Into words like line and volume.

Arche: the beginning, the origin, the commencement. Arche: place of power, authority. Arche: the command.

Dr. Hruška, archivist of memory, the archon of memory, building and organizing his files, his cases, my case, me. He called the clinic the "castle of memory," or, another time, "the archive of the psyche." This is why he had the diaries of Sidney Keter there. This is why he had Gabe Slatky's collected plays. This is why he had Daniel Cohen's novels and my translations of works by Anton Grassfeld, Horák, and the poets Ingrid Müller and Pepi Kafková. This is why he had the Cain responsa, Jacob Rodriga's letters from Prague, Momus's report, *The Book of Moonlight*, Dellman's novel about Nahum Griggs, Griggs's *Becoming Powerless*. And there was a story by a woman named Milena, or Mila, and there were the plays of Rosa Fuchsbein, and there was Fo's script for *Silence*. Archive of memory. Archive of psyche. An archive fallen out of time, out of place. *My word is like fire, like a hammer that shatters rock.* Cain. Julia's Cain. Cain as sister. Cain as innocent brother. Cain as framed, accused, driven from home by an angry, jealous God. Abel as spirit. Abel as breath. Abel as vapor rising from Eden's rich, mossy ground.

The noise drew me deeper into the castle, humming, vibrating, pulsating, the voice of Ida Fields. It's a snowy afternoon. Ida is sick. She's in the bathroom throwing up. I'm lying on the bed trying to work out a solution to a tricky scene in the translation of Grassfeld's *Trending Toward Zero*. Then, without warning, I'm in Berlin's Zoo Station. I board the train to Prague. I gaze out the window. It's gray. The icy rain is falling. Where is Ida now? She's gone north to a cabin in the woods, the cabin where I, as a boy, would paddle a canoe over to a nearby dock and eat ice cream on the porch with the novelist Martin Dellman. Ida has gone north to bury a child.

Deeper into the castle. I went toward the house, toward the eternal burning, the fire that should have lasted forever but is now extinguished. After burning the archive. After burning the castle. After burning the village to the ground.

Arche. Origins. It was late evening when K. arrived. Fog and darkness surrounded him. Nothing could be seen. Not even the faintest glimpse of a castle. Apparent castle. Across the bridge into the village. The desire to stay. Why have I come here to this desolate place? To find traces of an ending. *It was difficult to understand her, but what she said*

The cabin, dimly lit, fire in the hearth. Candlelight. She was in there reading a book. The cabin by the lake, Dellman's book about Nahum Griggs. Julia—she's reading my translation of *Blue, Red, Gray*. Milena, she's reading Cohen's manuscript called *Guests at the Hotel des Bains*. All of these readings are folded together, all readings becoming one reading, all texts merging into one text, and at the same time, everything pulling apart, disintegrating, spilling out of an ending without end, without the resolution of a period, into a pile of used-up words.

Arche. The command. I sat across from Hruška as his pen flew across the page. I knew he was writing a case study of a man who lost the ability to distinguish between real life and fiction, between a novel and its translation, between himself and his characters. How could it have gone this far? Hruška wonders. How could this person have gotten lost in this web of alleyways on what seemed like a straightforward journey from one point to another? Hruška gathered records. He drew a map, traced steps, plotted routes. When it was fully mapped out, Hruška thought he'd be able to lead the person to the exit, the way out of the maze. Words as fire—what is left but ashes? Words like a hammer—what is left but fragments, shards, dust?

NIGHT

I light another beeswax candle. K. Kostel, Keter, Kain. Kirschbaum. One path led from Berlin to Prague and into the twisted mass of Jan Horák's novel. The other path led in the reverse direction, from Prague to Berlin, to the house on Grunewaldstrasse, the twisted mass of the burrow, to death, to tuberculosis, a disease of the lungs, a collapse of the breath. The killing of Abel—the killing of breath. Abel as the breath of Cain. Cain, the wanderer, a body with no spirit, a being severed from God. There is a destination, but no path. What we call the path is only hesitation. Hesitation. Hesitation. Repeat. To repeat is to circle back. Thoughts no longer move forward or even in an arcing detour. They circle back into themselves. *The crows assert that a single crow could destroy the heavens. But heaven means the impossibility of crows.* A single crow. An impossible statement. The negative, a mirror, a reversal, Cain and Abel.

He arrived in Berlin at Anhalter Bahnhof. He took a room on Miquelstrasse but the landlady soon drove him out. He moved to another apartment on Grunewaldstrasse, an apartment above the basement laboratory of the chemist Dr. Kaesbohrer. In fact, Dora moved him. She carried his things from one place to another. She shopped for him, cooked for him, and fell in love with him, the eternal bachelor. She was the daughter of a Polish suspenders maker, an orthodox, conservative man. She fled her home for Breslau, and from Breslau, she made her way to Berlin. She spoke Yiddish and Hebrew, Polish and German. She found work with the Jewish Home, led the children in song, taught Hebrew. She cooked, cleaned. She took the children on vacation to the Baltic Sea. There was a family staying next door. A woman with three children was accompanied by her brother, a forty-year-old writer from Prague. A teenage girl in the group, whose family owned a bookstore in Charlottenburg, knew of him. He'd written a thin volume called *The Stoker*. His name was Franz Kafka.

Months on Grunewaldstrasse, on the periphery of a city spiraling toward death, ripping itself apart, crushed by godlike forces called "economy." One hundred marks became one thousand, then one million, one hundred million, one billion—one billion marks for a single egg. Riots, panics—gangs formed. A nation defined by fear and hate. Hate that could only end in death. The death drive. The death spiral. Death looking in at life. A writer in Stieglitz takes the train into the city center, then back to his life in the citadel, the castle keep, that magnificent, vaulted chamber, which he built through total dedication, with suffering, with pain and joy. The joy of creating oneself. The joy of creating safety for oneself. And peace. Peace? A place to be, to exist, freely, fully. How can he be free and full if he is confined to this cell? The freedom and fullness of self-imprisonment. Then came the noise. It started as soon as the last bit of wall was hammered into place. It was the noise of the mysterious antagonist—a hum, a vibration, a tremor in the earth. He could not have known that in the cellar below him, the chemist, Dr. Kaesbohrer, had developed the precise mathematical equation to represent the collapse of freedom, the deterioration of safety, the coming of death. Not only that, Kaesbohrer had mixed and experimented and had come up with an antidote. It was the only possible solution, a potion, a cloudy yellow liquid. The result of drinking the liquid was the utter disintegration of the real. There was no escape other than the utter disintegration of the real.

The winter of 1924 was brutally cold. They had no money for heat, no money to feed the fire to cook. His cough started to worsen. The disease crawled from his lungs into his throat. His weight fell: 125 pounds, 124, 123, 122, 121, 120. The beast approached, the beast of illness, the beast of poverty, the beast of politics. Ghosts rose from their slumber. They rose early from their winter hibernation—Prague ghosts, Vienna ghosts, Berlin ghosts. Years before, in a letter to Milena, he wrote about *playing tag with ghosts*. Ghosts chasing him, he chasing ghosts, a mutual haunting: 119, 118, 117—the dim countdown to nonexistence. How many days can the hunger artist go without eating? He corrected the proofs in his final days, barely able to lift the pen to make the marks. A letter comes from the Kurt Wolff Verlag: *not a single book has been sold since summer*. Due to *insignificant sales*, we are canceling your account. Joy in nothingness. Greatness in nothingness: a metamorphosis, a penal colony on an island, a torture machine that gives illumination in the sixth hour—116, 115, 114. An animal who builds a burrow. A mouse named Josephine. An ape who says hello: 113, 112, 111. Long, bony fingers. Dark eyes. Crow-like nose. Crow. Jackdaw. Corvid. Kafka. The winter darkness. His time in Berlin was up. He returned to Prague, then went to a sanatorium in Wienerwald, then to a lung clinic in Vienna. His throat was closing. He couldn't eat, could barely swallow: 110, 109, 108. To Kierling. Unable to talk: 107, 106, 105. Sleep. Chest rose and fell. *Kill me, or else you are a murderer.* Two injections. June 3, 1924.

NIGHT

Another beeswax candle flickers to life, illuminates the disintegration of the real, the obliteration of the real. I continue to move toward the interior of this structure that has no interior, that has no end. Room after room. Some are empty, others furnished with chairs, desks, and benches. Empty bookshelves. Where have the books gone? Did they burn them, as Dora burned his manuscripts in the winter of 1924? They watched, together, as the stories went up in flames. Fire as the antiarchive. Fire as *anarche*.

NIGHT

Two more beeswax candles. My supply is dwindling. Apart from gazing into their warm light, I can barely tell if I am awake or asleep, writing in wakefulness, writing in dream. Sleepwalking through the endless castle, the same scenes repeating over and over again. Stone walls. Desks. Ceramic ovens. Those large books on the tables, empty, their pages the size of unfolded sheets of newsprint. Often, I tell myself that I need to turn around and go back the way I came—meaning not only leaving the castle but finding the road down the hill to the village, crossing over the bridge, finding the trail which leads over the mountain ridge to Špindlerův Mlýn, locating the bus to Prague. It's no use. I have lost the sense of which way is back. There is no way of telling which way leads to the exit and which toward the citadel, the innermost chamber. One thing changes as I move from room to room—the textures of the sound. The hum or vibration. It is the sound of a swarm moving through the earth. It is the sound of a great beast circling. It is the sound of my breath. The sound of my heartbeat. It is the sound of my pencil scratching this page.

NIGHT

God has been defeated. Jacob has wrestled him to a draw on the banks of the Jabbok River. The crows say . . . The crows maintain . . . The crows assert that a single crow could destroy the heavens. Heaven is the impossibility of crows. An army of humans has invaded and burned the heavens. They have slaughtered the angels. God has fled to higher realms. God has receded so far that no belief can reach Him. Prayer falls back to the ground unheard. God continues to move farther from us, and the farther He moves, the greater is the evil on the earth. Only the ultimate evil can bring about the reversal of God's recession. *Rouse yourself*, the people will call out together, *rouse yourself, why do you sleep, O Lord?*

I have lost myself, a self that never was. I am not who I am. I am not anyone. I am becoming other than that self. I move toward the inner sanctum. The sanctum of silence. There is no God sitting on the castle's throne. There is no throne in the castle of Count Westwest, a count with no body, no voice, a count who was not a count, the count who was a steward, the count who was but a portrait of a substeward, a portrait of a man with his head bent, a portrait of a man in thought, a man asleep, the portrait of a man dreaming dreams of an endless concatenation of rooms containing folders with the cases of every villager, official records, and these official records with their stamps and numbers are falling out of the folders, becoming messy, disorganized. The dreamer tries to stop the disordering. He grabs handfuls of papers and stuffs them in folders, in the wrong folders, reports where there should be no reports, permits where nothing is permitted, deeds where there is nothing to own. The dreamer works until the end, until the papers are back in the folders, the folders back on the shelves. As he finishes, he notices one folder that has eluded his eye. It had slipped away into the shadows in the corner of the room. He goes to it, reaches down, picks it up, reads the label: *K.*

NIGHT

It was deep into the night when Julia started to tell me the story of the tiny kingdom of Eden. She had discovered bits and pieces about it over many years, she said, beginning with what she called the Girona documents. It was toward the beginning of the thirteenth century when a woman named Keturah led a group out of Barcelona to the west to settle in a lush valley along the Ebro River. The valley had been discovered by a scout sent by a cartel of Jewish merchants who had dealings with the Muslim princes to the southwest. The scout, Efraim, was a member of Keturah's circle, and when he returned from his journey, he gave her a map with a meandering line drawn from Barcelona to the valley. The line had to meander, Julia said, to jog this way and that, to double back, to circumvent, because these were chaotic times. Muslim power on the peninsula was

fractured into dozens of small states, which were always under threat from powerful forces coming across the straits from
North Africa. To the north, the Christian kingdoms were pressing down in spasms of violence. Areas could be ruled one year
by a Muslim prince, the next by a Christian king, and the one
after by a sultan. In such a realm, small spaces could open—
spaces beyond the control of the greater powers. And this was
fertile land, Julia said, she had walked it herself, picked lemons
and figs from wild trees—or trees in long-abandoned orchards
that were nearly consumed by tall grasses. The valley was not
directly on the river, of course not, Julia said, because the river
was the key to power in the region. The valley marked on the
map by Efraim was over the hills beyond the northern bank of
the Ebro, perfectly concealed by steep slopes all around. The flat
land in the valley was nothing much, a thin strip—just enough
for a small village of one hundred wanderers from Barcelona,
people in search of an almost unimaginable freedom, freedom
from Muslim and Christian laws, freedom from violence and
the threat of violence, freedom from the domination of the
closed structures of faith and reason—freedom, in other words,
to live an expansive and righteous life in poetic harmony with
the world.

There had been a council called by the pope that took place
in the Lateran Palace in Rome. A decree had come down that
Muslims and Jews in Christian lands must be distinguishable
by dress to prevent Christian from marrying Jew, Christian
from marrying Muslim. Jews were forbidden to hold public offices, and a Jew, once converted, should not slide back into the
former belief. Despite this deterioration of life in Christendom,

the rabbis of Barcelona strongly opposed Keturah's migration. For them, it was a demonic movement led by godless people, like Keturah's lover Solomon, who had tried and failed to cultivate an orchard of date palms on the outskirts of the city, a sure sign, the rabbis mused, that he had attracted the curse of Cain. Keturah was even worse in their eyes. She dressed in the fashions of Babylon—hair wild and uncovered. She wrote poetry in Arabic, or, even worse, in a Hebrew tainted with adulterations from unholy languages—Arabic, Aramaic, Latin, Greek, and even with those degenerate versions of Latin written in Hebrew letters. That Keturah would load the holy Hebrew letters with such foreign impurities was intolerable to the rabbis, grounds enough for excommunication. Keturah was still a young woman when her husband died, leaving her to care for three daughters. Many men had sought her out, but she had refused them. In Barcelona, she worked as a copyist, and she was able to copy works in every language, to translate between them when necessary. The Christian kings and nobility had great desire for written works, and Keturah was known to possess the most accurate eye and the most beautiful script—a script, one king's chief librarian remarked in a letter to his steward (Julia had this letter in her possession), *fit for the word of the Son of God*. Keturah's parents had brought her and her brother Abraham to Barcelona from over the mountains. They were fleeing the king's violence against the Cathars. Not that the Cathars were friends of the Jews—they maintained that the Hebrew Bible contained the writings of Satan, that Satan was an evil god, the dualist opponent and antagonist of the God of goodness, God, the father of Christ, God, the author of the new scriptures. From over the mountains, Keturah and her family brought a set of unwelcome ideas into the city, ones that read the holy books as patterns of color and light, that saw through to the roots of things, into the heart of the world, where instead of material reality there was divine force, instead of endless imperfection there was boundless perfection, harmony instead of partiality—and there was fullness, perfect fullness, the harmony of all—*ha male*. This was the primal element of poetry, the animating force of poetry in every language, Hebrew, of course, and Arabic and Latin and Greek. Keturah explored language down to its roots—pushed toward the substrate, because only there could a single word find its connection, its binding, to another. There was, for Keturah, as Julia described it, an energy in this binding of one word to another, an energy not of one type but of many types. It could be the energy of collision, starting with explosion, ending with trajectory. It could be an unraveling or dissipating energy, a fading, a becoming silent, an echo that slowly quiets. It could be the energy of friction, one word rubbing against another, making electricity, heat, fire—or, when cold, splinters, powder, dust. How to unlock this force, to unleash this energy? This required more than learning, more than understanding in a rational sense. It meant not study but embodiment—thrusting one's body and soul into the shells of words, infusing them with life, remaking the spirit through the quivering vibrations of language—but knowing that this remaking was at the same time a shattering, and that this shattering of the self through the pouring of its spirit into the vessels of language was but one step in the long, arduous process of preparing for the final confrontation with the divine force, that this confrontation would come when history came to its sudden halt, when time stopped, when the whirl of the world's energy became trapped in the eternal now. This potential energy was the living breath of poetry—the sonic key to the heavens, not the heavens in the sense of a domain above, but heavens as the triumph of goodness, of a time when flawed, partial, selfish, individual things would become joined in divine fullness, achieving the primal harmony that, ironically, the first act of creation unwittingly destroyed. From beyond the mountains, Julia told me, Keturah brought this impulse, and it was this impulse that she carried to the valley of the Ebro River, a valley they called Eden. It was perhaps the smallest state on earth, the smallest state ever to exist—one valley, one field. It was a community forged through poetry, through the mystical realm of language, a community that wanted only to remain unmapped, erased from the geographical imagination of the world, and thereby able to escape attacks from the north or south, the east or west, to disappear into peaceful, blissful nothingness—not forgotten but unknown.

In anticipation of the exodus from Barcelona, Julia told me, and continuing after she settled in the valley, Keturah composed a series of poems called the Eden Cycle. They told the history of the first years of humankind through the perspective of Eve, the first woman, from her creation from the body of Adam to her death in exile. Because one of the later poems covers the death of Abel and God's punishment of Cain, Julia considered it part of the Cain responsa. Julia had found a complete copy of this cycle in Girona during a year she had dug so deeply into the documents that she nearly lost herself. She had fallen backward into history, she told me, and it was as if history's forward motion had, for her, ground to a halt, the whole mechanism of time collapsing into a heap of twisted, broken shards and gears. A year in Girona—or two, or three, or a lifetime, a lifetime in Girona. Just as it was a month, or two, or three—or a lifetime on Grunewaldstrasse. She was young, early twenties—and I wonder how it could have been that such a being could have fallen into such a deep historical pool—or, rather, such a stormy sea. The only thing that can be said with any confidence is that the tiny Kingdom of Eden was, for Julia, the eye of the hurricane. It wouldn't last—it couldn't last. How could it have lasted? This is as clear as could be. A kingdom formed through a cycle of poems called the Eden Cycle. Ending in conflict. Ending in exile. It began with an act of rebellion. It ended with a spasm of violence. Cain and Abel. Abel and Cain—Keturah, K.—it ended in murder. I asked Julia why she went to Girona, how she found herself precisely there, there in the last years of the twentieth century, there in the middle decades of the thirteenth century as kingdoms rose and fell, as the power of princes and kings waxed and waned with the phases of the moon, as the Muslim and Christian warriors crushed between them the world of the Jews.

Julia told me she discovered the original texts of the thirty-six poems of Keturah's Eden Cycle in a crate of documents that was dug up from a construction site along Girona's outer wall. Or, in another version at another time, Julia told me she purchased the poems from an old man named Avram Daud, who appeared one day in the Girona book market, only to disappear the next. Or, she said, they were discovered in the city's municipal archive—or in an attic or cellar amid inquisitional sanbenitos, or fascist military gear, or soccer (she called it football) memorabilia, jerseys of the great stars of the Spanish league. No, she told me, none of this was quite right. She'd found the poems carved into the Jewish gravestones of the city, not directly, but in coded form. Sometimes every seventh word, sometimes every seventh letter. Or preserved in whispers—the whispered memories of ghosts, of those long vanished but still there. A poem called "Binah." Julia recited it. It is about a point of light, the original or first light, the dawn light. And this light is both a point and not a point, because it must emanate from a point and yet suddenly and completely covers the whole sky, the whole earth. It is the totality of the brightening of the dawn sky before the sunrise. Both singular and total. An emanation hewn from God's spirit—*binah*, light cast into a palace of mirrors, image bouncing off image, one image creating another, then another, then another in a seemingly infinite regress—image within image shrinking down in size until all light becomes a minuscule dot, a speck of dust, a grain of sand. As it shrinks, at every stage, it undergoes a slight distortion, distortion from one reflection to another because no mirror is perfect, all contain the influence of the fallible human hand. Wisdom multiplied until it becomes an abstraction, until it vanishes into the depths of the surface. A play of imagination. Imagination creating composition; relationships providing order and logic to a space that would otherwise be nothing other than flat—or that would fall apart into fragments, into pieces, the mirror falling forward and smashing on the stone ground. This light—binah—not invisible or white light. It is black.

Binah as the black reflection of wisdom. Black light split into a spectrum of pure color. One color unfolded from another, one idea unfolded from another. What is the first idea—the idea of blackness? What light flows into the palace of mirrors to begin the process of fracturing and fragmentation, of doubling and splitting and distorting? *Chokhmah*—the breaking of the dawn. The infinite and the infinitely small—the paradox of wisdom. Wisdom emerging out of the emptiness. *Wisdom from nothingness*—chokhmah from keter, wisdom from emptiness, wisdom flowing into the palace of mirrors, fractured, reconstituted as a reflection of a reflection of a reflection—yes, the poem's refrain! *Wisdom comes from nothingness / wisdom seeks its return to emptiness / the emptiness of existence.* The serpent's words: *God has lied to you.* You will not die if you eat of the forbidden fruit. He is afraid that if you eat from it, your eyes will open, and you will be like Him. Knowing evil. Staring into the heart of evil. Finding wisdom—finding wisdom in the space between good and evil. What is this, the serpent said to Eve, but choice—the choice of good over evil, evil over good—the beauty and chaos and horrors of the human will.

On her way to Barcelona from over the mountains, Keturah stopped in Girona. It was over 750 years before Julia was there. Seven and a half centuries separate one body from the other— bridged through language, through translation—like the poem "The End of Eden" from the Eden Cycle. A gravestone poem, a cellar poem—a poem buried under fascist uniforms and soccer scarves. The poem begins with *hesed*, the divine attribute of love, of the mercy of God, but in the very first sentence hesed is placed in relation to *gevurah*—God's strength, discipline, judgment, punishment—power. Power in tense coexistence with love. The opening: *The tree of life grows in Eden / Its long drooping branch of hesed / Tangled with the rising branch of gevurah.* Tangled could be "caught in"—caught in the rising branch, or maybe caught "by" the rising branch. These were the issues that kept us awake at night, those endless nights of poetry and sex, of open windows and gazes into the dimly lit street below my small apartment in the center of Prague. Julia looking out for Cain's arrival. What was I looking for? Wind. Emptiness. The last drunkards stumbling home from the pub? Or was it chokhmah, the blackness of all color, all wisdom combined into one impenetrable nothingness? And one night, I turned away from the window, left the apartment, walked to the bus station, and boarded a bus for Berlin, which ended instead in the mountain town of Špindlerův Mlýn—the closest station to the village of Z.

An army appears on the hill above the valley near the Ebro River. The plates of armor strapped to breasts and arms and legs glow in the morning sun. Then the sound of stampeding horses—the glint of swords, the heat of torches. In the center of the village, the tree of life, bearing its pomegranate fruit—ripe and red. Keturah has turned into a pomegranate tree, her branches pointing in all directions, intertwined with each other, tangled, laden with ripe fruit. Crack open a fruit and let its juices flow—let the juices stain fingers and drip down hands and arms. The tree's trunk, a movement stilled, a curve, a dancer half-turned and slightly bent—frozen at the point of maximal grace. Keturah's body, young, sturdy, rooted in *malkhuth*, the kingdom of God, the light of the moon (*luna*), containing the sap of *yesod*, the active force, and *tifereth*, beauty and compassion of the

Lord. On Keturah's wooden hips, the low branches of *hod* and *netsah*, majesty and endurance. The warriors descend the steep slope, the horses gaining speed. The people of the kingdom of Eden run for their lives. Some try to climb the opposite hills to disappear into neighboring valleys. They are caught quickly and chopped down. Others barricade themselves in the stone temple and perish as the warriors set it on fire. The last villagers gather around Keturah, the tree of life. One by one, they are killed—their blood flowing into Keturah's roots, into the trunk and branches and leaves, filling each seed of the pomegranate fruit. *Tiny vessels of life / teardrops of breath and blood.* What do the warriors chant as they set the tree on fire? It is, as Julia chanted, *bereshith bara Elohim*! And the flames seem to leap from the torches to the outermost branches. They race toward the trunk—and soon the whole tree is on fire. This is the heart of the poem, Julia said to me, as she read me those verses. The fire turning into light, the light splitting into color, the color becoming radiant, alive, until the very force of its beauty opens up a crack in the perceptible universe—a sliver as thin as a single sheet of paper, a single pomegranate leaf—and through this crack, the onlooker could see a point—a point that was also a word, but this word has never been read before, never uttered. It is a word with no sound, a word of fire and color and heat and light and darkness and fullness and emptiness, a word that cannot be contained by letters, a trembling and quivering word, a word of pure force held tenuously in a brittle husk. As the crack opens, widens, the word bursts through its husk—pours forth in a torrent of energy and light—*reshith*— the beginning—filling the valley with the ocean of *shekhinah*.

Nothing but the name of God, Julia said to me. All language is contained in the name of God, itself mysterious, unknowable, and silent. Is this why, she asked (but not me—perhaps herself?) God destroyed that tower of unity, the tower in Babel which was, after all, reaching up to Him—reaching up if only to whisper His name in His ear? The tower crashed to the ground, splintered into fragments, some as large as houses, others as tiny as a grain of sand. Layers of meaning, interpretation—ideas about how to put one piece together with another. Architects and theoreticians, grammarians and scholars seek an answer to the same question: how to piece together that which is broken? Smooth one edge down with the finest file and another edge will present itself in jagged roughness. The promise of unity. It is not the physical unity of the tower. It is not even the unity of the architect's plan—no, it is the secret truth of unity itself. That is the quest, Julia said. This is what Keturah meant by *raza*, by mystery.

NIGHT

It was late evening when K. arrived. It was late evening when I arrived. I wander deeper into the castle. Rooms unfold into rooms like the stretching of an accordion. A draft moves through the space—not a steady draft, more like a series of pulsing breaths. Like Julia's breath on my neck, hot, full. K.'s breath as he gazes up at the apparent emptiness, icy, thin. It was late evening. It—*es*. The beginning, marked by a yawning abyss of signification. It was. *Es war. Es*—ego. *Es*. Self. Late evening of the ego. Late evening of the self. Arriving at selfhood in the late evening, the late hour of life. Selfhood emerging at its end, the circle of the self finding closure in the darkness, in the snow, beneath the apparent emptiness of something greater looming above it. The castle—*Schloss. Schloss*—a lock. *Es—das Schlüssel*, the key. The key of selfhood, the locked castle, the opening, the splitting of the black light into visible color. Nothing could be seen. By whom? By *es*, this ego, this self. Late evening—night. It was night when the self arrived. Night as early morning, after the midnight hour, after evening crosses the border of day, which points to the coming of a new time. It was late evening when K. arrived. At the border of time, K. confronts his *es*—inscribes the circle of his selfhood in the newly fallen snow. *Umgeben*—to surround, to encircle. *Nebel und Finsternis umgaben ihn.* Fog and darkness surrounded it. *Schlossberg.* Castle hill. *Scheinbare Leere*, apparent emptiness, which is also fullness. *Berg.* The mountain. The mountain of locked secrets. Behind the veil. *Andeuten*—indicates, suggests, implies the existence of *ein grosses Schloss*. Great lock, a great but inaccessible structure for those who don't possess the key, the *es*, the self-as-key. Pull out the verbs. The first is *sein*, existence. The second is *liegen*—to be situated, located. Then *umgeben*—surround, enclose, encircle. Then *andeuten*—to suggest, indicate, to imply. Finally, *blicken*—to gaze. The picking of the lock with a stack of verbs: to exist/to be located/to encircle/to suggest/to gaze. Room after room. I make my new camp in a space so deep it could well be the center of the earth—the center of the earth or its most distant edge. There is no day or night here. It is a darkness beyond night, the elemental blackness of fire. Black fire—the ink that burns the scrolls. The ashen word of God.

NIGHT

I light two more beeswax candles. I have four left. My flashlight battery is also fading. When the candles are gone and the flashlight dies, I will be stranded here with no chance of making it out again. I push on with the wild belief that the core of everything lies at the center of the castle's structure, a core that contains the meaning of stories left unfinished, those like *The Book of Moonlight*, like Julia's story of Keturah, a woman becoming a pomegranate tree, its trunk bent into the shape of a dancer, leaves spread out like fingers, branches into arms, a crown of tangled ideas and desires, desires as earthy red spheres containing thousands of juicy seeds.

NIGHT

It could be that the castle is structured as a series of rooms and hallways spiraling inward—the tunnel of a snail's shell. The coil of a snake.

NIGHT

I wake up confused, disoriented from a nightmare. It trails away into the following thought: perhaps the spiral is winding its way upward like the stairs of a ziggurat, or it is twisting downward into the land of the dead.

NIGHT

After some minutes or hours of sleep, I wake up with thoughts of *The Book of Moonlight*, a book, which, with every reading (though it is impossible to "read" it in the traditional sense) breaks apart, collapses, becomes a ruin of a text, like this ruin of a castle, a castle with no end, a castle spiraling into eternal darkness, text into eternal meaninglessness. What is left? No light is left. No meaning is left. Movement is left, a search is left. Is hope left? No. There was no hope from the start. Or maybe hope was the only thing there was, and that's why I couldn't see it, because if it was the only thing there, it was also nothing, because there was nothing to relate it to. When my candles are gone and my flashlight burns out, is this the end of hope? A dimming light, a return to the medieval world, knights on horses descending on the valley of Z.

NIGHT

The last of the beeswax candles are gone. The flashlight is nearly out. I quickly take stock of my remaining provisions and am surprised to find that I have only two jars remaining—a large jar of blueberries and one of cabbage, which I can hardly bring myself to eat. The end of light. The end of food. The end. A person is not meant to survive here. The world has already ceased to exist here. It cannot be made to live again.

She held out her trembling hand to K. and had him sit down beside her, she spoke with great difficulty, it was hard to understand her, but what she said

She is the divine light, shekhinah. A trembling shekhinah, a nervous shekhinah, a light soon to be extinguished. Shekhinah has no voice, shekhinah tried to form words, to speak, but I cannot understand her. Her thoughts are not bound to language, even if her radiance gives birth to all language, filling the vessels of letters with the name of God. But what she said

What?

What?

DARKNESS

I am writing this in total darkness. I move through the space, a prisoner of walls of darkness.

Cain arrived in the village. This was the ending. The end of the village, the end of the world.

The history of the village is the prelude to Cain's arrival.

K. Cain. The stranger with a mark on the back of his neck.

I found Julia one day at the museum staring at a painting of Mary of Egypt. Tears of joy rolled down her cheeks. "All we need," she said, "is a loaf of bread." She had lost her mind—or found it.

Julia said that when she found the valley near the Ebro River there was a pomegranate tree. Its leaves and branches were on fire. Yet, the tree didn't burn.

Julia picked a fruit and broke it open. Its juices contained salty tears, blood, echoing cries from the deepest past. They stained her fingers. Painted her skin.

I took the book from her and wrote: *The crows assert that a single crow could destroy the heavens.*

What does heaven mean?

The impossibility of crows.

I move along the edges of the rooms, guided by my hands on the cold stone walls as I am guided on these pages by the tips of my fingers, which can feel the ever so slight indentation of letters on the page.

A scene. I'm sitting in the reading room in Berlin's Staatsbibliothek. I'm wearing a pair of white cotton gloves. On the table in front of me is the first issue of the journal *Milgroym*, published in 1922. A bird with a blue flower in its mouth and a pomegranate tree are on the cover. The tree's fruits hang like spherical jewels in various shades of red. This is the forbidden fruit.

The black moon, *luna negra*, the new moon, the inverse of moonlight, *The Book of Moonlight*, itself the inverse of the primary source of light. Is this what the Talmudists meant by black fire on white fire, black moon on white moon, emptiness as the obverse of fullness, letters defined by the blank sea of the page, sea of shekhinah, the *olam tohu*, the world of confusion?

DARKNESS

Darkness obliterates thought, only to make true consciousness possible. The slow rise and fall of my chest. Nostrils prickled by the frigid air. The coolness and smoothness of the stone slabs under me. Early tremors of a gnawing hunger. Sounds of soft pulses of air. Breath. Breath and a distant, almost-imperceptible whistling of the wind as it moves across the same crack through which I entered the castle. Traces of rotting wood. Scents of a fire extinguished long ago. Scents of dust and ash. In the darkness, I find each sensation, pull them apart, follow their pathways—pathways back, back, and away.

Cabins in the woods: one structure containing the entire village of Z. A structure a short canoe ride from where Martin Dellman took his last breath. My brother Henry told me to draw a line separating reality from fiction. But what side of the line is truth on? He didn't say. He didn't know.

I have wandered into this valley, which might as well be on the obverse side of the moon. I am no longer in the world.

The world no longer surrounds me. I haven't left it; it has left me.

Julia returns from her night wanderings. Her skin is cold. Her hands ache. She's been searching aimlessly throughout the city. There's nothing to find out there, I tell her. She laughs, a demon's laugh, though she is closer to angel than demon. She is an angel of light and darkness, one moon, two sides.

DARKNESS
Two tasks of the beginning of life: to keep reducing your circle, and to keep making sure you're not hiding somewhere outside it.

A bird stands on the curve of a pomegranate; it holds a blue flower in its beak. The blue flower of miracle. The blue flower of desire. The blue flower of hope.

K. laughed. He let himself be led through the darkness.

The only light in Gerstäcker's house came from a fire in the hearth and a squat stump of candle on the table.

The mother sat bent under crooked beams in an alcove.

She held out her trembling hand.

She spoke.

It was difficult to understand her.

But what she said

Gerstäcker—the coachman as Charon, ferryman of the dead. Son of Erebus, God of darkness, God of shadow, Erebus, born from Chaos. There are no words before creation, itself the result of language. And God said . . . The end is silence, the return to the world before creation, to the realm of emptiness, emptiness before darkness, silence as the parent of darkness.

When I sleep, I can see lit-up spaces. I see the blinding white of a blizzard from the cabin window as I wait for Ida Fields.

I boarded a bus bound for Berlin. The bus must have changed course while I slept, heading east instead of north, from normal time to a time long since ended. Ended in silence. In emptiness. In ruins. In Z.

In the space beyond the circle of the self—the wilderness of the other.

Inside mystery, darkness.

There is nothing to learn here. There is nothing to know. This place, this castle, is empty of knowledge. It is empty of history. History and knowledge vanished from here. They fled before the end came. This is the place after the end, but somehow it still exists. Inside mystery, silence.

It occurs to me, while emerging from a fitful sleep, that the castle is not a spiral. It is a closed system. If so, I am tracing the same walls over and over, passing repeatedly through the same rooms.

There is one closed letter in the Hebrew alphabet, the *samekh*. If one traces the path of the samekh, one is neither on the inside nor on the outside. One moves along the border, the border of in and out, the border of self and other, the border of order and chaos, the border of life and death.

A trembling border, the samekh, like the trembling hand of the coachman's mother.

I see myself walking through the forest with my father. It must be the fall, because the leaves are full of color and the forest floor is a combination of a dozen shades of brown. He's going slowly, often pausing to regain his composure, or balance, or breath. My own breath constricts as he struggles. Then the moment passes. He's breathing easily now, his face relaxes. He's a young man again, tall, lank, a head full of black hair. This younger man is inaccessible to me, even as I cling to his leg and force him to swing me around the room. The old man, on the other hand, can be read on the surface, the seemingly empty gaze, the wrinkled cheeks, the furrows on his forehead, the sagging jeans. He is pale, seems fragile. He comes around a bend in the path. The ocean opens up in front of us. I look down and see green-and-brown seaweed caught between the rocks. My father gazes toward the horizon—not at the sea, not at the sky, at the in-between.

The closed samekh. The infinite. The ein sof. The shattering of the vessels, the fractured body of God. One part of God is ocean, the other part is sky. The universe is the paper-thin gap between them.

K. let himself be led through the darkness.
    Through the darkness to find God—no.
    Through the darkness to discover himself—no.
    Through the darkness to obliterate the castle—no.
    Through the darkness to blend into village life—no.
    Through the darkness to grasp meaning—no.
    Through the darkness to the realm of death—no.
    Through the darkness,
    To the muffled voice,
    To the dim light,
    To the trembling hand,
    To silence.

Am I sleeping now? Am I dreaming these words, which, in this darkness, are not words but movements of my arm, the tensing and releasing of my hand, my fingers, pressure applied and removed by my thumb? Writing as a bodily act. Not words, not representations—material gestures, sensations, pain, arousal. And floating alongside these sensations, ideas and emotions. Ideas and emotions like clouds in the darkest sky.

I move along the walls slowly, feeling along with my fingers, careful not to crash into the stonework, the edges of rooms, touching the plastered corners as they chip and flake away under the slightest pressure, leaving gritty residue behind on my skin. Now and then, usually after sleeping, I eat a spoonful of preserved blueberries. They contain a hallucinogenic agent, or a poison, which launches me on the path to freedom, allowing me to break through to a new life, a life without walls, an edgeless, cornerless life, without Mondschein, without Kirschbaum.

DARKNESS

Another corner, another long wall, another border between here and there, present and past, reality and fiction. I'm on one side, my brother Henry is on the other. Castles exist on both sides, castle of light, castle of darkness. Life on one side, words on the other. On one side the samekh, on the other the *hay*.

I scrape my spoon along the bottom of the jar, pushing it back and forth, listening to the delicate chiming as the spoon collides with the glass, feeling the rhythmic reverberations. The blueberries are gone. My food is gone. I take everything out of my backpack and leave it on the floor. I keep only my notebook and pencil. Everything else is superfluous.

Julia appeared with a copy of the book. I took it and wrote: *The crows assert that a single crow could destroy the heavens.*

A single crow, a kamikaze flight, slamming itself into the glass gate, its beak making the slightest crack—but from that tiny crack, a larger one forms, and from that larger one, others appear, running like rivulets from the center to countless points on the edge. The cracks compose an intricate pattern, something like a snowflake—until the whole structure crashes to the ground.

Traces of Sidney Keter: the note in the file about Z., the Keter diaries showing up at Zelená Hora, the movement of Sidney Keter out of Prague in 1939, vanishing to the north into the Giant Mountains, traces of his path, traces of his life, intersections—in Berlin, in Prague, here. I am following his path, intersecting his life, becoming him, following him into Horák's *Blue, Red, Gray*, thereby merging my life with the novel's protagonist, Josef Kostel, thereby disappearing with Kostel into the forest, thereby leaving behind a book without a protagonist, leaving behind a book without an author, thereby leaving behind a jumble of words.

Esther Bird, blue flower of desire in her hand, blue flower of miracle, blue flower of hope, this was the flower pressed between pages one hundred and one hundred one of Dellman's copy of *Becoming Powerless*. I picked it up with my thumb and forefinger and felt its dried petals crumble into dust.

Kain arrived in the village. The end of days had come.

Cain has arrived in the present, Julia said, the end of days has come.

What can open the gates of heaven if not a bird with a blue flower in its beak?

Nothing can open the gates of heaven, because there is no heaven and there are no gates. There is only a castle on a hill above a village with no way out, no doors, no windows, only room after room of darkness.

There is one Hebrew letter without end—samekh.

The name of God—*yud*, *hay*, *vov*, *hay*—contains all language. But it is language as a series of cracked vessels from which meaning seeps out. Where does this substance go? It flows back to its source. And where is that? That place is nowhere. That place is what we call heaven. Heaven means the impossibility of crows.

GLIMMERING

I turn a corner and there is a faint light in the room. The light appears to come from above me, but I can't locate its source. As my eyes adjust, I can make out more and more of what is around me. The first thing that strikes me is that I have come to the end of the system of rooms. This is the final room. There is no door to the room other than the one I have just passed through. I close the door behind me just to be sure, to be sure I have truly arrived at the heart of the castle—the castle's keep.

There is a bed in the right-hand corner of the room, next to which is a small table with a lamp on it. On the wall to my left is a desk with a wooden chair. The desk has drawers on each side and a long, thin drawer in the center above the knees. There's more: an old armoire, its doors loose on their hinges and slightly ajar, a beaten-up Persian carpet, bookshelves. I make my way around the room. The shelves are full of books. The armoire is stuffed with clothes. The thin drawer at the center of the desk has a notebook in it. I take it out. I hesitate before opening it, thinking about the possibilities—Keter's diaries, *The Book of Moonlight*, the last words of Gerstäcker's mother, the story of the death of Cain, Hruška's case studies, Martin Dellman's unfinished final novel, Nahum Griggs's treatise, Cohen's manuscript, something, something that would start a chain reaction, leading to a final outcome. An explosion of fire—revelation. An understanding, a sensation of pure joy. Or the other way—a crushing despair, a vortex of hopelessness. I run my fingers over the surface. The brown leather cover is soft and smooth. This notebook has been left here for me, I think, placed here by Keter, or Kostel, it has been left here by Cain. This is Cain's accusation against a murderous God, his indictment of the evil that dwells in heaven, that dwells in the center of our world. This is what Julia desires, and this is what I need, the final piece of the puzzle, the piece of the puzzle that when set down will complete the image, complete the story, bring a stop to the unfolding of creation and usher in the end of time. An opening of a notebook, the end of the world.

Out of the corner of my eye I notice that a crack has formed in the wall next to the armoire. I move over to it and press my palm against the stones. Only the slightest pressure is needed to push through the wall. The stones give way, a gap opens up. Light floods in, forcing me to turn away and shield my eyes. When my vision adjusts, I gaze through the hole and out across the valley.

Then more cracks start to appear in the walls. This time the stones don't need pushing. They begin to tremble and collapse on their own, breaking away piece by piece, opening bigger gaps, letting in even more light. Soon the ceiling is falling. Wooden beams and ceramic shingles crash to the floor around me as I take refuge in the leg space under the desk. I crouch there as the castle of Count Westwest falls apart.

It doesn't take long before everything is over. I climb out from under the desk with the brown leather notebook tucked under my arm. There are heaps of stones and wood around me. Down in the valley, the village, too, seems to have collapsed. The schoolhouse, the church, the gentlemen's inn, the inn by the bridge, the small stone houses along those narrow streets—rubble.

An elaborate hallucination? Induced by a psychedelic agent that grew in the final jar of preserved blueberries?

I remember blueberries from another time. Those on the hills above our cabin on the lake. I am there with my brother Henry. We are each filling a bucket on a late August afternoon. Two brothers out in the field. An older brother named Henry, a younger brother named Sy, picking blueberries, eating blueberries, fingers and mouths stained purple, the color of life flowing through our veins.

A bed, a desk, an armoire, bookshelves. The modest furnishings of a small apartment in the center of Prague. A notebook left in the top drawer above the knees. Bound in brown leather. A gift from a friend long since passed away. I open the notebook. The pages are blank. I flip through until I notice he has written something on the last page. A note left as an epilogue to an unwritten novel:

The crows claim that a single crow could destroy heaven. There is no doubt of that, but it proves nothing against heaven, because heaven is just another way of saying: the impossibility of crows.

As I read these words, I see him here: his thick hair and large piercing eyes, his narrow face and bony nose, his ears flaring out like misshapen angel's wings, his wide eyebrows and thin lips, and his gaunt body, ill-suited to the demands of life. If I could reach out and touch him, I would know that it will turn out all right, that I'll survive, that I'll make it out of this valley. But he is gone, blown away by a gust of mountain wind. It could be that he is soaring high above me, testing whether heaven has the will and the strength to prevent this single bird, this *kavka*, from entering. Or it could be that he is not soaring. It could be that I am that bird, that I am soaring, but if I am that bird, I am not flying heavenward, I am heading instead toward the distant horizon where the sky and the ocean meet.